DOCTOR WHO

THE DEVIL GOBLINS FROM NEPTUNE

KEITH TOPPING AND MARTIN DAY

BBC BOOKS

First published in the UK 1997 by BBC Books,
an imprint of BBC Worldwide Publishing
BBC Worldwide Ltd, Woodlands, 80 Wood Lane,
London W12 0TT

Original series broadcast on the BBC
Format © BBC 1963
Doctor Who and TARDIS are trademarks of the BBC

ISBN 0 563 40564 3

Design by Black Sheep

Printed and bound in Great Britain by Mackays of Chatham
Cover printed by Belmont Press Ltd, Northampton

Doctor Who and the Devil Goblins from Neptune was initially an outline by Paul Cornell, Martin Day and Keith Topping. *The Devil Goblins from Neptune* is rather different, but many of the plot strands and characters hark back to that original synopsis. We would like to express our gratitude to Paul for his input, and for being happy for the two of us to go it alone.

Now, the usual suspects: thanks to Ian Atkins (computer boffin), Nick Cooper (military hardware and technology adviser, with special responsibility for photocopiers), Helen Day (sanity), Paul Griffin (original artwork), Jeff Hart (Minister for the Colonies), John McLaughlin (agenting), Richard Prekodravac (the man down under), Lily Topping (occasional helpful comments), Peter Wickham (Soviet ambassador) and Mark Whitney (in charge of the glonthometer); to Paul Berry, Paul Brown and Steve Purcell (structural advice and comments); to Tim Archer, Daniel Ben-Zvi, Steve Leahy, Richard Poser, Bill Rudloff, Michael Zecca and the other kind folk on rec.arts.drwho (political and technological queries); and to David Blenkinsopp, Colin Brockhurst, Lee Mansfield, Jackie Marshall, James Sinden and Paul and Tony Smith (early and ongoing encouragement).

Dedicated to Ian Abrahams, who made me do this.
KT

Dedicated to Emily
(a sort of fairy tale for when you're older).
MD

Soundtrack by Atomic Rooster, Badfinger, the Beatles, David Bowie, Captain Beefheart and his Magic Band, Jimi Hendrix, the Kinks, Led Zeppelin, John Lennon and the Plastic Ono Band, Van Morrison, MC5, Pink Floyd, the Rolling Stones, the Stooges, the Thirteenth Floor Elevators, the Velvet Underground, War and the Who.

Action by Havoc

FIRST PROLOGUE:
FROM RUSSIA

A steady drizzle fell from a gunmetal-grey sky against the pale buildings of Gorkiy. An eight-wheeled personnel carrier that had seen better days moved through a landscape otherwise devoid of movement.

The rain had started soon after they left Moscow, and Shuskin had shifted position more than once in an attempt to avoid the water that dripped through tears in the canvas hood. The two benches of rough metal afforded little protection from the bone-jarringly pitted road. In the front of the vehicle, just visible to Shuskin behind panes of reinforced glass, sat the driver and Colonel Katayev, enjoying the comparative luxury of a heated cabin. Rank has its privileges, thought Captain Valentina Shuskin, but what's the alternative? Being allowed in the front because I'm a woman? No, this seat would do. She thought of Prague, and of Uri and the double-cross that had, effectively, ended her military career. Until now.

The carrier made another harsh turn, Shuskin extending a hand to the roof to steady herself. Moments later the vehicle stopped, and the colonel turned to gesture through the glass. Shuskin nodded, and made her way to the rear of the vehicle.

The driver was already there. He went to offer Shuskin a hand down, remembered their respective ranks, and stood to attention. Shuskin jumped to the ground and brushed the grime from her dress uniform.

'You'll be quite familiar with the business end of a BTR-60,' said Katayev.

Shuskin turned and saluted. 'Indeed, sir.'

'Standard transport for the marines, I believe.'

'Correct, sir. I spent four years, seven months and twenty-seven days in the marines.' Katayev hadn't asked the question, but Shuskin was keen to remind the veteran of Stalingrad that she had seen some front-line warfare. And, of course, her share of *mokrie dela* – that unreal form of cold, faceless war.

Katayev set off at a brisk pace, Shuskin marching at his side. She glanced behind, and saw the BTR-60 cough into life and execute a three-point turn. The cloying smell of diesel hung in the air, despite the rain.

'Nearly five years of front-line duties in a number of Warsaw Pact countries,' said Colonel Katayev, nodding to himself. It seemed that it had been his intention to discuss her career all along. Shuskin didn't know much about Katayev, but her only previous contact with the man had been out of doors and off the record, so she wasn't surprised that he had asked the driver to drop them off some distance short of their destination. 'In 1968 you worked at the underground installation at Semipalatinsk. A cul-de-sac in an otherwise promising career, wouldn't you agree, Captain?'

'I imagine most soldiers' careers have ups and downs, sir. And it did at least bring me to the attention of the officers recruiting for UNIT.'

The colonel nodded. 'You enjoy working for us?'

'Of course.' Shuskin wasn't sure where the colonel's questions were leading.

'But you miss the excitement of more overt activities?'

Shuskin decided to temper her honesty, off the record or not. 'The unusual nature of the work makes up for the lack of more orthodox military operations.'

'A good answer,' said Katayev. 'I feel much the same myself. Wherever it is thought that I can be of most use, then there I am happy.'

They came to a halt outside an office block. The colonel pressed an intercom button, but ignored the clipped query from the tannoy. He turned to Shuskin. 'You seem surprised at our destination?'

Shuskin turned her face away in embarrassment, annoyed that the old man could read her so well. 'When I realised we were heading for Gorkiy I thought perhaps we were to visit the submarine yard. I admit I wasn't expecting this.' She indicated the dilapidated tower blocks and the nearby residential flats, studded now with just a few lights.

'Then it will perhaps satisfy your commendable curiosity to let you know something at the outset.' The door buzzed to indicate that it had been opened remotely, but again the colonel ignored it. Instead, he smiled for the first time. 'We're not here at the behest of the military or of the United Nations.'

'Then who...?' began Shuskin, just as the truth was dawning. 'The KGB?'

Katayev pushed open the door. 'It's best not to keep them waiting.'

The corridors smelt of dry rot and boiled cabbage. Paint peeled from every possible surface, and pipes and cables ran exposed over the walls. Only the security cameras, tucked into the darker corners, hinted at the building's function. If the new owners of the building wanted it to appear run-down, they'd certainly gone to extraordinary lengths, right down to the pool of urine in the corner.

They came to a door like any other, but here Colonel Katayev stopped and knocked. A man with the small, nervous eyes of a rat opened the door, indicated where they should sit, and then disappeared out into the corridor. Shuskin heard the door being locked behind them.

At first she thought they were in a lecture hall, as much of the room was dominated by steeply banked rows of seats. Then she noticed the large screen that the chairs all faced. She thought she could smell fresh glue and paint, an artificiality stronger than the stench of the corridors. Shuskin ran a hand over one of the seats. Her eyes widened. The covering was cream-coloured leather.

'If you ever wondered where the riches of the Soviet Union end up...' Katayev spoke in a whisper, a half-smile on his lips.

He nodded towards the front of the room. On two chairs were grey plastic folders. Shuskin followed him, and glanced at the papers in her binder.

Katayev nudged her with his elbow. 'Sit down. There is a protocol to follow at these meetings.'

The lights went out the moment she was seated. As her eyes struggled to adapt to the darkness she saw a figure shuffle into the room through another door. He made his way towards the back. Shuskin took her lead from the colonel, and stared forward at the screen, although she was itching to find out more about the mysterious man behind them, and the contents of the folder in her hand.

'I am grateful that two senior officers from UNIT have so willingly consented to meet with us,' said the man.

His voice was strong and clear, and Shuskin detected something of a regional accent. Baltic, perhaps?

'I am...' There was a pause, as if he were plucking a word from the ether. 'Mayakovsky, of the Narodnyi Kommissariat Gosudarstvennoi Bezopasnosti.'

So, thought Shuskin, the Soviet People's Commissariat for State Security rather than the KGB. This must be really important.

'Please observe the screen in front of you.'

It flickered, and a blurred test image appeared. This was replaced by a photograph of a building. Shuskin noted Renaissance architecture, grounds that spoke of western Europe, a winding gravel road with a small car, obviously travelling at some speed.

'Headquarters of UNIT in the United Kingdom, some three to

four months ago.'

Before Shuskin could really take it in the image vanished. Another slide was shown, this one of a modern building of glass and steel in a city centre. London, possibly?

'The alternative headquarters, used in conjunction with or instead of the previous building. They move around more than we do.'

Shuskin thought the final comment a joke, but it was delivered in the same emotionless tone. Perhaps it was just what it seemed, a statement of fact. Again, before she could dwell on the picture, it was changed.

Another bourgeois house, doubtless maintained by oppressed workers and servants. The lawn was dotted with white statues and human figures. Shuskin saw uniforms and, right at the back of the picture, a jeep. It was her first glimpse of her equivalents in the West.

'Current HQ,' said Mayakovsky.

The slide changed, but this time to a cropped and expanded version of the original image, homing in on the figures. Green army uniforms, a young woman, and a decadent Westerner, flaunting his capitalist wealth.

'The man in the frills and cape...'

With a click the picture changed, zooming in on his face. It was blurred, then computer-enhanced. White hair, lots of it, slightly curly. Strong nose. Sharp, mysterious eyes. Equally strong chin, atop a mass of lace and velvet. A fop, a dandy. Doubtless quite debauched and lacking in any moral decency.

'This is the extraterrestrial. You will bring him here.'

SECOND PROLOGUE:
THE SPY WHO CAME IN

Thomas Bruce walked towards the almost anonymous offices of Drake Chemicals on 53rd street. He wore a suit that cost more than most people pay for a car. His car cost more than most people pay for a house.

Everything about Bruce screamed of the trappings of wealth. His suit was tailored by John Smart of Savile Row, London; it suggested sophistication and a hint of danger. His shirt and tie – even the handkerchief, ironed and nestling perfectly in his jacket pocket – were silk, from Barrett's of New York. His shoes were Italian, the leather hand-cured and hand-stitched. He'd bought them in Rome on a recent trip; he'd been in the city for only thirty-six hours, but had still found time to attend the opera and do some shopping.

To those who passed, he looked like another rich businessman in his early thirties, going to a meeting with a client and enjoying the bright sunshine. In fact, Thomas Bruce was forty-three, and he killed people for a living. Despite his ostentatious attire, he'd spent most of his professional life walking in the shadows. It was dark in there, and he liked that just fine.

Bruce wore Ray-Ban Aviators against the harsh reflection of the sun on the Manhattan skyline, but he removed them as he entered the building so that he could wink at the receptionists behind the main desk. He took the elevator to the sixth floor, checking his watch – a Baume & Mercier, imported direct from Geneva – as the door opened. On time. Of course.

'Good morning,' he said to the secretary, smiling brightly as he strode across the room to sit on the corner of her desk. 'I believe Control is expecting me.'

'Of course. Go right in.'

Bruce stood, folding his copy of the *New York Times* under his arm, and slipped the shades into his pocket. He entered the office without knocking and sat without being invited. For a moment the occupant of the office didn't even raise his head from his papers to acknowledge Bruce's presence. A cigarette smouldered in the large cut-glass ashtray in the centre of the leather-topped desk. It looked as if it had hardly been touched, but had already burnt down close to the filter.

Then the older man snapped 'Situation?'

Bruce smiled as his eyes met those of his superior. 'Under control, if you'll pardon the pun.'

'I wasn't aware of one.'

Bruce noticed for the first time a glass of whiskey in front of him. 'You were expecting someone?'

'Only you, Tom.' Control nudged the glass across the table towards Bruce. 'I have confidence in your ability to minimise the threat and deal with matters expediently. He *has* been dealt with, I trust?'

'With extreme prejudice,' said Bruce without emotion, draining the glass. 'I assume you have another job for me?'

Control stood, and walked to the filing cabinet at the back of the room. He was a small, inconspicuous man in his early fifties who wouldn't have been out of place in a bookshop or behind a bar. Flecks of dandruff on his grey jacket created the impression that he'd been in the shadows too long and was gently crumbling away, but Bruce knew better than to make snap judgements. The hand that reached into the cabinet was well-muscled, and there was a fading bruise over the knuckle of the little finger, as if he had been in a brawl.

Control extinguished the cigarette when he returned to his desk and dropped a bulging manila file in front of Bruce. 'UNIT,' Control said.

Bruce gave a wry smile. 'Tin soldiers playing hunt-the-alien.' There was a poorly disguised hint of annoyance in his voice. 'Give me a break, we *can't* be interested in those guys. I've seen the reports on the New York HQ: it's amateur hour. A piss-ant operation.'

'True,' said Control. 'Set fire to their pants and they'd think it was Martians, but…' He paused, and it gave Bruce a chance to see something he rarely noted in Control's face: a trace of concern. 'The Agency has a specific interest in their work. And there are certain… considerations attached to the British end of the operation.'

'England?' said Bruce, cynically. 'More alcohol-induced flying-saucer sightings at Stonehenge?'

'Britain is strategically vital to the entire programme. You know that.'

'God alone knows why,' Bruce muttered. 'I've never met a more ignorant bunch of peasants. Goddamn country thinks it's still running the world.'

Control, well used to Bruce's outbursts, let him finish. 'That's partly the problem,' he said. 'The country's becoming unstable. They're a threat to the programme.' He opened the file and picked out the top sheet. 'This is a report from one of our men in London. The political situation has been a potential disaster area ever since the Liberal coalition took power.'

'I thought that suited our purpose,' said Bruce, remembering the shock waves that ran through the West some six months ago. The general election had seen an alliance of Liberals, various disenfranchised Tories and Socialists, and a group of minor fringe parties, enter power on a popular platform of social reform, the abolition of the death penalty, and a strong interstellar defence programme.

'In a manner of speaking.'

'Can't blame the Brits, I suppose,' noted Bruce with a thin

smile. 'Four invasions in the last four years. They always seem to get the bugs landing on their doorstep.'

'It's made them trigger-happy and reckless. Last night there was another National Front by-election victory.' Control glanced at a communiqué that sat in his in tray. 'Place called Walthamstow.'

Bruce nodded, having read a report on the subway. 'That's six now,' he said.

'Indeed. They give the people easy answers, and promise strength against the aliens. And, when you've seen Cybermen marching down your street, there's a lot to be said for easy answers.' Control picked up another report. 'That suits us, of course. Subvert the British space programme. Make sure they don't get their hands on any reusable technology.' He laughed, harshly. 'Let them play with their International Electromatics toys, their vid-phones and disposable transistors.'

Bruce shared in the joke, but he sensed there was something more serious coming. 'If Britain's such a disaster area, why not just leave them and concentrate on Paraguay? Surely the potential for a zero-option situation there is stronger?'

'Paraguay will be kicking-off big time, but not for another year. The Chinese and the Russians are still not ready for war, either with each other, or with anyone else.'

'Do we get involved?'

'Is Uncle Sam an American?' Control's eyes were grey and hard. 'We'll show no hesitation when the situation can be used to our advantage. Let Styles and that Texan jerk Alcott organise their conferences. *We* know where it'll all end.' Control flicked through the file. 'British UNIT worries us. They're the most experienced on the planet, and we need to get somebody in there.'

'Meaning me?'

Control didn't answer. He pulled three photographs from the manila folder. The first was of a woman with red hair and bright, lively eyes. 'Dr Elizabeth Shaw, born Stoke-on-Trent, 1943. Research scientist at Cambridge, seconded to UNIT last summer. Meteor expert, medical doctor, quantum physicist...'

'Pretty girl,' said Bruce, reaching for the photograph.

'...with an IQ of over two hundred. Dangerous.' Control released the photograph to Bruce, then tapped the second, a man in uniform. 'Brigadier Alistair Gordon Lethbridge-Stewart. Head of British UNIT. Don't let the reputation fool you. Brilliant career in Africa and Aden, a great leader. His encounters with extraterrestrials will make him an extremely dangerous opponent. If we're to stand any chance of cracking them, we need to dispose of Lethbridge-Stewart. With terminal force.'

'And the other one?' asked Bruce.

'Ah.' The meaningless interjection and the length of the ensuing pause were enough to pique Bruce's interest. 'Scientific Adviser,' said Control at last, standing and walking towards the window. 'As you'll see, we've not got much on him.'

Bruce stared at a typewritten sheet of six lines, attached to four reports with observations by agents in the field. 'This is ridiculous,' he said at length. 'There's nothing in this but speculation. "There are strong rumours at UNIT HQ that the Doctor is an extraterrestrial"...' Bruce looked up, and saw a dark shadow flicker across Control's face as he turned away from the New York skyline. Bruce shook his head. 'We don't even know his name,' he said.

Control gave a short, harsh laugh. '*We* know much more than that.'

PART 1: ANY FRONTIER

CHAPTER 1

With a dark, ominous drone of rotor blades, the helicopters buzzed over the festival site. To those inside, Viscount Rose's estate was a sea change of colour: bright, gaudy, Day-Glo shades of purple, yellow, and red, splashes of paint that ebbed and flowed to an organic rhythm.

The helicopters worried Nick Blair. There was something sinister and almost Wagnerian about the way they had appeared in convoy from out of the clouds, and scudded across the sky, swooping close to the stage.

Stoned Weekend, who had been entertaining the crowd with their interpretation of southern boogie, had stopped mid-song. 'Look, man,' the singer had said dismissively. 'I can't handle dive-bombing fascists. This isn't Vietnam. There weren't these distractions at Tanglewood…'

Half the crowd – those whose brains hadn't been numbed by the sun, the loud music, and the drugs – had coughed up a reaction that could have been a fists-in-the-air cheer of anti-establishment solidarity or a bemused murmur of 'Where the hell's Tanglewood, man?'

The entire festival was in danger of becoming a farce.

Nick Blair blamed himself. Well, no, he blamed the expectations of an audience who'd seen *Woodstock – The Movie* and thought *that* was what Redborough '70 was going to be all about. But, unfortunately, these things cost money. The bands who sang about peace, love, and freedom needed to support their country estates and heroin habits; the guys who'd built the stage were on union rates and the local council wanted a piece of the action just for allowing the thing to go ahead.

Nick, a veteran of two Isle of Wights, had been employed to bring Viscount Rose's vision to life. But even Rose's pockets had a bottom, and that had been reached long before Nick was anywhere near booking the Grateful Dead or Jimi Hendrix. The response from the Who's management team had been typical: the band would be half-way into a world tour and, incidentally, the fee's a flat quarter-of-a-million. The answer from Dylan's manager had been even more cutting: 'Where the hell is Redborough?'

So Nick had done the only thing he could: booked lots of second-division rock bands whose labels were keen to get them on to the prestigious festival circuit, a couple of folkie songwriters who wanted the exposure, and, of course, Glandring the Forehammer ('It's from *The Lord of the Rings*, man'). Quite how he'd secured the services of the leaders of the flowering Northampton sci-fi commune scene was still the subject of much debate. In truth, Nick had simply promised more money than was actually available, got them to the site, and then told them that if they didn't go on, he would announce that they were a bunch of uptight breadheads who were refusing to play. There was already a group of French anarchists going around trying to tear down the fences, so Glandring the Forehammer ('It's from *The Lord of the Rings*, man') wisely decided to take the stage and perform an acoustic version of their concept triple-album *Lederhosen, Restaurant, Benzedrine, Fusilier*.

The helicopters continued wheeling overhead.

'We're into the progressive scene,' said Glandring's singer/lyricist Zak Wigmore. Zak was in the middle of a rant about how Glandring's music was a product of society, the war, and of his being thrashed by his nanny as a six-year-old after she caught him trying on her underwear. He then introduced 'Gemini Descending', a free-form jazz workout in which

12

saxophonist Mac played whatever he felt like and Zak bellowed incoherent poetry at the audience. It was the closest thing they had to a pop single. Then, just as Zak was getting to the bit about Venus being 'like a penis' (that always got a good reaction), he pointed to the sky. 'Far out!' he said loudly. For a split second the rest of the band thought it was just the industrial-strength acid sucking his brains out through a straw, like that time in Doncaster when he confidently stated that electricity comes from other planets. Then they looked at the sky too. And stopped playing.

Nick Blair saw the lights a second after Zak. The sky was awash with colour, a shimmering pyrotechnical display. Some time ago he had watched a large meteor shower over America, but this was different, more magical and otherworldly. He stared until the diffuse patterns began to hurt his eyes.

On stage, Zak had the microphone and was taking a message from the planet Freak-Out. 'What you are witnessing,' he said, 'is the dawning of the Age of Aquarius. It's in Revelation, people. They're coming. They're going to wipe the Earth clean. And we can all live in the sea like dolphins. Or crabs...'

Everyone was looking at the sky now, a cloth of gold daubed with blood and fire. A ball of flame crashed into the sea with a gushing hiss that brought an ecstatic moan from the onlookers. And then the lights in the sky faded. The festival watched in awe as a mist began to reach out to them from the water.

Nick glanced at the stage. Zak picked up a fallen microphone and asked the band if they knew the chords to 'Fly Me to the Moon'.

Close to the edge of the festival grounds, Becky and Ray were holding each other. They were from Norwich, and it had taken them four days to hitch-hike here. By the time they arrived, every decent vantage point was taken and they were at the back of a two-hundred-thousand-person queue for the toilets. So, they did what any sensible young couple would do in the circumstances: they went down on to the deserted beach and made love during Glandring the Forehammer's set.

'Look at the sky,' said Becky, breathlessly.

'Yeah,' grunted a slightly underwhelmed Ray. 'Awesome.'

'Let's go for a swim, and be in harmony with the ocean,' continued Becky with a blissful look in her eyes.

Ray shrugged impassively. 'OK,' he said. They ran naked into the cool, frothing water, surging through the surf up to their thighs, then their chests. Becky giggled. Ray was cross, but curiously excited.

They touched in the moonlight, the gentle waves lapping around them, their skin like marble in the blue-white light. Becky's face was porcelain, with dark wet hair swept back out of her eyes. Ray felt a surge of sexual energy. He wanted her, here and now.

'Ow!' Her stifled cry shattered the moment. She looked down into the water, her face almost touching the rippling surface. 'I've just stood on a stone, or...' Her voice trailed away as she saw the water change colour around her. 'Ray,' she said, her voice trembling, 'there's something in the water –' She stopped again. Ray was gone, with hardly a sound – a small splash, no more.

'Ray!' she screamed. There was a sudden shooting pain down the side of one leg, as if numerous razorlike teeth were ripping at her flesh. The water rushed upward to cover her face. Her arms pinwheeled, thrashing at the sea, but the only replying sound – muffled and booming through the suffocating water – was that of a fully blooded Glandring the Forehammer ('it's from *The Lord of the Rings,* man') starting 'Journey to the Centre of the Sun', all eighteen minutes of it. Long before the first guitar solo, Becky was swallowed by the blackness that was all around her.

CHAPTER 2

Sergeant Benton and some of the men had a running joke about the Doctor's laboratory. Whenever anyone turned up at UNIT HQ to see Liz Shaw or the Doctor himself, they were pointed in the general direction of the lab and then advised to follow their senses. Almost without exception there would be a pungent odour to follow, or an explosion would rattle the building's foundations, or a creeping glow would advance down the corridor. At the very least one could normally hear the Doctor cursing in Venusian as another experiment went wrong.

But today the corridor that led to the Doctor's room was eerily quiet. The door was half closed, but Benton thought he'd better knock anyway. 'Doctor, are you in here?'

There was no reply. Benton knocked again, pushed open the door, and stepped gingerly inside.

As usual the room was packed to overflowing with oscilloscopes, flasks, soldering irons and Bunsen burners. It was quite impossible to tell exactly what the Doctor was working on. On a bench close to the door a spherical glass ball bubbled and pulsed, as if the Doctor's current interest was biological, but towards the back of the room Benton noticed a complex rigging of microphones, portable power generators, and a Marshall amplifier. Perhaps the Doctor was working on a countermeasure against sonic attack.

In the centre of the room was the old police box that housed much of the Doctor's equipment. He had stated on many occasions that this device – his TARDIS – could travel through time and space, and Benton had no reason to disbelieve him. Although much of what the Doctor claimed seemed to be impossible, he was almost always proved correct in the end. A strange bloke, then, but certainly someone to trust when an alien invasion force was heaving into view.

For some time now Benton had made sure that he was first in line for any assignment that involved UNIT's mysterious scientific adviser. Hero worship wasn't something that Sergeant John Benton, DSO, could really claim to understand, but he knew that he would have to wait a very long time to meet someone as remarkable as the Doctor again.

'Doctor?' Benton walked around the TARDIS to the doors on the far side. Both were open, and the Doctor's velvet trousers and sturdy shoes projected through the doorway at floor level. He looked to all the world like a mechanic under a Cortina.

'Are you flanging the whatsit on the glonthometer again, Doctor?'

'I'm fine, thank you, Sergeant,' came the muffled reply. It was as if he was in a different room. 'I'm a bit busy, you know – unless you want to help, of course. Liz is off somewhere, and there's only so much one pair of hands can do. You could start by passing me that perigosto stick on the bench over there.'

'Sorry, Doctor, bit pushed for time myself. The Brigadier told me to hand you this.' Benton looked down at the sheet of paper.

'What's "this"?'

'A report from the UNIT radar station in Sussex.'

'What does it say?'

Benton sighed. 'It says they picked up a large mass approaching the Earth, but it fragmented somewhere in the ionosphere.'

'Burnt up you mean?'

'No, not exactly.' Benton scanned the report again. '"Despite fragmentation, there was no measurable reduction in mass."'

'Really?' For the first time the Doctor's muffled voice sounded a little interested. 'That does sound most peculiar. Oh, well, put the report over there' – a finger emerged from gloom of the TARDIS doorway and pointed in the general direction of one of the benches – 'and I'll read it later.'

Benton cleared his throat. 'Actually, Doctor, the Brigadier was hoping that you could go over and investigate immediately.'

'Why? Nothing's landed, has it?'

'Not that we know of.'

'Then surely it can wait, Sergeant?'

'Well, you see, the Brigadier is more interested in you giving the radar station the once over.' Benton stared up at the ceiling, knowing what would come next. 'No one else picked up this meteor, and … The station is using special equipment that you designed after the Auton incident. The Brigadier thinks your radar must be up the creek.'

'"Up the creek"?' The Doctor suddenly appeared in the doorway, having jumped to his feet. 'I'll have you know that that station is now the most advanced on Earth! If it detected something, then there was something there to detect.'

'I'm sure you're right,' said Benton. 'But it's what the Brigadier ordered.'

The Doctor reached for the cape that hung behind the door. 'Come on, we'd better drive down there. But in future, do get straight to the point, eh?' He hurried towards the door. 'I can't stand people who dither.'

Dr Elizabeth Shaw glanced down at the scrap of paper in her hand for the hundredth time, checked it against the number of the terraced house, and rang the bell. The air was still and silent, and the noise of the buzzer seemed to echo some distance inside. Footsteps thumped down the stairs, and then the door flew open.

'Mark!' Liz blurted out; it was all she could say before her mouth went dry.

The man was in his late twenties, tall, to the point of almost brushing the door frame with his hair, and well built. A fading bruise around one eye – doubtless from intervarsity rugger – contrasted with small pebble glasses and the sort of cardigan that only students are ever seen in. 'Liz! Great to see you. Please, come in.'

The moment the door was closed he gave her an embarrassed but genuine hug, then led her towards the kitchen. It was narrow, and made dark by the shadow of the next house. Mark flicked on a strip light, and then filled the kettle.

Liz dropped her suitcase on to the floor and massaged her tingling hands. 'You've not changed,' she said at last.

'What?'

'The light.' Liz indicated the other neon tube, left off despite the gloom. 'Always Mr Frugal.'

'Mr Almost Zero Income, more like,' said Mark. 'It's all right for some people, swanning around the place with the UN picking up the tab, but the rest of us are still living in the real world.' There was laughter in his voice, but Liz knew it concealed a real criticism.

'But then some of us could have worked on one of the cheap electricity research schemes, rather than selling our soul to British Rocket Group.' Liz couldn't believe it: she'd barely said hello and already they were arguing in that coded way of theirs.

Mark smiled, and leant back against the cooker. 'You forget, my dear – I have no soul!'

Liz shook her head, blinking against the memories. 'I never believed that for a moment.'

'You always see the best in people. Sometimes that can be as blinding as prejudice.'

'*You're* always too eager to do yourself down.' Liz scanned the room: the fridge festooned with postcards from around the world; the shelves carrying exotic Chinese ingredients, doubtless bought as part of a short-lived attempt to enjoy a cuisine beyond scrambled egg and beans on toast; the general air of grime and cheerful neglect. Her eyes latched on to a girlie calendar in the little hallway that led to the downstairs toilet.

'Not mine, I hasten to add,' said Mark.

'Of course,' said Liz.

Mark handed her a cup of tea, and she began spooning in the sugar.

'You never used to take sugar,' he observed.

'Army tea – it's unique. After thirteen months I'm starting to acquire a taste for it.'

'And army life in general?'

'It's not like I've been conscripted or anything,' explained Liz. 'I can leave whenever I want.'

'Really? That's not the impression I get.'

'No, it's true. I'm always on the verge of leaving.'

'Then why don't you?' Mark came over, and for one awful moment Liz thought he was going to hold her hand or something. But he stopped short, and beamed his most disarming smile. 'You gave up your ground-breaking research to go off with some mad foreign professor who sees a UFO in every abduction and a primeval force behind every crop circle. Why do you stay with them, Liz? You said you hated it at first.'

Mark led the way into the sitting room, flicking off the kitchen light as he went. Liz followed, sipping her tea. 'I did hate it. But… Oh, I don't know. Perhaps I'm learning that there are important things going on, beyond the dusty halls of academia.'

Mark snorted, sprawling in a large armchair. Foam leaked on to the brown carpet. 'You were the one who used to disagree with me when I said there's more to life than books.'

'I was joking.'

'I'm not so sure.'

'Times change. People change.' Liz tried to get herself comfortable. 'It's like I said in my last letter. I suppose it's as simple as that.'

Mark smiled again. 'Same old Liz. You were saying that when I first got to know you.'

'I remember saying to Wellington one day – "Nosey," I said…'

John Benton would normally have allowed the mistake to go uncorrected. His respect and admiration for the Doctor knew no bounds, and he realised that, as with all good storytellers, many of the Doctor's tales were at best apocryphal and at worst utterly fabricated. But Benton felt curiously liberated by the wind rushing through his hair and the sun that painted the landscape on one of the first cloudless days of summer. 'Napoleon,' he interjected quickly.

'I beg your pardon?' said the Doctor, clearly annoyed at being contradicted in mid-sentence.

'Last time you told me this story, it was Napoleon,' said Benton sheepishly. He knew the Brigadier wouldn't have tolerated such an interjection, but then he didn't share the Doctor's fully developed sense of humour. Actually, that wasn't really fair on the Brig. Some time ago it had dawned on Benton that – underneath their vastly different exteriors – the Doctor and the Brigadier were remarkably similar in temperament and outlook. Both were men of integrity, passion and honour, and Benton would willingly have walked into a withering barrage of gunfire for either.

'Really,' said the Doctor huffily. He paused for a moment and Benton held his breath, fearing that he had caused offence. But the Doctor was just changing gears on his yellow roadster Bessie, the road having flattened out again. He dabbed the accelerator and turned to face Benton with a beaming smile. 'My dear fellow, I spent a considerable length of time in the Peninsula. I was with a British rifle brigade when I met Sir Arthur Wellesley. And I was a prisoner of the French at Salamanca – 1812 I think it was. I always find it's best to see both sides of both sides, if you see what I mean.'

'I didn't really think you approved of war, sir,' said Benton.

The Doctor turned his attention back to the twisting country lane. He sighed as he changed gear for another sharp corner. 'Sometimes it's inevitable,' he noted with genuine sadness. 'I'm a man of peace, but I seem to spend much of my time caught up in conflict. The central paradox of my life, perhaps.'

Benton leant back in the seat. 'What's the central paradox of mine?' he asked, fascinated.

'You're far too intelligent for your role in life, Sergeant Benton.'

Benton smiled. 'I'm not so sure, Doctor. I like to know where I stand, and what's expected of me. The army offers me that. Or at least it *did*, until I first bumped into you.'

The Doctor missed the last comment, his eyes far away. 'You know, I'm reminded of the time I met Puccini in Milan...'

Something flickered to their left, a bright light through the shadows of the hedgerows. Probably just the sun glinting off a greenhouse or a wing mirror, thought Benton.

The noise of gunfire came a moment later.

Liz sat on the bed and unpacked her suitcase, deep in thought. The spare room was right at the top of the terrace, the only room on the third storey. It reminded her of a suburban Rapunzel's tower, the roof rising to a mock turret just above the window. The house was as quiet as when she had first arrived, but Mark's new friends would be back soon. For the moment Liz welcomed the peace.

Mark Wilson had moved house soon after Liz had left Cambridge to begin working for UNIT: it was strange to see him in an unfamiliar location, stranger still when so much water had passed under the bridge. Or had it? Mark clearly seemed to think that she was just the same old Liz, and certainly their conversation had been as complex as ever. It was so difficult to tell when Mark was using humour to make a serious point and when he was just trying to make her laugh. Their relationship –

such as it was – had always been like that, as if they communicated in two different versions of the same basic code. Their inability to be truly honest with each other had finally scuppered any hint of something more serious and intimate, but, much as Liz would like to think otherwise, she still felt an attraction towards the man, for all his faults.

And it's not like you're little Miss Perfect, she reminded herself.

Still, it was good to be back in Cambridge, but she felt a certain melancholy that the place and the people she had once known so well had so successfully continued without her. She was an alien in a land made strange by the merest shift of time; perhaps that was how the Doctor always felt.

She left her suitcase half unpacked on the bed, and descended the two flights of stairs. Mark was watching the television in the gloom, a childlike expression on his face. He hadn't heard her come down, despite the creaking floorboards of the hallway. She watched him for a moment, his strong features standing out in profile, and wondered what would have happened if she had stayed.

She coughed self-consciously and walked into the room, returning to the uncomfortable sofa.

'Nice room, eh?' said Mark, still watching the television – one of his more annoying habits. 'We all agreed that the guest room should always be tidy and ready for use. And because we hardly ever go in there it is.'

A face appeared on the television, a face Liz recognised. 'Ah, I see now why you're so interested. Bernard's looking well,' she said.

'Indeed. He's changed a lot since you left.'

'I notice he's still dodging the questions about British Rocket Group's latest unmanned mission to Neptune.'

'You can't blame him, can you? He wants to make sure that everyone comes to the press conference he's organised. Anyway, we haven't finished analysing the data yet.'

'And you're clearly rushed off your feet.' Liz's comment

sounded a little more sarcastic than she had intended.

'They owe me far more than an afternoon off,' replied Mark, oblivious to anything but the news report. 'Anyway, you can only look at so many figures and blurred photographs in one day.' The newsreader's face appeared, and Mark got to his feet, walking over to the television to turn down the sound. 'I wish we could afford one of those new IE remote-controlled TVs,' he said, returning to his seat and looking at Liz for the first time.

'But then think of all that exercise you'd miss,' she said, smiling sweetly.

Four rapid shots took out Bessie's far-side tyres.

'Holy cow,' shouted Benton as the little car howled its own protest amid the squeal of punctured rubber. 'We're under attack!'

'So it seems,' said the Doctor without a hint of irony as he fought to control the car's steering. 'Brace yourself!' The Doctor swung the car towards the nearest hedgerow, gritting his teeth against the pull to one side. The steering wheel shuddered under his hands. He worked at the brakes, deftly avoiding locking the wheels, and Bessie skidded through the hedge. Both Benton and the Doctor were thrown forward as the car ground to a halt, the yellow bonnet wedged firmly into a freshly ploughed field.

'Damn it!' said Benton. 'My rifle's back at HQ. The Brigadier will give me hell about this malarkey.'

The Doctor glanced towards Benton and gave him an infuriating grin. 'Good job you haven't got it. Terrible things, guns. You look as if you've been dragged through a hedge backwards, Sergeant Benton.' He jumped from Bessie, patting the side of the car affectionately. 'There, there, old girl; worse things happen at sea.'

Benton went to step down on to the field, but the Doctor stopped him. 'No, Sergeant, you stay and get on the radio.'

With that the Doctor disappeared through the hole in the

hedge and stepped out on to the road. He brushed dirt from his velvet jacket as his eyes scanned the hedgerows.

He saw his attackers a moment before they emerged from their foxholes in the undergrowth. There were four of them, dressed completely in black, with boot-polished faces and balaclavas. Only one carried a rifle; the other three seemed to be unarmed. The Doctor watched with a mixture of curiosity, understanding, and anger as the dark figures came closer, their movements precise and balletic.

'Do I take it that you gentlemen were attempting to attract my attention?' the Doctor asked reasonably. There was no reply. 'I notice that your large friend is carrying a Simonov SKS automatic machine gun,' he said conspiratorially towards the closest attacker. 'In which case I assume you are members of the Spetsnaz. My congratulations, gentlemen, an almost textbook ambush.' Again there was no response.

The Doctor tried again, this time in Russian. The flicker of recognition in their eyes indicated that they understood him, but still they said nothing.

The man closest to the Doctor stepped forward, then, with catlike elegance, assumed an attacking posture, feet wide apart, one arm outstretched.

'You seem to be a martial-arts expert of some description,' the Doctor said, barely suppressing a smile. 'I should warn you that I am a tenth dan master in all of the major disciplines: Venusian aikido, Saturnian kung-fu. I trained as a Ninja on Quinnis in Galaxy Four. I'm not boasting, you understand. But I don't believe a physical confrontation is in either of our interests.'

No sooner had the words left his lips than the man attacked. It was a classic frontal karate assault, step-kick-grab, practised on a parade ground until the moves were automatic. The man's hands were doubtless considered deadly weapons in his homeland but the Doctor parried the move easily, chopping the man to the

24

ground with an exaggerated cry of '*Haiii*!'

The other men looked stunned by the ease with which the Doctor had dealt with their colleague, but before another could take his place they were distracted by a cry from further down the road. Benton had emerged with a large tree branch in his hands to use as a weapon. The attackers turned, and the man with the rifle raised it quickly to his shoulder.

'No!' the Doctor shouted. 'There's no need for anyone to die, gentlemen,' he added quickly. The two unarmed men turned back towards the Doctor, their companion continuing to train his gun on Benton. 'Sergeant,' the Doctor said with a resigned smile, 'you really do have the most irritating habit of doing the wrong thing at the wrong time. Drop the weapon and stay very still. We can sort this out peacefully.'

Benton complied. Although the gun remained on him, the armed man lowered it slightly.

The Doctor spoke to his attackers in Russian. 'You realise, of course, that the sergeant will have contacted the military by now. Within minutes this entire area will be crawling with jackbooted bully boys who fire first and ask questions later. UNIT are known for their shoot-to-kill policy. And you wouldn't want to die on a nice day like this for no good reason, would you?' As his voice trailed away, he could hear the distant sounds of a helicopter engine. He pointed to the sky. 'You've got two minutes. Run.'

The three men looked at each other, then back towards the Doctor. As one, they sprinted into the shadows of the road, and out on to the fields.

Benton stood rooted to the spot, watching the Doctor walk towards him as if nothing out of the ordinary had happened. 'What was all that about?' asked the soldier.

'Part rationalism, part hypnotic suggestion. I've always been quite good at that sort of thing. As I am at saving your life, seemingly.' His final words were drowned by the noise of the incoming helicopter. A tall, dark-moustached soldier dropped to the ground just before the helicopter landed. He carried a Browning 9mm pistol in one hand, and was followed by four heavily armed UNIT soldiers.

'Ah, Lethbridge-Stewart,' said the Doctor amicably. 'I'd appreciate it if you could have a few of your stout fellows get my car out of that field. Poor old thing.'

'Doctor, what on Earth happened?'

'A minor incident, Brigadier, nothing more,' said the Doctor.

'Sergeant Benton!' barked the Brigadier. 'Report!'

'Sir,' said Benton, snapping to attention. 'Some five minutes beyond the base we were attacked by four men, one of them armed. He shot at the car, hitting the tyres. The Doctor fought off this man' – he pointed to the prone figure of the Doctor's first attacker – 'and the other three… escaped, sir.'

The Brigadier inspected the man on the ground, and then stood up, shaking his head. 'We won't get much out of him, I'm afraid. He's dead.'

'That's impossible,' said the Doctor, horrified. 'I barely touched the man.' He knelt down, checked for a pulse, and then stared closely at the man's face and lips. 'Cyanide capsule,' he said flatly. 'He'd rather die than be captured.' He felt a moment's anger and slapped his palm on to the ground next to the body. 'I abhor needless death, Brigadier!'

'I agree, Doctor. And your death would have been particularly unnecessary,' replied the Brigadier.

'Don't be a fool, Lethbridge-Stewart. If they had wanted me dead they could have killed me at any stage. They could have shot me, instead of Bessie's tyres. No, they were trying to kidnap me.' The Doctor paused and looked into the shadows of the road as if the answers lay there. 'I wonder why…'

'I for one don't intend to give them a chance to satisfy your curiosity, Doctor. From now on you will be accompanied at all times by at least three armed men.'

'That's ridiculous!' protested the Doctor.

'You say that about most of my decisions, Doctor,' said Lethbridge-Stewart, turning back towards the helicopter as if the conversation was at an end.

'And I'm usually right,' commented the Doctor under his breath as the Brigadier clambered into the cockpit.

'I think we saw history last night,' said Billy Fleming. 'A vision of what's to come.' He gestured in the direction the lane was taking them.

Susannah smiled the same spaced-out smile she'd had since about 7.30 that morning. 'The Great Gig in the Sky. That's what they'll call it.'

'And, man, we were *there*,' said Billy. 'Right in the centre of it.'

Chuck nodded, deep in thought. 'I wonder what that sky thing was – literally, I mean, because I don't want to deny the validity of the subjective experience…'

Billy and Susannah glanced at each other and smiled. Both thought Chuck odd, but over the last couple of days they'd grown to like him. He was an American, slightly older than their nineteen or so years, and had claimed to be into the music more than the drugs. His detachment – his desperate attempts to force his 'square-peg' character into the round hole of the festival scene – was charming rather than embarrassing.

'It was, like, the ancient gods coming out of the stone circles and having a party.' Billy started coughing, which at least interrupted his free-form interpretation of the message of the lights in the sky.

Susannah giggled. 'No, I thought it was like the Earth Mother lying back and –'

'I don't think I really want to know this,' said Chuck. He stopped and looked around. It was now getting dark, and, he had to admit, one country lane looked much the same as any other.

27

'You sure we're going the right way?'

'Geographically or spiritually, do you mean?' asked Billy with a knowing smile.

'Geographically,' said Chuck, rising to the bait as usual.

'Yeah, of course we are.' Billy nodded confidently. 'I think.'

'Spiritually, we are *definitely* going the right way. No one's going to control the kids any longer,' said Susannah. 'We'll do what we want. It's like Glandring the Forehammer said –'

'It's from *The Lord of the Rings*, maaaaan,' said Billy, giggling.

'You've got to break down the barricades of your own soul before you can even think about –'

'We're lost,' announced Chuck finally. 'I hope your friends in the caravan will wait for us.'

''Course they will,' replied Billy. 'Faz and Justin are, like, totally together. Still, we ought to stop soon. We could walk for miles in the dark and end up off Rose's land. I don't wanna get hassled by the locals.'

'Look,' said Susannah helpfully, pointing a purple-nailed finger through the gloom. 'There's a barn. We could get some sleep there, wait for morning.'

It was the first sensible thing Susannah had said all day, and it took Billy by surprise. 'What, you mean, like, go for a roll in the hay?'

Susannah gave him a withering look.

'Well, we'll just have to hang loose, see how the evening progresses,' he mumbled, ever the optimist.

Chuck was the first to the barn. It was an old building right on the edge of a field, the holes in the ancient timbered roof having been hastily made secure with corrugated iron. The door was padlocked, but there was a large window around one side, the panes of glass long gone. With barely a pause Billy pulled at the rotten wooden frame until the whole unit came away in his hands. He laughed like a schoolkid as he tumbled backward.

'Well, I'm sure Mr Rose won't mind,' said Chuck. 'We'll try to put the frame back in place tomorrow morning.'

Susannah sighed, flashed Chuck a brief *you-haven't-got-a-clue-have-you?* look, and pulled her long tie-died skirt up around her waist. Chuck found himself staring at her shapely legs as she disappeared into the barn, then realised what he had been doing, and was grateful that no one could see his red-faced embarrassment in the dark.

Billy had no qualms about staring at the girl. 'I think I'm bloody in here, mate,' he said.

Hours later, Billy woke from a crazed sexual fantasy with an unbearable pressure on his bladder.

He groped around in the dark, knocking into Chuck, who was snoring loudly. Susannah was right at the far end of the barn, having found some straw to sleep on. He vaguely remembered her making some heavy threat along the lines of 'Either of you comes near me in the night and I'll have your goolies for breakfast', and decided against trying his luck.

He walked towards the window, the grey hedges and dark sky glimmering against the pitch-black interior of the barn. He pulled himself through without injury – no mean feat – and walked a few paces around the side of the barn. Unzipped his flies. Felt waves of relief. Man, something he'd drunk over the last few hours had gone straight through him.

He made the usual patterns against the stones and then, bored, stared upward at the sky, watching the clouds passing over the pinpoint brightness of the stars. Being a lad from the city, he'd never seen the stars as bright and as close as this.

He was doing up his flies when he heard something land on top of the barn. He glimpsed inky-black, flapping wings. There was a guttural noise not unlike a cough, sounding like a gunshot in the still darkness. Probably just a crow.

Billy walked back towards the empty window frame. There was a scrabbling sound from the roof, as if the crow was keeping pace with him. He glanced up, but could see nothing. For some reason his heart was pounding. Perhaps it was just the thought of going back inside, close to where the gorgeous Susannah slept.

He placed one foot on the windowsill, about to push himself through.

Without warning something smashed into his back. He lost his balance, swayed forward – then felt what seemed like a claw on his arm, pulling him backward.

He tumbled on to the grass, face up. Night sky. Comforting clouds. Just a bad trip. Perhaps –

With an otherworldly screech a creature, dark and flapping, arced down towards him from the sky, talons outstretched.

CHAPTER 3

One of the disadvantages of having to change UNIT HQ with the regularity that befitted a secret organisation was that you were never truly at home anywhere. At least, that's the way it seemed to Brigadier Lethbridge-Stewart. No sooner had the dust settled from one move than they would be off again. It made continuity a big problem.

And few things irritated the Brigadier more than discontinuity.

The daily file of normal UNIT business, brought to him by his adjutant Corporal Bell, was the usual mixture of interesting oddities, absurd speculation, and sensationalist rubbish. He glanced at the reports with disinterest. The first was from a police chief superintendent concerning several strange crop circles found over the last few months around Polesworth in Warwickshire. Could they, the policeman wondered, be connected with recent alien threats to Britain? The Brigadier scribbled a quick note to the effect that the chief superintendent would be better employed checking out the activities of young farmers after closing time at the local. A similar query from a constable in Wiltshire was also dismissed. A much more interesting report came from an RAF base in Leicestershire. Two pilots flying back from a night exercise near the town of Coalville had a close encounter with a bright, glowing object. Radio communication between the Harriers and the ground was lost for over a minute, and both RAF men reported that after having encountered a blinding light they had no memory of the ensuing period.

Lethbridge-Stewart noted the file for further investigation. The reports were remarkably similar to those UNIT had received at the time of the Cyber invasion. 'Get the Doctor to have a look at that one, I think,' he said, and moved on to a report on increased radiation levels in the Solent just as his intercom buzzed.

'I have Professor Trainor on line three for you, sir,' said Carol Bell.

'Put him through,' said the Brigadier. Another distraction. As a favour to Ralph Cornish, who had recently been appointed to overall command of the British space programme, UNIT were to provide security for a press luncheon which was to announce the results of British Rocket Group's latest unmanned mission to Uranus and Neptune. Professor Bernard Trainor was the man under whose direction the mission had provided much valuable information about these two mysterious planets. The Brigadier had met Trainor once, at the launch of the spacecraft the previous year, and had found him to be a charming if somewhat absent-minded man.

'Good morning, Professor,' he said brightly. 'What can I do for you?'

'Brigadier?' replied Trainor, as though expecting someone else. 'How are you?'

'I'm well,' said the Brigadier, casting his eyes towards the ceiling. 'Is there something you need?' He didn't really have the time for pleasantries. At this moment, Captain Mike Yates entered the office and the Brigadier threw him an exasperated glance.

'I was just… That is… The press luncheon…' said the professor.

'Of course, Professor,' soothed the Brigadier. 'The arrangements are in hand. My liaison officer should be with you shortly to deal with any last-minute problems that you, or we, may have.' He covered the telephone mouthpiece with his hand and growled at Yates to have a seat.

'Professor Trainor, sir?' asked Yates with a mischievous grin.

'Third call in the last two days,' said Lethbridge-Stewart before returning his attention to the professor. He was asking, in his own unique way, whether an old student of his who was, he understood, currently working for UNIT, could be spared for the luncheon. 'You must appreciate, Professor, that UNIT's work has security implications, and that I'm not able to give specific details

32

about any of our staff. That information is classified.' He was about to begin quoting the Official Secrets Act when he detected disappointment in the professor's voice and asked who the person in question was.

'Dr Elizabeth Shaw,' said the professor. It was the straightest answer that Lethbridge-Stewart had ever heard the professor give.

'That's a coincidence,' he said. 'Dr Shaw *is* my liaison officer. I imagine she'll be with you quite soon. Good day, Professor.' And with that he put the phone down before the old man could add anything further. 'No wonder she was so keen to do this,' said the Brigadier, half to himself. 'I expected a lecture on how it was demeaning for someone of her abilities to have to trail up to Cambridge like an errand girl...' The Brigadier stared at Yates with a suspicious look on his face. 'Did you know anything about this, Captain?'

'No, sir,' said Yates. 'I wasn't even aware that Liz was working this weekend.'

'Well, anyway, I have a small job for you, too.'

'If you want me to go back to my old school, sir, I'm afraid the answer's no: I don't think they'd be too thrilled to see me!' Ice formed on the upper reaches of the Brigadier. 'Sorry, sir, just a joke.'

'No one enjoys a good joke more than I do, Captain,' said the Brigadier. 'But...' He paused. 'Was there a specific reason why you came to see me?'

'Two reasons, sir,' said Yates, clearly relieved to have escaped the wrath of Lethbridge-Stewart with his rank intact. 'Firstly, I've just received this memo from the Home Office. I'm afraid they've turned down your request to D-notice that pop record you were concerned about. The one about Mars, sir.'

Lethbridge-Stewart tapped the desktop angrily. 'Bureaucratic oafs. That song's obviously based on leaked information concerning the Carrington fiasco.' The Brigadier took the memo from Yates and scanned it for a moment, searching for loopholes.

'Yates, I want this Bowery chap placed under twenty-four-hour surveillance. If he so much as sneezes I want to know about it.'

'Understood, sir,' said Yates, saluting. 'And sir, I have Bruce Davis outside.'

'Who?'

'The new crash retrieval officer from New York.'

Lethbridge-Stewart nodded. 'Well, you'd better show him in, Captain. We don't want the Americans to think we're all bungling incompetents, do we?'

The morning after the attempted kidnap, the Doctor was again travelling down the country lanes between UNIT HQ and the tracking station. On this occasion the journey was uneventful, if less comfortable: the rigid metal seating of an armoured personnel carrier was no match for Bessie's forgiving, leather-clad seats. The conversation, too, had taken a turn for the worse, Benton joining in the ribald banter of the accompanying UNIT troops and seeming to have little time for the introspection of the previous day. When they finally reached the radar station, the Doctor was both relieved and delighted to find that one of the technicians working at the station was Sam, a young American whom he had personally recruited to UNIT's research-and-development wing during a lecture tour of the United States the previous year. 'I see they've given you the most boring job imaginable,' said the Doctor.

'It could be worse, Dr Smith,' said the young man. 'I could be making the tea!'

The Doctor immediately set about examining the equipment, Benton looking over his shoulder. 'This machinery is working perfectly,' the Doctor concluded triumphantly after several minutes.

'Never doubted it,' replied Benton with a hint of sarcasm.

'Ah, but the Brigadier did. I really wish that man would listen to what I say once in a while.' He turned to face Sam. 'Were you here when the large mass was picked up?' he asked.

'Yes. It frightened me to death. At first I thought it was just a meteor, but it was about the size of Rhode Island. If that had hit the Earth…'

'I know,' said the Doctor sympathetically. 'What happened next?'

'Well, this is the really interesting thing. The mass began to disintegrate, just as you would expect with a meteor. But the fragmentation seemed too uniform – as if it was choreographed. I remember what you said at MIT about looking for anomalies when watching the skies, so I logged it immediately.'

But the Doctor wasn't listening. His attention had been drawn to the copy of the *Sun* that Benton and Private Harrison were busy reading. 'Give me that,' said the Doctor, snatching the newspaper from the hands of the startled soldiers.

'Hey, I was reading it!' said Harrison sulkily, but the Doctor shushed him to silence as he stared at the front page, a huge photo of a pop concert with a headline that screamed NAKED RAVERS SEE STARS!

'Evidence,' said the Doctor, tucking the paper into his pocket.

'What's up, Doc?' asked Sam, suppressing a grin when the Doctor shot him a filthy look.

'What is it, Doctor?' added Benton, slightly more respectfully.

The Doctor removed the paper from his pocket and began to read from it. '"Thousands of half-naked hippie kids, enjoying high temperatures at the Redborough '70 pop festival on the south coast yesterday, claimed to have seen unusually bright shooting stars…" Blah, blah, blah. This is appallingly written.' He glanced up at Benton. 'Do you read this regularly?'

'Very popular with the lads, sir. Tells us what's going on and lets us get on with our lives. And the sports coverage is very good.'

'Hmmm…' The Doctor sounded unconvinced. 'Anyway, the report goes on to say that the crowd witnessed this meteor shower at around eight o'clock in the evening.' He glanced at the date.

'This is yesterday's paper, describing the evening when you reported the meteorite. About what time was that, Sam?'

'Just before eight... Ah.' Sam purred like the cat with the cream. 'I see where you're coming from.'

'And where *it* was going *to*,' said the Doctor with a flourish. 'Now, this pop festival took place on the Earl of Norton's land. Old Norton's been an invalid for decades, so I imagine that permission for this thing would have been given by his son.'

'That would be Viscount Rose,' interjected Benton.

'Very good,' said the Doctor with surprise. 'You know the family?'

'No, sir,' said Benton. 'I read it in the paper yesterday.'

'I know Peter Gillingham-West, the Viscount Rose – or, rather, I've been introduced to him on a few occasions. Always struck me as something of a decadent young man, but I'm sure he'd be keen to help in an investigation of such importance.'

'Investigation?' asked Benton.

'But of course, man,' said the Doctor, as though he were attempting to explain quantum physics to a lobster. 'There may still be evidence at the site of this festival. I would go straight down there but it's probably wise to speak to the viscount first. Now, if I remember correctly, this being Saturday, he's likely to be at the Progressive Club in Mayfair.'

'Do you want me to get the Brigadier to pull a few strings, Doctor? I've heard that the place is quite exclusive.'

'Nonsense,' replied the Doctor. 'I've been a member for thirteen years! I'd better go alone, though, they don't allow riffraff on the premises.'

'Of course not,' said Benton sadly. 'Silly of me...'

'Not to worry, old chap,' said the Doctor, seemingly oblivious to the hurt he had just caused. 'Can you get one of your men to run me into the station? I've got a train to catch.'

* * *

The man Yates showed into the room appeared to be in his mid-thirties, tanned, with short, dark hair. He removed his expensive-looking sunglasses as he entered, and shook hands with the Brigadier.

'How do you do?' said Lethbridge-Stewart matter-of-factly.

'An honour, sir,' replied the man. 'Bruce Davis. I've been looking forward to meeting you for some time.' His smile seemed genuine enough.

'Have you, by jingo?' asked the Brigadier. He had never particularly got on with Americans: by and large he considered them loud people, with far too great a sense of their own importance. But this fellow seemed perfectly charming. He motioned Davis to sit and nodded to Yates, who saluted and left the office.

'Quite a place you have here,' said Davis.

'We've only just finished moving in. One of the drawbacks of the job, I'm afraid. Constantly being on the move. I expect the New York office is the same.'

'Actually, no,' said Davis. 'We've been in the Bronx since we became operational.'

'Isn't that a slightly… inappropriate area?' asked the Brigadier, remembering his own experiences in the Big Apple as a twenty-one-year-old on his way back from Korea.

'It has many advantages, sir,' said Davis. 'And if there ever were a situation, you just count to ten and run for cover.'

'I have your file here,' said the Brigadier, again drawn to Davis's bewitching smile. 'You've seen a lot of action since joining UNIT.'

'Not as much as you, sir, or your British boys. You guys are highly regarded in the US for your personal experience of Alien Life Form situations.'

Lethbridge-Stewart nodded contentedly and allowed the American to continue.

'Your Classified Action report on the Auton invasion was breathtaking.'

'Thank you,' said the Brigadier with just a trace of satisfaction. 'Of course, our scientific adviser was largely responsible for the finished document.'

'Oh yes, Dr Smith. He's something of a legend, too. Will I be able to meet him at any stage?'

'Yes, quite likely.' The Brigadier tapped the file confidently. 'Your record is, nevertheless, impressive.'

'I'm flattered to hear you say that, sir. Some of the mopping up at the second Silurian chamber in Oregon was good work. I also partnered Bill Filer investigating the International Electromatics West Coast Division.'

'I've heard of Filer. Good man?'

'Yes, sir: I'd trust him with my life.'

'I also see,' noted the Brigadier, 'that after university you worked for a controversial businessman in Washington.'

'I did, sir.'

'Why was that?'

'If you mean why didn't I go straight into the military, sir…?'

'No, no,' said Lethbridge-Stewart quickly. 'No implied criticism. I'm just interested in why you chose such a dangerous line of work.'

'I was young, sir,' said Davis. 'And stupid. The money was good, but it was a blind alley. Lifestyles of the rich and famous. Serious danger but ultimately no reward.'

'I think you're going to enjoy your time with us here, Mr Davis,' said Lethbridge-Stewart. 'I'll take you down to your office. Captain Yates will be available to help you should you need anything. In the meantime, welcome aboard.'

They stood to shake hands, and the Brigadier felt an empathy with a fellow soldier. He noticed for the first time that there was a hardness behind the smile, a very necessary ruthlessness. He was clearly a man of hidden depths.

'Thank you, sir,' said Davis. 'I hope I won't let you down.'

CHAPTER 4

The Progressive Club was an imposing building of some five storeys in the leafy heart of Mayfair. To one side stood the headquarters of an obscure but influential government think tank (rumour had it that there was a connecting corridor between the two to facilitate the easy transfer of shared members); to the other the consulate of a diminutive but ambitious southern European state. Some years ago a wealthy Middle Eastern government had made overtures to purchase the consulate for their own purposes, and the powerful members of the Progressive Club had fought tooth and nail against the plans. This opposition was not so much an act of racist bigotry as a response to that nation's refusal to condemn terrorism: when one was finally admitted to the Progressive Club, one undertook to stand firm against vulgarity of any kind.

The dichotomy of the club was further illustrated by the gilt-framed paintings that adorned the foyer of polished marble. In ancient oils: red-jacketed huntsmen, resplendent on impossibly splay-legged horses, bugling across the shires of Little England. In modern acrylics: photo-realistic whales butchered in choppy seas, the blubber being stripped away as the seas turned red. In gently faded watercolours: a victorious batsman applauded from the village green, bat raised aloft in a cerulean sky. In the artist's own blood: 'The slaughter must stop!', scrawled over a photograph from Vietnam.

The Doctor found himself wondering what the man had used to fix the painting's various elements into place – and what that work must have cost the club. A shade under half a million, perhaps – and it had been placed in the foyer, just next to the series of hat stands that serviced the club's occasional guests. The Doctor had once slipped into the Progressive Club's

39

kitchens – their canapés were rightly famous throughout the capital – and had noticed an original Van Gogh just above the cavernous refrigerator. Moments later, he'd been thrown out by the burly French chef, but this insight into the opulence that underpinned the club's social activism had stayed with him.

The Doctor strode briskly towards the reception. Bertram was there, as usual – the Doctor had never known the man take a day off – and he smiled as he took the Doctor's cloak. 'Good day to you, sir. Trust you are well?'

'Indeed, old chap.'

'Uneventful journey?' Bertram rotated the signing-in book to face the Doctor. It was leather-bound and covered the last thirty years of the club's existence. Its contents were both irreplaceable – there was no other record of the members, their election to high office within the club's bizarre hierarchy, and their unpaid fees – and probably subject to the Official Secrets Act. Twenty-one grey-suited valets patrolled the club at any one time, and the two permanently stationed in the foyer were there not just to observe those who came and went but also to guard the precious book.

'Reasonably,' said the Doctor, signing in with a flourish. 'Bessie's had a prang. I had to come by train.'

'Bad show.' Bertram nodded. 'Delayed arrival?'

'We were ten minutes late into Victoria.'

'Cow on the line at Hurstpierpoint?'

'Something like that.' The Doctor smiled. 'Then I noticed someone following me on the Underground. Damned man stood out like a sore thumb. Probably the Brigadier's idea of heightened security.'

'Lose him at Green Park, did you, sir?'

'That's right. I dived through the doors just as they were closing, left him standing on the platform. You should have seen his face.'

'A veritable picture, I imagine.'

The Doctor took one last glance at the book before Bertram whisked it away. 'I notice Viscount Rose is here today.'

'You'll find Mr Gillingham-West in the Kean Bar on the third floor.'

'Thank you, Bertram.'

'Not at all, sir.'

'Anything else I should know?'

'All eastern rooms on the top floor are operating a policy of strict silence.'

'Oh dear,' said the Doctor. He'd once seen a man expelled for clearing his throat in a room where the strict silence rule was in force.

'And the second floor is largely closed, sir.'

'Redecorating?'

'That's the official reason,' said Bertram, with the merest hint of a smile. 'And I'd probably avoid the banqueting hall if I were you, sir. There's some sort of competition going on in there.'

'Competition?'

'Competition, sir. Paper aeroplane, longest flight thereof.'

'Longest, as in distance?'

'Indeed, sir. My money is on the clerics.'

'Really?'

'Yes, sir. Rest blotto. Sending out for more champagne even as we speak.'

'Which reminds me – I'll have a bottle of your best vintage Krug, up on the third floor.'

'Consider it done, sir.'

The Doctor nodded at the valet positioned just outside the lifts, but decided on the stairs. The carpet underfoot was rich and deep; the brass banister impeccably polished. Despite the Progressive Club's name, and its committed principles, many of which the Doctor shared, it was almost comforting to see the old place so firmly keeping at least one foot in the past. On the second floor the Doctor noticed thick red ropes closing off many of the rooms. He couldn't detect any drilling or hammering. Redecorating indeed.

The third-floor corridor was comparatively modest, the decor more nineteenth century than eighteenth. Closed doors of stout oak let through laughter and occasional hints of whispered conversation. The bar was at the end, one windowed wall overlooking the street. A few men lounged in the corner, smoking; at another table, half smothered by the drooping leaves of an enormous *Monstera deliciosa*, two men read extracts from that morning's *Times* and *Telegraph* to each other. And under a peasant scene by Brueghel the Elder sat a casually attired man in his forties, staring down into the road. He turned the moment the Doctor approached. 'One of the club dullards said you wished to speak with me.' Viscount Rose indicated the ice bucket towards his feet. 'And your champagne has arrived.'

The Doctor was slightly taken aback. 'I do hope I'm not intruding.'

'It's a free country,' said Rose. 'So they tell me.'

The Doctor sat facing the man. 'I wanted to ask you about the recent festival on your estate.'

Rose snorted. 'It should have been today. Saturday makes sense. But I was prevented from holding a weekend festival *on my own land*.'

'With respect, it's not actually your land yet.'

'I forgot you knew my father.'

'How is he?'

'Not well. He sits there, waiting to die. You can almost see the dust settling on him.' Rose nudged the ice bucket with his foot. 'Better enjoy yourself, while you still can. Wealth isn't particularly helping my father at the moment.'

'I'm very sorry to hear that.' The Doctor nodded to one of the grey-suited valets, who came over to uncork the champagne. 'I'm

42

told some revellers saw a meteorite shower –'

'Revellers?' snapped Rose, suddenly irritated. 'Is that all they are to you? Children frolicking in the fields? Pat them on the head – there, there, you'll grow out of it?'

'I meant no offence,' said the Doctor hurriedly. 'I'm only really interested in the lights in the sky.'

'I can tell that. You have no idea what's happening, do you?'

The Doctor's unblinking eyes caught Rose's. 'My dear fellow,' he said levelly, 'I know that very many things are happening at present. Some good, some dangerous. I believe that the meteor shower might be significant.'

Rose suddenly looked away. 'I don't know anything about a meteorite shower. I'd blame the heat and the drugs.'

The Doctor rubbed his chin. 'A moment ago you criticised me for doing down the young people – now you're claiming that this light show was all in their minds.'

'Who's to say?' Rose picked up his glass, holding the stem between surprisingly delicate fingers. 'What's real anyway?'

'Come, come, man, this is no time for cheap philosophy.'

'I'll tell you who knows all about cheap philosophy,' said Rose, animated and tense again. 'The fools in Westminster. Governments throughout the Earth. A few years ago the world's youth were on the verge of something marvellous, something really new and beautiful. But the governments have snatched that away from them, sold them false dreams of utopia and plastic nightmares of deadly aliens. I don't buy their lies for a moment, and neither do the people I associate with.'

'Then why come here?' The Doctor's hand encompassed the whole club in an elegant gesture.

'The older the ties, the more difficult they are to break,' sighed Rose.

'This club was founded on honour and decency, tempered by a belief in progress and change. The founders weren't any more

43

interested in revolution or quick fixes than you are.'

'So?'

The Doctor stared at Rose. 'I think you're hiding something.'

'And I think you're a management stooge. The established order that you unthinkingly serve will soon be a thing of the past. It's just a question of time.'

'I sympathise with the anger of young people,' said the Doctor. 'But order must be maintained.'

Rose jumped to his feet, stabbing a finger in the Doctor's direction. 'You sound just like a Nazi!'

'No, old chap, I –'

'I'm tired of apologists for the establishment, Doctor.' Rose began walking across the room. 'Maybe I'll see you around,' he called over his shoulder, his voice heavy with sarcasm.

The Doctor glared at the floor, angry at the way the conversation had gone. He drained his glass, and wondered if there was still a way of appealing to Rose's better instincts. There had to be.

The Doctor stood up, and made his way towards the door. Perhaps if he told Rose something of his involvement in the recent alien invasions then the man would see that he was serious and –

A man with a machine gun stepped into the Doctor's path. 'Do not move,' he said in a thick Russian accent. He jabbed the gun forward for emphasis. 'You are a prisoner of the Union of Soviet Socialist Republics.'

FIRST INTERLUDE:
UP IN THE SHY

The man introduced himself as Jimmy Ferro, researcher into the paranormal. Bob Campbell was tempted to shut up shop there and then, but something told him that the scruffy man had more money than sense. And Campbell was always happy to relieve the foolish of their excess wealth – especially if they had long hair and had clearly never done an honest day's work in their life.

'Please,' Ferro said. 'I need to charter a balloon flight. Immediately.'

Campbell scratched his chin. 'I don't tend to do charters – a quick flip around the local barrows and circles, that's my forte.'

'I'll make it worth your while.'

'And it's lunchtime. I really should be getting back to my good lady wife.' Campbell teased him closer, like the expert angler he was. 'If I'm late she'll think I'm having a fling with some bird down at the White Hart.'

'Whatever you would normally charge,' said Ferro, 'I'll pay double.'

'Well…' Campbell affected deep thought.

'Twenty pounds?' offered Ferro.

It was like taking sweets from a baby. 'Just the figure I had in mind.' Campbell glanced at his watch. 'Where would you like to go?'

'Over the Earl of Norton's land.'

Campbell's face blanched with fear. 'Oh, sir, you don't want to be going there.'

'Sorry?'

'Only joking,' said Campbell. 'I'm quite a fan of them horror films. *Dracula in India*, *The Haunting of Toby Jugg*, *Raiders of the Stone Ring* – I've seen 'em all. I expect you have, too, what with your interest in the supernatural and all.'

'I don't bother with rubbish like that.' Ferro looked hurt by the very suggestion. 'I'm a serious scientist.'

'Of course you are.'

'Is going over Norton's land a problem?'

Campbell bustled about behind the counter, looking for a map. 'I wouldn't have thought so. What's Hippie Pete going to do? Shoot us down?'

An hour later, Campbell was beginning to wish he'd obeyed his instincts and flipped over the 'closed' sign. Ferro had been poor company, the journey had so far been monotonous, and even the pleasant feeling of the sun on his back did little to lighten the mood. Still, he kept telling himself, think of the money.

'Were you here for the concert?' he asked, desperate for some sort of communication with Ferro.

Ferro shook his head, his eyes fixed firmly on the instruments cradled in his lap.

The balloon flew over a small river, bordered by thick hedges. A cow had somehow pushed its way through and stood in the muddied water, a forlorn look on its face as if it didn't know what to do next. Campbell smiled. 'I sometimes think I'm the only one not swept up in this new way of looking at things.'

Ferro grunted; it was impossible to tell if it was in affirmation or disagreement. He probably couldn't give a monkey's either way.

Campbell continued regardless. 'I don't know what to make of young people these days,' he said. 'Nothing's sacred: they want to have their cake and eat it.' Campbell let some more hot air into the balloon, and the basket rose higher into the sky. 'Call me old-fashioned, but I never even thought about "freedom" when I was their age. Just got on with the job at hand. But these young people, they go down to London, they take drugs, and they become homosexuals. That's the permissive society for you, isn't it?' He paused for a moment, thinking. 'Those hippies who saw fireworks in the sky? I blame the drugs.'

'I suppose it's a matter of interpretation,' muttered Ferro. It was the closest they'd come to a conversation since taking off.

'What is?'

'The lights in the sky.' The young man glanced up for a moment. 'I heard all the reports, and that's why I'm here. I believe those people saw something, something real and measurable and scientifically provable.' He fiddled with his instruments again, and made a few notes in a spiral-bound notepad.

'And what *did* they see, then?'

'The "stars" were the result of the warp engines of a flying saucer reacting with an atmosphere unusually rich in carbon.'

'A flying saucer? Oh, I see. Our little green friends get on well with the hippies, do they?'

'Grey. Most authenticated sightings of alien life forms have indicated a grey skin colour.'

'Doesn't have quite the same ring to it, though, does it?' pondered Campbell. 'Little grey men, I mean. Makes them sound like chartered accountants.'

Ferro stared blankly back at Campbell.

'Oh, never mind,' muttered Campbell under his breath. He glanced at his watch. 'We ought to be thinking about landing soon.'

'Just a few more minutes, please,' said Ferro. 'I've picked up some interesting readings, but nothing's very clear here. Probably the effect of the coastal breeze.'

Campbell looked down at the landscape again, the fields etched by darkening shadows. They flew over a small village, and for a moment the twisted church spire seemed close enough to touch. But Bob Campbell never misjudged heights, and they flew comfortably over.

Something flickered in front of the sun.

Campbell turned to the side, expecting to see a small cloud, but there was nothing there. Must have been a bird.

There it was again. Something tiny and dark, dancing in front of the sun, then swooping down towards the coppice of trees near Bradley Hill. A rook, perhaps? Whatever it was, it almost seemed to know how best to conceal itself, like a fighter plane during the war, using the burning sun to blind the eyes of its enemy.

Campbell squinted at the sun, but could see nothing against its glare.

Then a shadow passed over the sun again. There was a muffled sound from towards the top of the balloon, as if something had landed. The wicker basket swayed slightly.

'Nothing to worry about,' said Campbell. 'Probably just a –'

There was a scrabbling at the fabric of the balloon, an awful tearing noise. Something that sounded almost like laughter.

The ground began to rush upward.

PART 2:
BLOOD OF THE LAMB

CHAPTER 5

'Do not move!' The stock of the machine gun rested against the Doctor's side. Two more men appeared, hands on pistols concealed inside tweed jackets.

'Honestly,' said the Doctor, more irritated than surprised. 'There was a time when nobody could get in here without either a lot of money or proof of genealogical descent from royalty. Or preferably both.' He paused and cast a quick glance at his three assailants, realising for the first time that they were the three men who had attacked him and Benton the previous day. 'You *are* persistent, aren't you?' he noted drily. With a mixture of resignation and genuine curiosity he raised his hands and smiled warmly. 'I'm aware of the protocol in these situations, gentlemen. In my time I have been threatened by experts. So... Take me to your leader!'

The Doctor was marched along the corridor to the staircase and literally carried down to the back door by his two burly guards. The man with the machine gun gave a few curt orders in Russian, which the Doctor understood to mean they should wait until he had checked that their escape route had not been compromised. Then the Doctor was forced out into the sunlight, and bundled into the back of an unmarked van before he could take stock of his surroundings. A blindfold was slipped over his eyes by what seemed to be female hands and his arms were tied behind his back. The van moved off at an inconspicuous pace. The entire kidnap operation had taken only three minutes to execute.

At first everything was silent. Then he heard a woman's voice asking one of his guards if they had encountered any difficulties. The man began to reply that the mission orders had been carried out with precision when the Doctor chose his moment to ask the most obvious question that occurred to him.

'Excuse me?' he said in flawless Russian. 'Do you mind taking off this blindfold? My skin is very delicate and I bruise rather easily.'

His only reply was a brief grunt of what he took to be surprise. And then silence. After a pause he tried again.

'Hello,' he said brightly. 'I trust, since you've gone to all this trouble, that you want something from me. I should advise you that I can prove to be very uncooperative if I'm trussed up like a sack of potatoes.'

Again there was no reply, although the Doctor thought he could detect a small ripple of ironic laughter from the other side of the van.

He stretched out his feet and felt them come into contact with something solid. He sniffed the air, detecting a faint odour of oil and an even fainter smell of soap. When he next spoke his voice was light and chatty in a way that belied his situation.

'I expect the Progressive Club will have reported my abduction to UNIT by now. They're a snobbish crowd, but hardly unobservant. Three clodhopping chaps can't walk in off the street and snatch a member in broad daylight without somebody noticing.' The Doctor's voice levelled out. He was attempting the same steady, regular speech pattern as he had used during the Soviets' first attack. Hypnotic suggestion, a way of extracting oneself from potential harm with merely the power of the spoken word.

'I was in Russia in 1917 during the October uprising,' he said simply. 'I love your country, such a proud people, so noble under tyranny. I met old Lenin in Petrograd, as it was then known. Splendid chap, loved cricket you know. He was exiled in London for fourteen years, hardly missed a day at Lord's during the summer…' He allowed his voice to trail away whilst he took deep regular breaths, and then resumed at the same pitch. 'Of course, I never agreed with what you did to the Romanovs – that struck me as a frightfully bad show. They were a decent-enough bunch, just a bit stuck in their ways. You'll find most royal families are like that, really: underneath the privileges and the pomp and circumstance, they're just as ordinary as you or I. Of course, I met the Old Tsar at the Dri Kaiser Bund in 1871. I remember I said, "Nicholas," I said, "it's all very well you being Tsar of all the Russias, but you must use your despotic powers in a benevolent way. The Liberation Movement is a powerful one. Listen to Tolstoy and Stakhovich." But he wouldn't –'

'Enough.' The voice that stopped the Doctor in his tracks was high-pitched and angry.

'Madam,' the Doctor said bluntly, 'you have me at a disadvantage. In fact, you have me at several disadvantages all at once. I request that you at least allow me the decency of knowing to whom I am speaking.'

'*Niet*,' said the woman angrily, and the Doctor felt the jab of what he took to be another Simonov in his solar plexus.

'Very well,' he said. 'I'll just sit here and shut up then, shall I?'

'*Da*,' came the reply.

'Wonderful language, Russian,' muttered the Doctor coldly. 'So expressive.'

The man's eyes stung from the fumes of Oxford Circus. He picked up the warm telephone receiver, and rested a coin against the slot. Several times his fingers slipped on the dial. He felt sick. One job, one foul-up – one posting to Antarctica coming up.

'Good afternoon, Ministry of Defence.'

Pushing in the coin, the man cradled the receiver closer to his lips. 'Custodian Seven to Watchtower. Authorisation: Juvenal.'

The line crackled for a moment, and a polite male voice

inquired, 'All right, what's happened?'

'Captain Yates,' said the man, 'I'm afraid things haven't gone according to plan.'

'Meaning?'

'The Doctor lost me, sir, but I went to the club, and he's not there.'

'Not there?'

'Not there, sir. He signed in, but no one's seen him since.'

The Doctor estimated that he had been in the van for ninety minutes when it finally stopped. As the doors were opened a variety of smells hit him all at once: the vague salty tang of a none-too-distant coast, the much more pungent odour of manure and hay. 'Lovely day for a drive in the country,' he said brightly as he was half dragged and half pushed from the van.

Hitting the ground, his cramped legs gave away beneath him and he found himself lying on his side on a dampish patch of grass. Then he was abruptly pulled to his feet and, without warning, the blindfold was ripped from his face. The sunlight momentarily overwhelmed him and he sank to his knees even before the rifle butt slammed into his midriff.

'This is correct use of protocol, yes?' asked a male voice in halting English. The Doctor, winded and in terrible pain, couldn't answer, but thought he heard the man cry out during the pause for a reply. The next voice he heard was the woman's again, and it rang out as clear as a bell.

'You are my prisoner,' she stated, then adding, as much, the Doctor suspected, for the men's benefit as for his own, 'You are being treated with the dignity that befits a soldier of the United Nations Intelligence Task Force. If you are mistreated, I will have the man who abuses you shot. Am I understood?'

'I am...' the Doctor began, but he was unable to finish his sentence.

'I know your rank and designation, Doctor. Please do not insult my gathered information with lies.' She snapped her fingers just as the Doctor was recovering enough of his sight to stare at an attractive woman in camouflage fatigues. 'Take him inside.'

The Doctor found himself being marched into what seemed to be a ramshackle abandoned cottage or farmhouse. He was taken into the kitchen, pushed into the corner of the room, and told to sit. With his hands still firmly bound behind his back, the Doctor complied and allowed himself to become accustomed to his surroundings. There were two doors of solid oak, the Doctor guessing that one must lead to a pantry. A guard was on permanent duty behind the other, through which he had been brought. Although shut, there was a window high up in the door which allowed the Doctor to observe events.

He counted some three or four soldiers in addition to the three men who had captured him at the club. All came along at varying intervals to check on him, although rarely did they bother to open the door. There was always at least one soldier stationed there, his head just visible through the pane of glass. The Doctor saw nothing further of the woman, although at one point he heard her raised voice, shouting instructions in some other part of the building.

The Doctor watched the shadows lengthening across the wooden floor, all the time turning over what little information he had on his captors and location.

He glanced up and listened intently as another soldier conversed with the guard at the doorway. He caught only six or seven words from a long back-and-forth discussion in hushed whispers, but it was enough to tell him that the Soviets were waiting for nightfall, and that a light aircraft was on its way. The last time the Doctor had visited Russia, he had been a hero of the October Revolution. Now, it seemed, he was to be flown in, secretly and in chains, to an uncertain fate.

The Doctor leant forward, relaxing the muscles in his arms, just as Erich Weiss had shown him all those years ago. He felt the coarse rope shift slightly, but still wasn't sure he would be able to get free. He glanced around the room, taking in the bare walls, the low stainless-steel sink and broken pine dresser. Perhaps if he could get to the sink and soak the ropes... No, that was sure to attract the attention of the soldier behind the closed door.

The Doctor clambered to his feet. 'Just stretching my legs, old chap,' he announced loudly. 'Pins and needles, you know.'

The soldier grunted and turned his head away.

The Doctor had noticed a number of rough metal nails in the walls, bright patches of plaster indicating the former position of hanging pictures and ornaments. If there was one down at his level he could use it to saw through his bonds. He walked carefully along the wall, feeling with his hands. Eventually he found a nail, somewhere towards the centre of his back. He had to raise his hands uncomfortably, but this seemed to be his best hope of freedom. The nail was securely fixed, and within moments the individual strands of rope were becoming frayed.

The soldier looked in a few moments later; the Doctor immediately glanced away, lowering his arms and yawning extravagantly. The man turned around, and soon the Doctor was working at the rope once more. At times the iron nail seemed to be making a better job of cutting the Doctor's wrists than his bindings, but eventually one link of the rope gave way. The Doctor immediately returned to the corner where he had been bundled originally, and called out to his guard. 'I say, how about some food? I wasn't able to dine at the club. I'm feeling a trifle peckish. Some cheese, perhaps. A little Brie would do nicely.'

The soldier considered, and vanished from sight, but was back at his position moments after barking out some orders. Eventually a second soldier came into view, and the door opened. He entered the room, carrying a tin plate. He watched the

Doctor intently, placing the food on the floor. Then he came over to the Doctor, bending down to untie his bonds.

The Doctor thrust his elbow into the man's face, catching him completely by surprise. As the soldier crumpled to the floor the Doctor flew across the room, kicking at the door. It smashed open, flinging the other guard to the ground.

The featureless hallway was deserted. It terminated in an open door, which led to a lean-to greenhouse. Shadows were lengthening in the garden beyond as twilight approached. He risked a glance behind, saw one of the guards simultaneously shouting a warning and preparing to the fire his rifle. The Doctor dived for the door, trying to close it as he passed, just as the first shot was fired. He felt a stinging pain in his side, which knocked him off balance, but his momentum carried him forward.

He threw himself at the panes of glass, rolling into a ball in midair. The greenhouse walls exploded around him, blotting out the percussive thuds of bullets behind him.

The Doctor hit the ground running despite the pain in his side, and found himself on a lawn of ragged grass, now illuminated as all the lights in the farmhouse came on. In front of him was a garden wall, with a lane just beyond.

The Doctor swerved as best he could to avoid the gunfire, then threw himself over the low stone wall. He risked a backward glance – saw the Soviet soldiers spilling out from the remains of the greenhouse – then sprinted across the lane, vaulting a gate into a field. He could hear the sounds of the soldiers coming after him.

'Please be seated, gentlemen,' said the Brigadier, striding into the vast conference room.

Captain Yates and Bruce Davis exchanged glances as they sat in two of the twenty-five available chairs.

'As you are no doubt aware, the Doctor is missing. We therefore must presume that he has been abducted. The question is, what are we going to do about it?'

Yates cleared his throat. 'I was hoping you were going to tell us that, sir.'

'I think, Captain, that we might start by considering the future of that nincompoop you suggested for the surveillance mission.'

'Boggs was trying his best, sir.'

'"Trying his best"?' exploded the Brigadier. 'Captain Yates, my grandmother could have done a better job. And she's been dead since 1955.'

'Sir,' said Bruce, 'I realise I'm only an observer at the moment...' His voice trailed away.

'That's quite all right,' said Lethbridge-Stewart. 'Your input would be appreciated.'

'Well, sir,' continued Bruce, 'it seems to me that our options are limited. We have no information to go on, no reason to expect anything as mundane as a ransom note. Can we not inform the airports and put up some road blocks?'

'My thoughts exactly,' said the Brigadier. 'Unfortunately, we don't have anything like enough information to warrant a Green Door alert.'

'Then it looks like we're just going to have to wait and see what happens,' said Bruce, a wry smile on his face.

The Doctor did not allow himself the luxury of slowing down until he knew he was clear of the farmhouse and the Soviet soldiers. Only then did the pain from his wound wash over him. He located the point where the bullet had clipped him, concluded that there was no real damage – but his hand came away stained with blood just the same.

The stars overhead were untouched by cloud, and the temperature had dropped alarmingly. The cold was keeping him clear-headed, for the moment, but he knew he must get back to civilisation soon. The Doctor paused again, listening intently. A fox yelped somewhere in a field, but beyond that it was completely silent. Except... Yes, just the merest hint of traffic, a swish of rubber on tarmac. Very distant, but still his best hope. Not a busy road by any stretch of the imagination – especially not at this time of night – but the Doctor counted about a car every five minutes as he strode purposefully towards it.

He moved across the fields towards a lane, and then followed that to a junction with the main road. It was just as quiet and desolate as he'd feared. If he started walking – he glanced swiftly overhead, establishing which direction would be best – then he assumed that someone would eventually find him.

The first five cars to pass him didn't even slow down – one gleaming Jaguar even seemed intent on running the Doctor off the road – but the sixth driver at least had the courtesy to slow a little before deciding against giving him a lift. Encouraged by this slight sign of interest, the Doctor gestured with his thumb enthusiastically when the next vehicle passed. It was a clapped-out old Volkswagen van, its pockmarked, rust-etched surface covered with poorly painted flowers against a purple starscape. It screeched to a halt, then backed up at such alarming speed that the Doctor began to fear for his life. The brakes slammed on again just in time. The passenger door flew open. 'Get in, man,' came the strangled-sounding voice from the front.

The Doctor hauled himself into position with his most winning smile fixed to his face, but found he had little need to impress.

'Wow, man,' said the hippie at the wheel, staring at the Doctor's clothing. 'Dig the groovy gear.'

The Doctor smiled and thanked the man profusely, pulling the door shut. Next to him, on the double-sized passenger seat, was a young pregnant woman who wore similar beads and loose clothes to those of the driver. Both seemed happy to see him – the woman immediately started talking, as if they were long-lost friends – and the Doctor's relief at getting out of the cold was genuine.

'So, you're coming back from the specially extended happening, too?' asked the woman, cranking up the van's heater another notch.

The Doctor smiled. 'Let me put it this way – I had quite an experience today.'

'Far out,' sighed the girl. 'Good to see the breadheads didn't win out today. Why shouldn't Rose do what he wants on his land?'

'Absolutely.' The Doctor nodded. 'Decent enough chap, Rose.'

'That's what they reckon,' said the driver.

The young woman noticed the red patch on the Doctor's jacket for the first time. 'Hey, man, are you all right?'

'Oh, don't worry about that,' replied the Doctor. 'I just caught myself on some barbed wire, that's all.'

'Bad karma,' replied the driver. 'Man, me and my chick were at Tamworth for the Byrds. It was heavy: wire everywhere. Too many day-trippers. We had to blow the scene, the vibes were wrong.'

The girl rummaged in the pockets of her kaftan. 'Smoke?'

'No, thank you, my dear. I've had quite enough excitement for one day.' The Doctor held his hands in front of one of the warm air vents. 'Tell me, did you see the lights in the sky on Thursday night?'

The couple both grinned like children, nodding furiously. 'It was, like, so together,' said the driver, tapping with the wheel to a half-remembered beat. 'The lights were groovy stars, all dancing their thing.'

'Really. And did these "stars" fall to Earth?'

'Yeah,' said the woman. 'Right at the end. They came down in the sea.'

'They?'

'The dwellers in the celestial temple, man,' said the driver, smiling, as if stating the obvious. 'They wanted to communicate.'

'Talking of which,' said the Doctor brightly, 'I see from that sign there's a phone box coming up. I'd be most grateful if you could just pull up over there and allow me to contact my friends.'

'Sure,' said the man. 'Whatever you want.'

The Doctor waited by the phone box, somewhat anxiously eyeing his new friends. He still hadn't told them whom he'd phoned, or the nature of the help they were able to offer, and was unsure how they'd react when the Brigadier steamed into view. He'd suggested that they leave him, but some misguided loyalty ('Just to see you're OK, man') kept them with him.

A rusting old van, a phone box in some benighted lay-by, two charming but ultimately rather irritating hippies. The perfect tableau with which to end a frustrating couple of days, thought the Doctor rather sourly.

Sometime later a convoy of jeeps and APCs appeared. The Brigadier stood in the front of the lead vehicle, swagger stick under his arm. Even from a distance the Doctor could see the man's moustache bristling.

The Doctor risked a sideways glance at the couple. They seemed frightened now, rabbits before headlights, considering a break for freedom but impotent before a greater power. 'There's nothing to worry about,' counselled the Doctor.

The man turned on the Doctor in a sudden rush of bravery. 'You never said you were with the pigs, man. We've only got our stash; you can't bust us for that.'

'They're *soldiers*,' muttered the girl in wide-eyed awe.

'Just pigs in different hats,' spat the man. He hadn't turned his gaze away from the Doctor; his anger was accusatory. 'And we tried to help you.'

'I'm really very grateful,' said the Doctor. 'All they'll be interested in is the "stars" that you saw at the concert. Nothing else.'

'*Gig*, man. It wasn't a concert.'

'Trust me.' The Doctor pointed out one particular figure, who seemed to share the Doctor's embarrassment at the over-the-top scenario. 'That's Captain Mike Yates. Go and see him.'

'Not a chance, man. I don't speak fascist.'

'Please,' said the Doctor. 'They can force you if you make them.'

The couple paused, then walked towards the captain, glancing back at the Doctor occasionally with ill-disguised contempt.

'Interesting company you keep, Doctor,' said the Brigadier, staring at the night sky as intently as if it were the cricket pages of *The Times*. There was precious little humour in his voice.

'Whatever you're going to say, Brigadier, can't it wait until the morning?'

'No, it cannot,' replied Lethbridge-Stewart. He still couldn't bring himself to look at the Doctor, like some schoolteacher struggling to come to terms with a favourite pupil's abuse of trust. 'I didn't authorise your little jaunt into London. You knew you were under strict instructions to be accompanied at all times.'

'I'm terribly sorry,' mocked the Doctor. 'I will try harder *not* to lose your plain-clothes chap in future.'

'Listen here, Doctor!' exploded the Brigadier. 'This isn't a game, you know. Two attempted abductions in under forty-eight hours. You were lucky enough to escape from them both – but with this constant emphasis on placing yourself in danger, it wouldn't have surprised me if you'd have been in Siberia by now.'

'Now, Brigadier, the point is –'

'The point is, Doctor, that I can't afford to be without you,' said the Brigadier levelly. 'If you're missing the next time the Autons invade or the Yeti terrorise central London, we'll be defenceless.' He nodded towards the vehicles, the soldiers spilling out on to the lay-by, the Lynx helicopter droning overhead. 'I've got good men and equipment. But any soldier is only as good as the intelligence reports he acts on. I simply can't afford to have you AWOL.'

The Doctor smiled. That was the nicest thing the Brigadier had said in weeks.

'Therefore,' continued the Brigadier, raising his voice a notch just as Benton strode forward, 'from now on, Doctor, everywhere you go, you will be accompanied by Captain Yates or Sergeant Benton. I can't order you to do anything, Doctor, but, by heaven, I consider that an order. Do I make myself clear?'

'Perfectly,' said the Doctor.

Benton saluted. 'We've surveyed the area. Nothing.'

'Of course there's nothing,' said the Doctor, irritated. 'I was kept in a house miles from here.'

'Where?'

The Doctor pointed back down the road. 'A farmhouse, about twenty or so...' He rubbed his chin. 'I wouldn't worry about it. They'll have gone by now.'

'Very well,' agreed the Brigadier. 'Benton, get the men ready to move.'

'Yes, sir.'

The Doctor and the Brigadier watched Benton as he ordered the men back into their vehicles. Yates was questioning the hippie couple, pointing to something written on the side of their van and joking.

'I do have one piece of good news, Doctor,' announced the Brigadier.

'What's that?'

'As you know, Miss Shaw is in Cambridge, liaising with Professor Trainor.'

'Yes?'

'Well, she's asked me... to invite you to a party.'

'Splendid. You'll come along too, won't you, Brigadier?'

Lethbridge-Stewart appeared horrified by the suggestion. 'I've got rather a lot on my plate at the moment, Doctor.'

'I understand,' said the Doctor. 'When is this party?'

'Tomorrow night.' The Brigadier checked his watch. 'Actually, I mean tonight. Nineteen hundred hours.'

The Doctor jumped into the back of the jeep. 'Plenty of time to get ready then.'

CHAPTER 6

The Glass Onion used to be a coffee bar, back when the world was a little more sane. Then the Cybermen marched down Noel Street towards Covent Garden, and things were never quite the same again. Now it had been rechristened the Apollo Café, and its small, white, iron, outdoor tables were largely unoccupied on this particular Sunday morning. A man in a blazer and an MCC tie read *The Times*; another sat with a Pan Am flight bag and a cup of weak coffee. He sipped from the mug between occasional heavy drags on his Guards cigarette. He disliked the brand but Bulaks were difficult to come by in this godforsaken country. Sometimes he agreed with Tom Bruce: coming to England was like taking a step into the Third World.

'The weather is unusually inclement for the time of year,' said Bruce in a mock upper-class English accent as he approached the table.

'Don't be a jerk, Tom. Just sit down and assure me you weren't followed.' Control glanced nervously around. He hated meeting in the open like this. 'I can't believe I allowed myself to be persuaded about the viability of this particular option.' He shuffled about in his flight bag and then withdrew a small manila envelope. He slid this across the table; Bruce left it where it was.

'I've been in this game almost as long as you have,' he said, with a hint of irritation. 'My methods are rarely beyond reasonable denial.'

'Just so,' said Control, glancing across to the man in the blazer. The man nodded, slipped on a pair of Polaroid sunglasses, and folded away his newspaper. He moved off up the street without a backward glance.

'One of yours?' asked Bruce.

'Deep cover. He's been here so long even the cousins believe he's one of the chaps.' Control glanced at his watch. 'You think you'll enjoy this assignment?'

'I've pulled worse special projects than this,' Bruce answered. 'You remember that game in Istanbul?'

'Oh yes, the little girl you found in bed with a cultural attaché, or five. Biographical leverage. And to think I used to believe you weren't cut out for covert actions.'

Bruce clicked his fingers, ordering a coffee from a bored-looking girl in the café. 'And don't be giving me any of that cappuccino crap,' he snapped. He returned his attention to Control, who was nearing the end of his cigarette. 'They're very bad for you, you know.'

'John Neuberger told me the same in Prague. I'm still here. He isn't.'

This seemed to amuse Bruce. 'Yeah, right. And, of course, you're ready to equate me with that one-man Bay of Pigs. Remind me to rain on your parade at the first given opportunity. Sir.'

Control stubbed out his cigarette. The small talk was over. 'Get your goddamn coffee, Tom, and then make sure this game isn't blown, or you'll be shuffling files in Virginia until the next Ice Age. Capiché?'

Bruce walked into the café and then returned to his seat with the coffee. 'The objective has been attained,' he said, spooning in some sugar.

'You've encountered no problems?'

'No, sir,' said Bruce with a grin.

'Impressions?'

'You want the good news, or the bad?'

Control breathed out slowly. 'This had better be pertinent, Tom. I've got better things to do than come to London to watch the changing of the guard.'

'The pudding club is, as we suspected, run like a branch of the Junior Campers. I've yet to meet the extraterrestrial, but the trigger man, Lethbridge-Stewart, is a dork. The rest of his staff are what you'd expect: inbred clowns from the shires. They're a joke.'

'Sure,' said Control, annoyed that Bruce's prejudices were getting the better of him again. 'Anything else?'

'At least they're all right-minded politically. Those that have any mind to be right-minded with. And they say the scientific adviser's assistant's photograph doesn't do her justice!'

'Well,' Control continued, 'I'm not here to be your counsellor, but, where Miss Shaw is concerned, I'd stay clear if I were you.' Control noticed, with not a little concern, that Bruce was wincing openly. 'We have matters of greater priority to deal with.' He pointed to the still-unopened package in front of Bruce. 'Look at it.'

Bruce flipped open the envelope and examined an out-of-focus surveillance photograph.

'Comrade Valentina Shuskin,' said Control laconically. 'The Bitch Queen of Leningrad.'

'Nice,' purred Bruce.

'Don't even think about it. She'd probably eat you alive. Fascinating background. A Little Daughter of the Revolution. Superstar activity in Prague, until her boyfriend chose to defect. Then... Soviet UNIT.'

'What? The puddings are letting anybody join their gang these days.'

'It's a free world, Tom.'

'Not if I can help it. What's the deal with the sister?'

'She's the leader of the *apparatchik* unit that are trying to take the Doctor out of the game.'

Bruce nodded, remembering the previous evening's meeting with Lethbridge-Stewart and Yates. 'I like these rules. Do they want to take your ET to Mother Russia for any specific reason, or are they just planning a party with the vodka and the rebel songs?'

'You know the reason they want him.' Control paused, and

drained his cup. 'Christ, but this place makes bad coffee.'

'I know,' replied Bruce, 'but the location's pleasant enough.'

'I like the idea of the Doctor being out of the main picture,' said Control. 'Perhaps the best place for him *is* the Soviet bloc. Our... contacts tell us that the Siberian operation is not what it seems.'

The yellow roadster pulled up with a disproportionately vulgar screech of brakes. Captain Yates immediately jumped on to the pavement and looked up and down the road, as if expecting trouble.

Liz watched from the window before moving towards the front door. Mike had clearly been in the Brigadier's company for too long. 'It's all right,' she said, pushing open the door. 'I guarantee there are no aliens in Cambridge.'

Yates turned round, almost embarrassed. 'Oh, hello. To be honest, it's not aliens I'm worried about at the moment.'

The Doctor walked up the steps towards the front door, a small case in each hand. 'Hello, Liz,' he said. 'I've missed you, you know.'

'So it seems,' said Liz. 'What on Earth is going on?' She pulled closed the door after Yates, and ushered them both into the sitting room.

The Doctor lounged in an enveloping armchair while Mike perched on the edge of a moth-eaten settee. 'Well, you see, Captain Yates has very kindly offered to look after me while I'm in Cambridge,' explained the Doctor.

There was a mocking tone to his voice which Liz recognised instantly. 'Offered?'

'Well, ordered, actually,' stated Yates. 'The Brig's idea. Increased security.'

'I've been the subject of two kidnap attempts in as many days,' said the Doctor, seemingly with some degree of pride. 'Soviet soldiers. Probably a group of crack Spetsnaz troops.'

'What can they want with you?' asked Liz.

'I'm really not sure. But they knew who I was. Maybe they want my advice for some reason.'

'Why not ask for your help?'

'Why not indeed?' The Doctor smiled. 'Anyway, don't let it worry you. I'm sure we weren't followed, and I have every faith in Captain Yates's ability to protect me should our friends put in another appearance.'

'I'm surprised to see you so readily agreeing to something the Brigadier suggests.'

'I'm never too proud to ask for help, Liz, you know that.'

Liz laughed. 'Of course, Doctor.'

'How are the arrangements for the press luncheon going?'

'Fine. Everything's under control. I'm hoping you'll meet Professor Trainor at the party later.'

'I'm looking forward to it.'

A young man poked his head into the room. 'Good afternoon,' he said brightly. 'I'm Mark Wilson. Can I get anyone a coffee?'

Both the Doctor and Yates shook their heads.

Wilson collapsed into a huge beanbag in the corner of the room. 'I saw your car outside. Can't say I've ever seen anything like it before.'

'I'll take that as a compliment,' said the Doctor.

'Please do.'

'And I'm told that we have you to thank for arranging this party?'

Wilson nodded. 'An informal prelude to next week's press conference. And I've arranged rooms for you and the captain tonight.'

'That's very kind,' said the Doctor. 'Liz has told me that you work for Professor Trainor. May I ask, in what capacity?'

'The professor was interested in my doctoral thesis on the use of cobalt-60 in radiotherapy,' said the man proudly. 'Of course, British Rocket Group use my expertise in an altogether different way. Calibrating instruments, minor power sources, that sort of thing. Ultimately, though, we're expected to be Jacks of all trades at BRG.'

'I read a paper of yours on sustainable power supplies,' said the Doctor.

'Really?' exclaimed Wilson, genuinely surprised. 'That magazine has a very small readership; I didn't think –'

'An excellent piece of work. Personally speaking, though, I'd have liked some discussion of the social impact of such energy sources.'

'Not really my field,' said Wilson defensively.

The Doctor smiled, but his eyes suddenly seemed cold and distant. 'None of us should ever forget the human context that surrounds what we do in the name of science,' he observed.

The room was full to overflowing with people, and Liz found the noise and bustle curiously restful after the introspection of the last few days. She sipped from her glass of Rocamar red wine. 'I see you have one of those newfangled eight-track cassette machines,' she said.

'Your point being?' asked Mark suspiciously, but with a hint of mocking humour.

'It's just that a few weeks ago I was talking to a friend of mine who works for Philips' R and D,' replied Liz brightly. 'And he was telling me that it's a technological blind alley. The music companies don't want the format to succeed because their *raison d'être* is records.'

Mark scowled openly, his hackles rising at the suggestion that, once again, Liz was making fun of his inability to know which new trend to follow. It was exactly the same as that time he'd told her confidently that there was no future in colour television because the technology was too expensive. 'Look,' he said in a voice that was higher-pitched that normal, 'the sound quality is infinitely superior to a long-playing record. And the system's easier to work than a Dansette. Just listen to it …'

The sound of the Alan Hawkshaw Orchestra rippled gently across the room from a pair of Quad speakers.

'Hmmm,' said Liz, putting down her glass and then settling into one of the armchairs. 'I remain to be convinced.'

'I thought quadraphonic sound was going to be the next big thing,' noted Gavin Hyde, one of Mark's housemates, a first-year philosophy student. He sat down on the floor next to Liz, cradling a brown-ale bottle in one hand and fingering his CND medallion as he tried, very obviously, to look anywhere but at Liz's shapely legs.

'Rubbish,' said Fay, another of the house's occupants. 'I agree with Mark,' she continued, with a look at Liz that said *I hate you and I want you to die*. 'What with the current vinyl shortage, LPs and those horrible little forty-five things are going to be dead in a couple of years. There's an oil crisis, you know. It's hard to make vinyl without oil!'

Liz, uneasy at suddenly being the centre of attention, stood up and crossed the room towards Mark's stereogram, a mahogany affair that was housed beneath a teetering bookshelf which overflowed with technical journals, copies of *New Scientist*, and a stack of dog-eared American super-hero comics. She passed two knots of party guests chattering happily and drinking extravagantly in the ambient splashes of light created by three lava lamps.

'Comics insult your intelligence,' she said picking up a copy of *The Brave and the Bold*. She knew that Mark would have followed her. She sensed his frustrated tension behind her.

'But comics are all I read,' he said, again in that high-pitched half-chuckle that told her that he was embarrassed and not a little drunk.

'I like the music,' she said, holding the cassette case of the

Studio 2 Stereo collection currently filling the room with its shimmering mood music and sweeping orchestral passages.

'No you don't, you'd prefer some Stravinsky or Stockhausen. Something unlistenable.'

'I don't think your friend likes me very much,' Liz announced. 'She seems very uptight. I wouldn't have really thought she was your type at all.'

'Fay's not *anybody's* type,' said Mark. 'She's a radical feminist.'

'So am I,' said Liz, with a cheeky grin that seemed to ruffle all sorts of feathers on Mark.

'I ought to put you over my knee,' he said between gritted teeth, looking away from her and back towards his friends, who were now talking among themselves.

'Not in front of the army, darling, they look after their own. They'd probably shoot you!'

Mark's fingers dug into Liz's arm. 'Sometimes I think you enjoy winding me up.'

'No, honestly, I've got better things to do with my time,' she said in her sweetest voice, pulling herself free. One or two heads were beginning to turn in their direction, though she saw that the Doctor was completely engrossed in conversation with Professor Trainor.

At that moment she and Mark were joined by two former colleagues who were also now working on the Neptune project. The conflict drained away.

'I think you should come back and join us,' said John Gallagher, one of Liz's oldest friends.

'At the party, or on the project?' she asked with a wicked grin.

'Both,' replied Gallagher. 'They're far too dull without you!'

Chris Hughes nodded in silent agreement. In all the time that she had known him, Liz had never known Chris use a word when a mute gesture would do.

'I'd love to,' she said, lightly touching John's arm. 'But...'

'I know, I know – Official Secrets Act. I suppose after the stuff you get up to with Dr Smith over there, rocket fuels must seem a bit namby-pamby?'

'You've met the Doctor?' she asked, as John began looking through Mark's cassette collection. She caught Mark out of the corner of her eye, slipping back towards his friends, looking alone and crushed.

'Yeah. Curious bloke,' said John. 'Told me I reminded him of somebody he knew years ago. I asked who and he said Joseph the Second of Austria-Hungary! Bit of an obscure joke, wouldn't you say?'

'That's the Doctor,' noted Liz.

'Hey, Mark,' called John to the other side of the room. 'Haven't you got any Rolling Stones, or the Who? Something with a bit of volume?'

'No,' said Mark, moving back towards Liz but avoiding looking at her. 'What you see is what you get.'

'Ah,' said John, picking up a copy of *A Saucer Full of Secrets*. 'This'll do. The Floyd are mellow.'

Mark seemed to nod and shake his head at the same time. 'Whatever you like,' he said, and turned his attention to Liz. 'There's a good discussion going on over here,' he said, indicating where Fay, Gavin, and others were sitting. 'We're talking about nuclear disarmament and utopianism.'

I bet you are, thought Liz with a wry grin. 'Sounds fascinating,' she said.

'Your input would be greatly valued,' said Mark, sounding not unlike a wounded puppy.

Oh God, David Mercer-on-Acid. Liz's eyes flickered towards the ceiling. After a brief hesitation, she smiled. 'I'd be delighted,' she said, and brushed past Mark, her eyes catching those of Mike Yates, who was chatting to a very pretty girl in a bright-yellow miniskirt who Liz didn't recall having been introduced to. Mike

70

gave Liz a broad wink and she grinned back at him. Good old Mike: even among these people, in these surroundings, he didn't find it difficult to be himself.

Welcome to the world of the middle-class intelligentsia, she thought. Look upon their works, ye mighty, and despair.

'I know what you mean,' said Mike, giving the girl a cheesy grin. 'I think hot pants are a very ugly fashion, too. I much prefer a girl in a dress.' Or out of one, come to that.

Her name, she said, was Valerie. She had a beautiful soft voice with a hint of Scandinavian or something in it. Mike Yates had always been a sucker for foreign girls, ever since he had been seduced by his French mistress at boarding school as a fourteen-year-old. There was something exotic and exciting about them. A mysterious quality that appealed to Mike's love of danger, sports cars and handguns.

The girl was very pretty, with dark hair, bright-green eyes and a charming smile. She hadn't been introduced to Mike but had simply walked up to him and started talking. 'I hope you do not mind me being so forward,' she had said, 'but I do not know many people here. You look as though you are in the same boat.'

Mike admitted that he was, and they had struck up a conversation about food and drink and clothes. Mike found himself asking her about music, though his knowledge of current popular trends was limited to watching *Top of the Pops* once a month or so when his duties allowed.

'I love that new group, the ones who wear leaves and vines in their hair. They are really freaky. I saw them on television last week. The singer is lovely.'

'Don't think I know them,' said Mike, before quickly adding, 'I'm sure they're far out.' (He groaned inwardly. Had he really just said that?)

'And I love the Beatles,' she continued.

'Ah yes,' said Mike, on surer ground now. 'It was such a pity about Paul, but I really dig the German guy.' In truth, when the new Beatles line-up of John, George, Ringo, Billy and Klaus had been announced, he'd been as horrified as everyone else by the prospect of listening to "She loves you, ja, ja, ja".

She put a hand up to his cheek and stroked his skin gently, swaying to the music. 'Michael,' she said, 'what do you do?'

'I…' Yates paused. (Plan B: lie your head off.) 'I'm a racing driver,' he said, turning his head slightly away from her and putting an arm around her shoulders.

'Is that not dangerous?' asked the girl.

'I suppose so,' said Yates, desperately trying to keep a straight face. 'It's a dirty job, but I guess somebody's got to do it.'

The song ended and Valerie whispered something, but Yates didn't quite catch it above the general hubbub of the party.

'I'm sorry?' he said.

'I asked if you would like to go to bed with me,' she replied.

For a split second Yates couldn't decide if he'd had too much to drink, or not enough. 'If you're sure,' he said.

The girl didn't reply, but took his hand and led him towards the door. They passed Mark Wilson and Liz, by now dancing together, holding each other closely and talking softly. Mike and Liz exchanged surprised glances and then Yates disappeared up the stairs.

'Good old Mike,' said Liz softly.

'Sorry?' Mark's head jerked backward, suddenly snapping out of dreaming reminiscence.

'He's a bit of a lad,' she added helpfully, watching the UNIT captain and the woman.

Mark inclined his head in their direction too. 'Oh, I see. Well, I hope they pick someone else's bedroom. I was hoping to get a little sleep myself tonight.'

'Pity,' said Liz with a mischievous grin. Just for the moment, she felt happy and relaxed, able to enjoy the minutiae of life rather than struggling to capture the bigger picture. The détente that existed between her and Mark had lasted for five minutes, but she knew in the pit of her stomach that it probably couldn't go on much longer.

'I'm sorry I dragged you into that rubbish discussion about the problems of youth,' said Mark. 'Sometimes Fay can be a real cow.'

'Maybe you should try being nice to her,' said Liz. 'That normally works.'

Mark stopped dancing. 'Liz, I –'

'Shhhh,' she cooed, taking his arms from around her neck. 'Don't spoil it, or say something you don't mean. Now, you'll have to excuse me for a minute. I'd better go and break up the Doctor and Professor Trainor, or else they'll still be talking at daybreak.'

The Doctor had been introduced to Professor Trainor by Liz right at the start of the party, and, once she had flitted off somewhere else, conversation had swiftly turned to the Doctor's and Liz's work for UNIT. Never one to let the Official Secrets Act get in the way of a good story, the Doctor had given Trainor an insider's view of the Cyber invasion, the Nestene attack, the Eocene crisis, and the aborted Inferno project, all of which Trainor knew little about.

'So, you have actually had direct contact with alien life forms?' asked the professor. 'I've heard Ian Chesterton talk about you often, but I always took some of his ideas with a pinch of salt.'

'Chesterton's problem was his scepticism, funnily enough,' said the Doctor fondly about his old friend. 'I ran into him at Greg and Petra Sutton's wedding earlier in the year, but we didn't have much time to talk. Is he still working for NASA?'

'Yes,' said the professor. 'I met him and Barbara in London last month. I told him that I hoped to meet you soon, and he said I should ask you about Vortis.'

'He did, did he?' asked the Doctor with a stifled laugh. 'I always said he was a rapscallion. How's their little boy?' he asked, changing the subject with indecent haste.

'Very well.' The professor began to ask him about something else, but the Doctor's attention was distracted by the model of the Neptune probe that was on Mark Wilson's mantelpiece.

'A very impressive piece of work,' the Doctor noted.

'You should see the original,' said the professor. The Doctor appreciated Trainor's sense of humour. He always found himself drawn to intelligent people who had a spark of personality about them. Too often he'd encountered academics with lots of brain but little soul.

'I'm fascinated by the propulsion system,' noted the Doctor as he and the professor moved towards the model.

'Indeed. I worked for almost five years on the specifications, but to be fair much of what we achieved is down to Rachel Jensen. An unsung heroine on the project and, I don't mind telling you, a genius on the quiet.'

'I don't think I know her,' stated the Doctor.

'Really? She speaks highly of you,' replied Trainor. 'Anyway, once we'd created a system that could handle the fuel load, the actual design of the craft was easy. We used some of the Russian data collected by their German scientists, and the rocket specifications of the Americans and *their* German scientists...'

'And they gave it to *our* German scientists,' continued the Doctor with a resigned smile. 'I met Von Braun in Texas last year when I did a recruitment tour. Sordid little man, I thought. Brilliant mind, of course...'

'I know what you mean.' Trainor nodded. 'Isn't that often the way with great thinkers? The scope for abuse of their knowledge is enormous. I still remember seeing the photographs of Dachau and thinking: One day, I could be responsible for something like this.'

'It's a risk we all take,' said the Doctor. 'Science is the domain of the naive and consequently prey to the tyranny of evil men.'

'Exactly,' replied the professor. 'And we have to be so careful these days. The media have created an artificial hysteria where space exploration is concerned. The public are uncertain if we should be restarting manned space flights for fear of what we'll find. They now expect every scientist to be governed only by the very worst motivations imaginable. I mean, after the Carrington debacle we've had to reassure them that we aren't all power-crazed megalomaniacs who want to rule the universe!'

At this point Liz joined them with a broad grin. 'Glad to see you two are getting along,' she said.

Trainor smiled, but took this break in conversation as an excuse to glance at his watch. 'Ah, I really should be going. It was so nice to see you again, my dear.' He stretched out his hand to the Doctor. 'A pleasure, Dr Smith.'

'No, the pleasure was all mine, my dear chap. I'm privileged to have made your acquaintance.'

'So, what do you think?' asked Liz after the professor had said his goodbyes and left.

'I see now where you get your independent turn of mind from,' said the Doctor jokingly. 'You had a remarkable teacher.'

Mike Yates and Valerie removed themselves to one of the bedrooms. Mike was somewhat confused by the evening's events, his carefully rehearsed moves and speeches having been rendered redundant by Valerie's pre-emptive strike. They sat on the bed for a while, saying little, then kissed, hurriedly. Both seemed coy and unsure how to proceed. It was not a situation that Mike was used to at all, but each attempt to get the show on the road was met by curious disinterest. Valerie, having gone this far, seemed to be having second thoughts.

They talked, fittingly, about trivialities. Mike got the impression that some of her hesitation was deliberate. He asked her if she felt uncomfortable.

'I am fine,' she said, standing and moving to the window. 'I… I am sorry. What must you think of me?'

Mike was trying to work out exactly that. 'I think you're frightened,' he said, trying to reassure her.

She was silent, staring out into the night with a glassy-eyed look of indifference that baffled Yates. She was pale and lovely in the naked moonlight, but with a quality of aloofness that Yates found puzzlingly attractive.

He turned away from her, bending down to pick up his discarded shoes. 'There's no pressure. If you don't want to –'

And then he felt the dull thud of the butt of his gun slamming into the base of his skull.

After Trainor had left them, the Doctor told Liz he was going outside for some fresh air. She watched him go, and then turned to find herself on the periphery of a conversation dominated by a rather overbearing professor of semiotics.

A few moments later Liz moved away to follow the Doctor through the patio doors. He stood, silhouetted in the light spilling out on to the lawn, staring up at the heavens. There was something noble and yet powerfully melancholic about his strong outline, bright against the cascading arc of stars. He was alone and lonely, a stranger in a very strange land, as he had often told her.

She moved behind him and coughed lightly to let him know she was there.

'Penny for them,' she said.

'You can keep the change,' said the Doctor sadly, not turning to look at her, his eyes still fixed on the myriad stars.

'When I was seven, I got a telescope for my birthday,' said Liz. 'It was the greatest thrill of my life to find Venus at the first attempt.'

'A beautiful planet,' said the Doctor wistfully. 'I was there, long ago of course. These days it's most inhospitable.'

'Are you thinking of home?' asked Liz.

The Doctor gave a short, cynical laugh. 'Home?' he asked. 'I may never see my home again.' He pointed towards the small cluster of stars that formed Sagittarius. 'She's somewhere out there. Gallifrey. In the constellation of Kasterborous.'

'You never told me the name of your planet before,' noted Liz, fascinated at this new information.

'You never asked,' replied the Doctor. 'It's close to the galactic core.'

'That's thousands of light years away,' Liz said, aware that she was dealing with staggering concepts of time and space.

'About thirty thousand, give or take a parsec,' confirmed the Doctor.

'You said the constellation was Kasterborous,' she asked. 'Is that another name for Sagittarius?'

Again the Doctor chuckled, and Liz thought for a moment that he was treating her like a child, sugar coating the more difficult concepts. But his answer surprised her.

'Constellation means something rather different where I come from – although the notion becomes somewhat redeemed by science in the far future of this planet. It's not a concept fixed by actual location, of course: it has elements of time and relativity involved. When I call an arbitrary cluster of stars a constellation, I do it in the knowledge that in a million years some of those stars will be long gone, and others will have been created in their place. I'm sorry to have to explain it in such pompous terms.'

'No,' said Liz, fascinated. 'I think I understand.'

'So much of what is, and what was, and what shall be, are governed by concepts which humans – even brilliant ones like you – can have no rational understanding of.'

Liz was blushing now, thankful that her face was hidden in the shadows of the warm summer night. 'I think that's the nicest thing you've ever said to me,' she said.

'This seems to be my week for telling people what's what,' the Doctor replied. 'I was saying to Sergeant Benton only the other day –' Suddenly his head snapped to his right. 'What was that?'

Liz followed the Doctor's gaze. 'I don't see anything,' she said, staring into the inky darkness beyond the garden.

'I thought I heard something.'

'Maybe the wind?'

The Doctor continued to look in the direction that the sound had come from. He was silent for a moment and then said, 'The Kagananaga Botizoids of the planet Logomundopsi in one of the Magellanic Cloud galaxies have a word to describe the effect of time and dark matter on the subjective position of stars. That might be a better descriptive term than "constellation". Unfortunately, to pronounce it, you would have to have your tongue surgically removed.'

'Oh.' Not for the first time Liz couldn't tell whether the Doctor was being facetious or not.

The Doctor's voice was curiously flat and unemotional, his eyes unblinking. 'I remember once, on the Volputic plains of Casuragi Three in Tau Ceti, I met an old Janus Lynonite. He was orange, with three eyes, and a head in the exact shape of a – Good evening, gentlemen.'

From out of the darkness stepped a group of black-garbed men whom the Doctor seemed to recognise.

'Do not move,' said a voice behind Liz. She spun quickly to find herself facing the girl who'd been with Mike. She was holding Yates's Browning 9mm in her hand.

'Not again,' said the Doctor. 'Young lady, I'll have you know I've had a very trying couple of days.'

'Shut up,' said the woman, moving to the Doctor's side and pointing the gun at his head, dramatically.

'What have you done with Mike?' Liz blurted out.

The Russian woman ignored her. 'Bring the female as well,' she ordered. Two soldiers walked towards the petrified Liz.

'This is utterly pointless, you know,' said the Doctor. 'Your masters must want me very badly indeed to have sent you on such a fool's errand, but you haven't made a very good job of it so far, have you? To botch one kidnap attempt might be regarded as misfortune, to botch three would look like carelessness!' He stared at the woman, speaking slowly to underline his point. 'There is no way you will succeed in getting me out of the country.'

She said nothing in reply, but Liz could see embarrassment and frustration etched on to the woman's face.

'You don't want to be doing this, do you?' the Doctor asked sympathetically, but he got no response other than the immediate attention of the rest of the troops.

The woman turned away. 'Sergeant?' A man snapped to attention. 'Where's the van hidden?'

'Two hundred yards down the road,' he replied. 'Leyonev's driving.'

'Then let us get out of here,' ordered the woman. 'Bring them both.' She glanced at her prisoners. 'Shoot to maim if they try to run or cry out.'

Liz and the Doctor were marched around the side of the house, through a gate, and out on to the road. The Doctor turned to look at Liz. 'Don't worry,' he whispered. 'They won't hurt you.'

The group reached the road, which was deserted. They could hear the sounds of the party, but the curtains were drawn. The neighbouring houses were in darkness.

The Doctor turned his attention back to the Russian leader. 'Why go to all this trouble?' he asked.

'There will be time for talk later,' she replied. It was the first time she had acknowledged the Doctor directly.

'Nice to see you can be civil,' he said bitterly.

'I am Captain Valentina Shuskin of...' She paused. 'Of the Spetsnaz. And I do not enjoy being lectured on protocol by an alien. Get in.'

As the door to the van was held open for him, the Doctor stared back at her blankly. 'How could you possibly –?'

'Get in, Doctor,' she said, and pushed him into the vehicle.

Liz followed the Doctor into the van, and the doors slammed shut. They sat in virtual silence as the vehicle moved off, a look of great concentration on the Doctor's face. Liz was too worried to think about anything. She stared at the soldiers who surrounded them. She noted their commando-style clothing, their impassive faces. Most, but not all, carried guns.

She could see the driver and another soldier in the front of the van, and through the windscreen observed the terraced housing give way to the newer houses on the outskirts, and then to country roads. Now clear of the city, the van picked up speed.

Suddenly the Doctor whispered something through gritted teeth.

'What?' asked Liz.

'I said "Brace yourself",' repeated the Doctor. He was using his hands to cling on to the rough wooden seating.

Liz followed suit just as the noise of the helicopters began to penetrate the van.

The soldier sitting in the passenger seat swivelled to address Shuskin. 'Three helicopters,' he said.

'What?' Shuskin clearly hadn't anticipated this development.

'Two Gazelles and a Lynx gunship in standard two-one formation to our right.'

'Motorcycles,' said the soldier at the back of the van, staring through the rear window. 'And an APC. They've got firepower.'

Shuskin swore openly in Russian as the first helicopter came into view. It swooped low, hugging the country lane for a moment, then ascended, spitting a rapid burst of machine-gun fire over the roof of the van.

'Just a friendly warning,' said the Doctor, unhelpfully.

Shuskin made her way to the back of the van and settled herself on the floor between two seated soldiers. She raised her assault rifle, braced herself, then booted open the rear doors. Immediately she started firing in the direction of their pursuers.

'That will just make them angry,' said the Doctor.

The headlights of the slow-moving armoured personnel carrier illuminated the motorcycles as they swerved from side to side in an attempt to protect themselves from the gunfire. The hail of bullets, picking fragments away from the tarmac road, swung closer to one rider, just catching the front tyre. It exploded, the bike pitching forward and throwing the soldier over the handlebars. Another motorcycle swiftly slotted into place.

Shuskin stopped firing, and turned to shout to her second-in-command. 'Komarov! Where are we?'

The man stood behind the driver and navigator towards the front of the van, legs braced against the bucking motion as the vehicle careered round another sharp bend. 'Miles from our destination,' came the reply.

'Suggestions?'

'Stand and fight.' Komarov's response was immediate and unequivocal, and appeared to go down well with the men, who nodded in agreement.

'Not an option,' said Shuskin.

'Then you've really got no alternative but to surrender,' butted in the Doctor.

Without warning the van swerved alarmingly, throwing the Doctor and Liz to the floor in a tangled mess of arms and legs.

'What is going on?' demanded Shuskin, clinging to the door frame.

'Smoke bombs,' replied Komarov.

Liz looked up from the floor, and could just make out a mist spilling around the periphery of the windscreen. She pushed herself into a more stable sitting position, then turned her attention back to Captain Shuskin. All eyes were on her.

As if aware of this, the woman cursed viciously, then barked out an order. 'Stop the vehicle! It is time to end this.'

'A very sensible decision,' said the Doctor softly. 'If you want me to talk to them –'

'Shut up,' said Shuskin. Even the Doctor was stung by the menace in her voice.

The van slowed to a dead stop, and for a moment there was a standoff. The helicopters continued to circle overhead, lights pinning the van to the spot like an impaled moth. Liz could see UNIT soldiers moving into position to block the roads. Somewhere to the left, a Chinook CH47 transport helicopter was coming in to land, presumably bringing in reinforcements.

'Captain…' one of the troops began.

'Quiet! I am thinking,' snapped Shuskin. She turned to find Komarov beside her. 'It has gone sour, Sergeant,' she stated.

'Not your fault,' replied the grim-faced sergeant. 'I have heard that British prisons are comfortable.' He paused for a moment. 'We have an alternative course of action, sir.'

Shuskin nodded. 'To be used as a last resort. Which it is.' She placed her Kalashnikov AKMS on the floor of the van, and turned to the Doctor. 'You will come with us, please?'

'Gladly,' said the Doctor, moving towards the van door. 'Do you wish me to mediate?'

'That will not be necessary.' Liz watched as the door swung open and Shuskin, Komarov, and the Doctor stepped out. Shuskin's hands were raised above her head to indicate that she was unarmed. As the sergeant followed her a shot rang out from the UNIT lines. Shuskin spun around to find Komarov collapsed in the Doctor's arms, spewing blood. There was a terrifying look of utter bewilderment on his face.

Shuskin screamed. 'Pavel!'

Liz moved quickly to the Doctor's side. There was massive bleeding from the man's chest; she bunched up the jacket in an attempt to staunch the flow, but knew that it was already too late.

Komarov tried to say something, but his froth-flecked lips moved silently. A moment later he was dead.

Shuskin turned towards the UNIT soldiers. Liz thought for a moment that she was going to lunge at the nearest man, but her anger merely came out in her voice. 'You murdering bastards!' she shouted, and then lapsed into Russian.

The Doctor was beside her, a look of dejected failure on his face. 'Lethbridge-Stewart!' he said angrily.

The Brigadier emerged from the cockpit of a Gazelle and strode across towards the pair, his gun in his hand.

'This was your idea,' continued the Doctor, 'and you assured me there would be no casualties!'

The Brigadier looked embarrassed, and turned away sharply. 'Sergeant Benton!' he snapped. 'I want a report on who fired that shot on my desk by ten a.m. tomorrow. All of you men carry the Yellow Card, and you all know the procedure for the firing of weapons in this kind of situation – and the consequences if those procedures are not carried out to the letter. Corporal Laine, take a duty of men and arrest everyone in that van.' He spun back towards the Doctor and Shuskin, his voice hushed. 'I will have the man who fired –'

Liz noted a sudden and complete look of surprise cross the Brigadier's face.

'Wait a minute,' he said, staring at Shuskin. 'I know you. It's Captain Shuskin, isn't it?'

'Yes, you murdering pig,' she replied.

'You know each other, then,' said the Doctor, somewhat pointlessly.

'This woman is, or was, a leading member of the Soviet UNIT

force,' growled the Brigadier. 'We met in Geneva last year. Captain Shuskin, stand to attention when in the presence of a superior officer.'

Shuskin barely moved.

'Do you know what you're saying?' asked the Doctor.

'I believe so,' said the Brigadier. 'I'm saying that one group of UNIT troops have invaded a sovereign state and committed acts of aggression against the local UNIT force. I believe I'm saying that this incident could be the end of UNIT. And the beginning of war.'

CHAPTER 7

The corridors of UNIT's United Kingdom HQ rang with worried voices and strained conversation. The adrenaline rush of combat was fading away, replaced by an uncertain tension as it became clear that a foreign branch of UNIT had been involved in the skirmish.

It was dark outside, but even in the middle of the night the entire building had snapped into wakefulness long before the Brigadier's return. Lethbridge-Stewart paced the hallways anxiously. The mixture of standard army troops and UNIT men had handled the situation well, had it not been for the unfortunate incident towards the conclusion. As he approached his office he saw two soldiers talking conspiratorially. He had a fair idea what about, and could hardly blame them. What a disgraceful and shambolic end to an otherwise well-executed operation.

The two men snapped to attention as Lethbridge-Stewart strode towards the room. He pushed open the door. The Doctor sat, seemingly so deep in thought that he did not see the Brigadier enter; standing in front of the desk were Captains Yates and Shuskin. Both came to attention as Lethbridge-Stewart entered, as did the two soldiers stationed to the side of the room. Both carried Sterling sub-machine-guns, but it was clear from the prisoner's attitude that her righteous indignation, and potential to be any sort of direct threat, had now receded.

Lethbridge-Stewart nodded to the men, who stood at ease. He walked solemnly around to his chair in silence; even the Doctor failed to make a flippant comment.

The Brigadier sat, glanced down at the papers on his desk, and cleared his throat. His voice, when he spoke, was quiet and deliberate. 'Captain Shuskin, I would like to begin by assuring you that every effort will be made to discipline the individual responsible for the death of Sergeant…' He paused. 'Kramerev.'

'Komarov,' said Shuskin flatly.

'Ah, yes. I will keep you informed as matters progress, but rest assured of my intention to pursue this matter to the satisfaction of us both.'

Shuskin nodded, but said nothing.

The Brigadier indicated the seats in front of his desk, glancing up at both Shuskin and Yates. 'Please sit down.'

Yates went to sit, but Shuskin remained where she was. 'I prefer to stand.'

Yates hovered uncertainly for a moment, glancing between the Brigadier and the Soviet woman, and then straightened. Whether it was out of solidarity with a fellow soldier or down to macho pride the Brigadier didn't have the time or the inclination to speculate.

He turned to the Doctor. For the first time Lethbridge-Stewart could remember, he wasn't lounging with his boots on the desk but sat hunched and leaning forward slightly, as if expecting to be called somewhere at any moment. He seemed both excited and concerned. He returned the Brigadier's faint smile.

'Your comments on the operation, please, Doctor.'

'With one great exception, it all seemed to go smoothly, Brigadier. Mike was excellent – he recognised Captain Shuskin for who she was almost immediately.'

The Brigadier glanced at Yates, who for some reason was staring stoically at the floor.

'I think their decision to make a move that very evening surprised us both,' continued the Doctor. 'But at least we now know who we're dealing with. *Why* might be a more pertinent question.'

The Brigadier nodded, but decided to keep Shuskin waiting a little longer. He turned his attention to Yates. 'Your preliminary thoughts, Captain?'

'Much as the Doctor said, sir.'

'And Captain Shuskin?'

The Brigadier noticed Yates glance away momentarily. 'She's done a lot of homework, sir. Good grasp of English, adequate working knowledge of the life and culture of contemporary Britain. She almost had me fooled, sir.'

Finally the Brigadier turned to Shuskin, who was staring at him with a hint of defiance in her eyes. 'Under different circumstances, I'd have said that congratulations were in order, Captain. You've shown extraordinary determination. But given that the aims of your mission almost beggar belief I can't really find it within myself. We all ought to be grateful that only one life was lost.'

'I can explain, sir.'

'I was hoping you would. I assume that you are acting in some sort of official capacity?'

'Very much so, sir.'

'And your aim was to take the Doctor back with you to the Soviet Union?'

'Yes, sir. We need his help.'

'Then why in heaven's name didn't you ask?' exclaimed the Brigadier angrily, thumping the desk. 'You must know that the Doctor's role as scientific adviser isn't one that restricts him to –'

'We did, sir. Or, rather, Colonel Katayev did. He has been petitioning UNIT HQ in Geneva for two months.'

'Any request for assistance from the head of Soviet UNIT would have –'

Again Shuskin interrupted. 'Each request was turned down, sir. Blocked, you might say, at the highest level.'

The Brigadier's eyebrows arched. 'Really?'

'Yes, sir.' Shuskin unzipped a pocket and withdrew a folded sheet of paper. 'Colonel Katayev said I should bring this and show it to you if there were… complications.' She handed the sheet over to the Brigadier.

He unfolded it carefully, switching on his desk lamp. It was a copy of a telex – thankfully in English – from Geneva UNIT HQ to the national headquarters in Moscow. He scanned it quickly, catching more than one reference to his name, and then read it again.

He looked up. 'According to this telex, I was consulted before these men came to their decision. I attended a meeting in Geneva, examined the evidence that your office had provided, and concluded that – and I quote – "There is little reason to believe that the Doctor's presence would in any way accelerate the speed of your investigation or the likelihood of its reaching a successful conclusion".' The Brigadier snorted. 'Doesn't even sound like me.'

'Sir?'

'I wasn't there, Captain. Haven't been to Geneva for eight months. And I certainly wasn't made aware of any request for assistance.'

'Then something is rotten at the heart of UNIT,' said the Doctor.

'You could say that,' said the Brigadier. He passed the telex over to the Doctor, indicating a list of people in supposed attendance at the meeting. 'Some of UNIT's top brass have effectively countersigned this refusal.'

'Or appear to have done,' observed the Doctor.

'But certainly it seems that at least one senior UNIT commander has been fabricating information and obscuring the truth.'

'It's called lying, old chap, and it means that somebody, somewhere, was desperate for me *not* to travel to the Soviet Union.' The Doctor turned to Shuskin. 'What is it I'm not supposed to help you investigate?'

Shuskin smiled. 'I am told it is as if a black hole has appeared in the heart of Siberia. Animals, people – even soldiers – who went in have never returned. A Red Army regiment was sent to investigate. We never heard from them again.'

'Then I'd better pack my thermals,' said the Doctor.

'You mean you're going?' said the Brigadier.

'Of course. And Liz is coming with me, too. If the Soviet authorities were prepared to go to these lengths to secure my services then it's only sporting that I comply.'

The Brigadier considered. 'Captain Shuskin, why didn't your superiors order you to come straight to me with this?' He indicated the telex.

'They didn't know if you were implicated, sir,' said Shuskin. 'Far easier to retrieve the Doctor by force, explain the situation to him, and risk even the wrath of the UN. As I hope to be able to show the Doctor, this isn't a small-scale problem.'

The Brigadier nodded. 'Indeed.' He glanced round at the Doctor. 'Very well, you and Dr Shaw will return with Captain Shuskin and her troops to the USSR.' The Brigadier stood up. 'And if someone has gone to the trouble of faking meetings in Geneva just to keep you away, then I feel a certain response is expected of me.'

'Meaning?' queried the Doctor, a look of delighted surprise crossing his face.

Lethbridge-Stewart smiled. 'I'm told Geneva is beautiful in the summer.'

Bruce had been woken by the clamour of troops leaving the base. He'd gone to the window, seen helicopters taking to the air and soldiers jumping into the back of canvas-covered trucks. Were the Russians in the process of ghosting the Doctor away? It seemed so, and there was nothing that he could have done, even had his orders been to protect the alien. But his orders were to spy, to steal secrets. And to cause a bit of collateral damage.

He'd stood there, wondering whether all the confusion could be used to his advantage. No, balls to that. Better by far to wait for the grunts to return, start running around like headless chickens. That would be perfect.

And so Bruce now strode around the base with a smile almost permanently etched on to his face. The atmosphere of tension and uncertainty was palpable, and Bruce found it strangely thrilling. You wait until you see what I've got lined up for you next, he thought.

He bumped into the Brigadier's adjutant in a corridor. 'It's Corporal Bell, isn't it?' asked Bruce, switching on the charm in an instant.

'That's right, Mr Davis.'

'Please, call me Bruce.' You stuck-up bitch.

Bell smiled sweetly. 'I wasn't expecting the Brigadier to drag you in tonight as well.'

'Couldn't sleep.'

'I'm not surprised.' She paused. 'Is there something I can do for you?'

Drop dead, perhaps? 'I'm looking for the Doctor's laboratory. I thought I might as well start tomorrow's work tonight. There's something I need there.'

Bell gave Bruce the directions, then rushed off towards Lethbridge-Stewart's office.

Bruce strode along the corridors, a file under his arm. He'd been collecting Photostats of top-secret information since his arrival – after all, why use miniature cameras and the other trappings of cheap spy fiction when he was currently above suspicion and allowed virtual free access to everything that UNIT most wanted kept hushed up? But this time he carried a few uncopyable memos. They'd be missed, of course. But it was almost time to go.

Time to go out with a bang.

And he'd only just arrived, as well. Shame.

'The sooner I'm out of this pudding club, the better,' he muttered under his breath.

The Doctor's lab was a room made oppressive by equipment and overstacked shelves. A large blue box stood in the centre, humming slightly. Flexes snaked across the floor from the object, running to banks of electrical devices, still switched on. The points of light that flickered reminded Bruce of the monitoring equipment in a hospital emergency room.

Bruce swore as he pushed the unbidden image to the back of his mind, then swept an armful of papers and journals from a cluttered work surface on to the floor.

Christ, thought Bruce, I don't think you'd even notice a bomb going off in this dump.

He got down on to his hands and knees, drew a small detonator from his pocket, and set about fixing the plastic explosive against the metal legs of one of the benches.

SECOND INTERLUDE:
THE GREAT SNAKE AT THE BOTTOM OF THE WORLD

No one had realised that the Doctor and Liz had been kidnapped until a wild-eyed Mike Yates staggered down the staircase, bleeding and shouting hoarsely. As most of the people enjoying the party were as dazed as Mike, they'd left him to it. Only when the soldiers came did they start to pay attention.

Fay Hardy watched everyone else being helpful, answering questions dutifully, making the men cups of coffee. How square. Suddenly it was difficult to tell the fascists from the kids.

She glanced over at Mark. Despite the assurances of a young and amused UNIT lieutenant, he was desperate to make sure that Liz was safe. Mark rushed off, having offered a lift to the still-shaken Captain Yates.

At 3 a.m. the military left. Most of the guests soon followed; the atmosphere was tainted. A small knot of Cambridge students and British Rocket Group scientists remained, sitting cross-legged on scatter cushions in the centre of the room, drinking red wine. *The Velvet Underground and Nico* murmured from the stereo. Fay sat with her head obstinately close to one of the speakers.

'All right, Tony,' said John Gallagher forcefully. 'I know you've got some stash on you, man. The John Waynes have all gone home to bed now, so you can start passing it round.'

Professor Anthony Leman giggled in a girlish, high-pitched squeal. 'But… It's, like, illegal, Johnny!'

Fay watched the others collapse in fits of drunken laughter. Leman was a popular man on campus, known to his fellows as 'Candlestick Tony', on account of the fact that he'd been present at the Beatles' comeback gig in San Francisco. Fay was the only one who seemed to find his after-dinner story of taking acid and talking to God in the middle of 'It's All Too Much' boring.

'Cut the crap,' she snapped.

'Cool it,' muttered John quickly, turning back to Leman with a knowing glint of evil intent in his eyes. 'C'mon, Tony, I know you've got some. Gimme a bang, man.'

'You're too eager, Johnny. Too quick into the five-bar-gate jumping,' said Leman softly. 'I think, I mean, you know...' He paused, aware that he was talking gibberish. 'Take off your crushed velvet, man, you're giving me a headache. Can you dig it?'

Gavin Hyde seemed to find this the funniest thing that had ever been said by anyone in the history of the world, but no one else was laughing. Fay stared at the crazy-eyed philosophy lecturer angrily. 'What you got, Tony? Speedballs? Twenty-Five?'

Leman fished in his pocket and pulled out a small red and yellow capsule which he held up to the light. 'Dymoxyl Lybegen Amphetamine-Sulphate. "909" to the trade. Synthetic, odourless, colourless, tasteless...'

'What's it do?' asked Fay.

'Do? It does your bloody head in, that's what it does.'

John reached out for the capsule but Leman snatched his hand away.

'Careful, sonny. This isn't weed. It's a possible cure for cancer, but it's said to *really* open the mind. I'm talking floodgates, baby. I'm talking about other realities. Turn on, tune in, freak out.'

'Yeah?' said Fay, quickly. 'I'll have some of that.'

Leman shook his head. 'It's twenty times stronger than anything you'll have ever had before.'

'Big deal,' said Fay, and grabbed the drug from Leman's upturned palm. 'Reality's boring. I try to avoid it whenever possible.'

Fay looked down at the pill. It didn't seem anything special.

'Careful,' warned John.

Fay ignored him. He was probably just annoyed that she had got the drug instead of him, but she detected a more genuine concern in Leman's eyes. 'Think hard about this,' he said quietly.

Fay slipped the drug between her teeth, swallowing it with a mouthful of wine.

The room was as silent as a midnight church. Fay stood up, pacing the room. She noticed absently the first flickerings of dawn through the dark window panes.

'Well?' asked Gavin.

'Give it time,' said Leman quickly.

Fay glanced around the room. Familiar patterns and shapes. 'Nothing,' she said, slumping in disappointment next to Leman. 'You're a frigging rat, Tony. Tell me the truth: this is a bloody antihistamine or something, isn't it?'

'No,' said Leman. 'No, it isn't. It'll happen,' he said, almost sadly.

Fay took him at his word, and looked around the room again. No change. Then she became aware of her own breathing, the blood pouring through her veins, the scratch of fabric on every inch of her skin. She forced her eyes open – she hadn't even noticed them close – and felt reality *bend*. Leman was saying something, but his voice came towards her in a wave. It was as if four thousand Zen Buddhist monks on a hillside were chanting at her and she was the Dalai Lama.

She swallowed hard. Darkness shrouded the periphery of her sight, then it blossomed blindingly in every direction, like a switch from tunnel vision to Cinemascope. She felt like she was a hundred feet tall. 'Oh,' she heard herself saying. 'I think…'

And then, rather than looking at the room, she looked inside herself, at the world contained within, at the snake wrapped around its apple-green purity, at the gaping mouth beginning to open, spilling dark shapes.

Somewhere, a world away, she could hear herself screaming.

* * *

Fay threw herself to the floor, her arms thrashing about wildly. She screamed again, ranting incoherently as her astonished friends sat motionless around her. Finally, John dragged himself out of his stupor and grabbed hold of Fay's flailing arms, taking a whack in the face for his trouble. 'Help me, for Christ's sake,' he said angrily.

Slowly, Gavin and Chris pulled themselves together and shuffled over to his side.

'Fay,' said John urgently, 'Fay. Listen to me. It's all right. You're with friends. Fay. Calm down.'

'No!' screamed the banshee he was holding. 'Don't let it open its mouth! The snake's opening its mouth.'

'What can you see, Fay?' asked Gavin, pinning her right arm to the ground. 'Can you hear me?'

'It's the snake,' she cried. 'The serpent. It's… It's so big. It's as big as the world.' Then she threw herself up from the floor with an astonishing strength that hurled the others across the room. Her eyes were wide and she stared malevolently at Tony Leman, who sat cowering in the corner. 'They're out,' she said simply. 'They're out and there's nothing you can do to stop them. They're going to kill you all.'

'Who?' asked a terrified Chris.

Fay turned to him, her eyes as black as the pits of hell. Screaming laughter bubbled from the back of her throat. 'They're everywhere.'

'Who are, Fay?'

'The devil goblins from Neptune,' she answered.

PART 3:
I, SPY

CHAPTER 8

Liz stepped down on to the tarmac, nervously pulling her coat tighter around her shoulders. A harsh wind ripped across the runway and surrounding flat grassland. The few buildings that dotted the airfield were indistinct against the watery sky and dimly glowing sun.

Liz turned to see the Doctor joining her under the belly of the Antonov An-26 tactical transport that had brought them to East Germany. She raised her voice against the whining turboprops. 'Not quite what I had in mind when the Brigadier told me to pack for a trip across Europe.'

The Doctor smiled. 'We're not here for the sightseeing, Liz.' He surveyed their surroundings. 'And that's probably just as well.'

The airfield seemed almost entirely deserted, the buildings dilapidated and crumbling. Even the tarmac of the runway was cracked, tufts of grass poking up in search of the weak sunlight. There was only one other plane, an enormous Tupolev Tu-126 in silver and red-starred PVO Strany livery. On the back of the plane, between the sweeping wings and the tail section, towered the enormous rotating saucer shape that housed the radar. The four engines were coughing into life, the eight-bladed contraprops whirling.

'Impressive, no?' Captain Shuskin came alongside them, watching the mechanics making the final pre-flight checks.

'I've never seen one up close,' said the Doctor.

'The basic design dates back almost twenty years. The

96

wingspan of this AWACS version is over fifty metres.'

The Doctor nodded. 'The Soviet Union has never lacked firepower and technology. It makes the disappearance of the soldiers in Siberia all the more disturbing.'

Shuskin nodded. 'Come, let us board.'

They walked across to the other runway in silence. The wind, even stronger away from the protection offered by the first aircraft, whistled shrilly despite the bassy drone of the Tupolev's engines.

The Doctor helped Liz up the steps of the plane. One end of the cavernous interior was given over to rows of radar screens and communication equipment; the other had been hastily filled with seats and a projector and now resembled a miniature lecture theatre.

Shuskin indicated that the Doctor and Liz should sit, which they did, grateful to be out of the cold. One or two of the chairs were already occupied: Shuskin made no attempt to introduce the men, and neither did they seek eye contact with the new arrivals.

The huge door slammed shut. A calm Russian voice crackled over the intercom, and then the engines began screaming. It was clear that the plane was taxiing into position.

Liz turned to the Doctor. 'Shouldn't we strap in or something?'

The Doctor shook his head. 'Don't worry, the take-off will be quite smooth.'

There were few windows in the plane, and it was difficult to tell at what point the massive craft finally lumbered into the air, but a few minutes later the interior lights dimmed still further and the briefing session began. The slide projector hummed gently, and Shuskin began to speak.

'In early March of this year our spy satellites uncovered evidence of what appeared to be a massive mining complex in Siberia.'

The screen glowed to show the garish colours of an artificially enhanced photograph. Twisting blue rivers arced around a region of green, like the outline of hands holding a precious jewel. Right in the centre was a rust-coloured circle, surrounded by tiny ruler-straight lines of black, like a spider's web of fracture marks.

'This uninhabited region is just to the north of the Central Siberian Plateau, well inside the Arctic Circle.'

A second photograph showed the area in more detail, the site resembling a cleaned bullet wound. The dark lines now seemed to be criss-crossing roads, extending some distance into the dark coniferous forests and then stopping dead.

'We dispatched a Yakovlev-26 high-altitude reconnaissance craft. Contact was lost immediately over the area in question, although the pilot confirmed that both construction and mining seemed to be taking place.' Shuskin paused. 'You are familiar, Doctor, with the Mikoyan MiG-25?'

The Doctor turned slightly. 'Yes. The prototypes broke numerous closed-circuit speed, payload-to-height and rate-of-climb records.'

'There is no better plane in the world,' said Shuskin proudly. 'We are already flying with impunity over Israel and Iran on reconnaissance missions. The MiG-25 is simply too fast for your F-4 Phantoms.'

'Madam, please don't equate me with any army or national government,' the Doctor pointed out sharply.

'It is of little importance, Doctor. We sent in three MiG-25s. We barely had time to monitor the battle in which all were lost.'

'Do you have any idea what shot them down?' asked Liz.

'No,' said Shuskin. 'They reported multiple enemy targets, flying in close formation – then nothing.'

Shuskin clicked a button, and the projected image changed to a photograph of what seemed to be a road running through the taiga. Instead of concrete or tarmac, the surface was smooth and silvered, like a long line of mercury. The trees had been harshly but precisely cut away to make way for the road, creating a monotonous edging of green and brown.

'We tried approaching the site by foot, an entire regiment of the Red Army. One soldier was ordered to return to base with these photographs of the road long before the site was reached.'

The picture changed again and again, showing numerous different versions of the road, its smooth-metal surface, and the surrounding area.

'He is the only survivor. If anyone else was sent back with further evidence, they never arrived. And we must presume that the rest of the soldiers died in battle.'

'And you think that alien life forms are behind the construction and all these deaths?' asked Liz.

'Late last year our radar systems reported multiple targets approaching the area.'

The Doctor turned to look at Shuskin, a silhouette against the white light of the projector. 'Multiple targets? Originally one mass, breaking up during the descent?'

'Indeed. This sounds familiar to you?'

'I'm rather afraid it does,' said the Doctor.

'Business or pleasure, sir?' the man at Geneva airport had asked. For the first time in as long as he could remember, Brigadier Lethbridge-Stewart had been lost for a reply.

The ensuing ride through Geneva was lifeless and silent. Normally, with the practised eye of a combat veteran, Lethbridge-Stewart would have been constantly alert, looking around him for potential ambush sites. But now he just slumped in the back of the car, grunting occasionally in response to the young Swiss UNIT captain who was driving him. They passed the Musée d'Art et d'Histoire and the captain tried to start up a conversation, but after three failed attempts he gave up and drove the grateful Brigadier in silence to the meeting place.

The alfresco Royamune café, overlooked by the old League of Nations building, was a regular spot for 'informal chats'. UNIT's structure was such that, because officers often felt unable to go through official government channels, they would, instead, fly to Geneva on leave and 'look up an old friend'. It was a tried and tested method of passing on information without the need to fill in forms, answer awkward questions or, possibly, compromise sources. Lethbridge-Stewart had used it before and knew its effectiveness. Hence, his message to Major-General Augustus 'Tubby' Hayes.

Lethbridge-Stewart and Hayes went back a long way. They had served together at Suez, and then in Aden, where Lethbridge-Stewart's reputation as a superb leader of men had been made. The newspapers called 1967 the 'Summer of Love'. All Lethbridge-Stewart could remember about the year was being a young colonel, fresh from his first close encounter with alien beings, shooting a machine gun at Arabs. Hayes was his commander then, and both had been seconded to UNIT soon afterward. Hayes, the initial government liaison officer to Lethbridge-Stewart as the nominal head of British UNIT, soon climbed the promotion ladder, and was now within the top echelon of the United Nations hierarchy.

Hayes was waiting for him when the Brigadier arrived and stood to greet his old protégé with a friendly handshake and bland questions about shared acquaintances. They sat and began to talk about Aden, and the Yetis in the Underground. Then Hayes snapped his head around to check that they weren't being observed.

'What's it all about, then?' he asked quickly.

'I have concerns. I'm worried about UNIT's internal security.'

'Aren't we all, old man?'

Strangely, despite their many years together, the Brigadier felt unable to entirely confide in Hayes. But vague questions were only going to get vague answers, so he plunged in with both feet. 'Some... information has come into my possession that leads me to, well, perhaps "suspect" is too strong a word...'

'Spit it out, man,' said Hayes harshly.

'Very well. I have specific reason to believe that Geneva HQ has been compromised.'

Lethbridge-Stewart sat back, a huge weight having lifted from his shoulders. He waited for the expected reply from Hayes that this was a ridiculous suggestion and, anyway, what evidence did this jumped-up junior officer have to cast aspersions on the integrity of the dedicated men and women of UNIT? But it didn't come.

'We all run the risk of cuckoos in the nest, don't we, Alistair?' said Hayes, standing and picking up his gloves. 'I expect we shall have cause to speak of this again. Enjoy your holiday, old man.'

The journey seemed to last for ever, and Liz found it increasingly difficult to get comfortable in her seat. After the briefing, Shuskin had handed out various documents and hard-copy photographs, which Liz had glanced at but could make little sense of. Indeed, she was feeling increasingly out of her depth. The comparative speed with which she had been whisked from Cambridge to East Germany and beyond hadn't helped, but really it came down to a growing realisation that this was a purely military problem. And she hadn't become a scientist to help soldiers fight wars with nastier toys than they'd had before.

Of course, she was concerned by the deaths of the soldiers, and the potential threat posed by this mysterious construction site, but it seemed to Liz that this 'mission' was little more than an excuse to watch the Soviets throw increasing amounts of military hardware at what seemed to be an unknowable and deadly alien threat. And she was surprised that the Doctor seemed to be involving himself at that level, discussing military matters with Shuskin towards the rear of the AWACS plane.

Anyway, what could Liz do? She was adaptable, and learnt quickly – it surprised and somewhat depressed her how swiftly she'd picked up the jargon and even the hardware specs of much of the British army – but she wasn't sure how much help she'd be to the Doctor over the coming days. She turned to him as he returned to his seat.

'Why did you ask me to come, Doctor?'

'Two heads are almost always better than one, Liz.'

'But this…' She indicated the craft interior, the officers who worked at the various screens, the accompanying MiGs just visible through the windows. 'It's all so "Come outside if you think you're hard enough".'

'I know,' said the Doctor. 'I'm very aware of the military mind, its predictable response to alien aggression. Just think for a moment. What will the Soviets do if they can't sort this problem out fairly swiftly?'

Liz paused, deep in thought. 'You can't mean…' she said at last.

The Doctor nodded. 'A nuclear strike has already been discussed. It's not an option the military and civil leaders will put off using for much longer.'

Liz gulped. 'But the damage, the fallout… If the wind's in the wrong direction then somewhere like Yakutsk would get roasted. And they don't even know what they're attacking.'

'Exactly,' said the Doctor. 'I'm going to suggest something a little more subtle. They might not listen to me, despite all the trouble they've gone to to get me. But perhaps if both of us shout loudly enough…'

Liz to smiled, ashamed that she'd thought the Doctor was getting too embroiled in the military's distinctive approach to problem-solving. 'And you think there's a link with that meteorite in the UK?'

'Almost certainly.'

'You had an idea there would be, didn't you?'

The Doctor smiled. 'I've never been a believer in coincidence, you know that.'

'Then why come all the way out here?'

'To stay and defend Britain alone would be parochial in the extreme, Liz. Anyway, the aliens – if that is what they are – have only just landed in Britain. They've been in the USSR for a number of months. If we can work out what's going on here, we'll have a pretty clear idea what to expect back in England, won't we?'

Liz nodded, leaning closer to the Doctor. 'And you believe the Soviets?' she whispered. 'You don't think this is all some elaborate trick?'

The Doctor shook his head. 'No. They're frightened. I'm inclined to trust frightened people.'

Mike Yates had volunteered for further duties as soon as it became clear that he hadn't suffered any long-term damage from Shuskin's blow to the head. Although the plan to allow the Doctor's kidnap had worked, and the entire operation was completed with minimal fuss or loss of life, Mike couldn't help but feel that his own rampaging hormones had let the Brigadier and the Doctor down.

The Doctor, of course, harboured no resentment, and, thankfully, Lethbridge-Stewart seemed preoccupied and had dispatched Yates with Sergeant Benton to the site of the festival to see if any further information could be gleaned from 'those young people'. From the reaction of the couple in the van two nights before, Yates suspected that there was very little chance of a pair of army officers, however nice and 'with it' they might seem, getting much frankness from the peace-and-love freaks.

He'd decided that they should travel in civvies and pose as journalists from the underground press.

'Remember,' he said, as they parked his Datsun close to the entrance to the festival grounds, 'If anybody asks, just say you're with the *International Times*, and say "man" a lot. It'll be a breeze.'

'Yes, sir,' said Benton.

'John, for goodness sake, stop calling me "sir" – that's a bit of a give-away, wouldn't you say?'

'Yes, sir… Mike.'

'That's better.'

As they walked through the near-deserted grounds Yates became increasingly aware that they probably stood out amongst the litter and the occasional clump of windswept youths like a pair of stolen cars. Oh, well. Standard army procedure: press on regardless.

'Check out the squares,' said one boy as they passed his tent.

'Hi, man,' said Yates with a cheesy grin. 'Me and my mate are from *IT*. We heard there was a happening going down?'

'Your hair's too short,' the boy said with disinterest. 'Make like a drum, and beat it till you've got yourself together, man.' He turned and scuttled back into his tent, muttering about 'weekend hippies'.

'Not very successful,' said Benton, straight-faced.

'No,' agreed Yates. 'Still, I suppose that proves we're never going to convince anyone we're part of their scene. We'd better just say we're from the *Daily Mirror* or something. At least that's left-wing. Let's try over there…'

They headed towards a group of dirty Transit vans with a large bonfire roaring away in front of them.

'Not a very inviting bunch,' said Benton as they closed in on a group of suspicious-looking long-haired people in flowing kaftans.

'First impressions aren't always reliable,' said Yates, turning on his most charming smile as he approached the group. 'Hi,' he said, 'I'm Mike Yates from the *Mirror*. Nice day, isn't it?'

There followed a long period of silence before one of the group, a woman, answered. 'Every day is a beautiful day on God's Earth,' she said.

Oh great, thought Yates. The Jesus Freaks. 'Good way of putting it,' he said. 'Listen. We've been sent down to find out what was going down at the gig on Thursday. You know, the lights in the sky and all that.'

'Why?' said another of the group.

The question floored Yates. 'Why what?'

'Why do you want to know about the lights?'

'Knowledge is good,' said Yates. 'Anything unusual should be publicised, so that people can learn what's going on.'

'People don't want to learn anything,' said the woman, sitting cross-legged next to the fire. 'They can't accept simple truths so they've got to invent their own meanings for the obvious. The signs are there, and have been for months.'

'Meaning…?'

'We're the Venus People,' she continued. 'You've heard of us?'

'Should we have?' asked Benton sarcastically.

'Not if you're too blind to see and too deaf to hear,' said a tall man with wild blond hair who had just emerged from one of the vans.

'What do you believe in?' asked Yates.

'We believe that God has seen the sick and sorry state of this planet and that he's gone to Venus,' said the newcomer. 'But mankind can't get its act together so he's gonna come down with his angels and wipe the planet clean.'

Yates nodded. 'Armageddon…'

'Too right,' said the man. 'But before he does that, he's gonna send the Saucer People to take us away to Eden.'

'On Venus,' continued another of the group. 'Just us, and the bands. *They* know. The Beatles, Floyd. That's what "Astronomy Domine" is all about, right?'

'Shut up, Crispin,' said the blond man angrily. 'They don't give a toss about all that. They're just here to suss out the scene and give it back to the Man, right?'

'Not exactly...' began Yates.

'Don't give me that crap. You're MI5, or Special Branch, or the military. You stink of it, man. I can smell you from miles away.'

Neither Yates nor Benton said anything. With their cover seemingly blown, their choices were limited. Yates chose to try to bluff it out. 'What makes you think that?' he asked.

'Before God found me, I was like you,' said the man. 'He sent the Saucer People to me. They said, "Arlo, it's coming down big time, baby. It's gonna be the end of everything."'

'You don't say?' muttered Benton.

'You're too uptight to dig anything, man,' said Arlo. 'So you just run off back to the cats in charge, and tell them what the Saucer People said: Earth's days are numbered.'

'I shan't be telling them that, or anything like it,' said Yates. 'What I will tell them is that I met a bunch of hippie dropouts who've had one too many herbal cigarettes. Come on, Sergeant, let's get out of here. Can't say I like the smell.'

Yates turned and hurried away. Benton, looking nonplussed, eventually caught up with him. 'What now?' he asked.

'I go to that pub in the village and have a very large drink,' said Yates. 'You can join me if you want.'

Benton smiled broadly. 'Now you're talking my language, sir.' He paused, glancing back over his shoulder. 'I take it you didn't believe what those freaks were dribbling on about?'

Yates stopped suddenly. 'Of course I believe them. But I don't want them to know that.' He smiled. 'I'm just trying to work out how on Earth I'm going to report it.'

* * *

106

Moments after they landed at a Soviet military base, the Doctor, Liz, and Shuskin had been escorted to another part of the airfield, where a fleet of helicopters were waiting for them. Liz felt a vague sense of disappointment: the overlapping runways and low buildings looked not unlike those they'd left behind in Germany. She'd always wanted to explore eastern Europe – the USSR in particular – but it looked as if her first and only glimpse of life behind the Iron Curtain would be from the windows of various aircraft.

The Doctor nodded approvingly at the helicopters arranged before them. 'We're actually very privileged, Liz.'

'We are?'

He pointed out the differing types for Liz. 'That huge beast over there is a Mil Mi-6, NATO codename: "Hook". It's a basic heavy-transport machine. Those smaller ones over there are Mi-8s, general utility helicopters.' Liz noted that most had external pylons fitted, bristling with rockets and gun pods. 'Now, here's the really interesting thing.' He pointed to a pair of helicopters towards the rear of the airfield. They were the smallest of all, almost insignificant as they faced her on the tarmac, were it not for their menacing crouch and their weapon-loaded stub wings almost as wide as the motionless rotors. 'Very early examples of the Mil Mi-24, the first true Soviet helicopter gunship, if I'm not mistaken. I wasn't aware any had been built yet. You can clearly see, however, the debts owed to the Mi-8 and –'

'I'm really sorry, Doctor,' said Liz. 'I never got round to finishing *Jane's Book of Helicopters.*'

Despite Liz's interruption, Shuskin appeared pleased with the Doctor's knowledge. 'I am glad you feel privileged. No other Westerner has been permitted to see the prototypes.'

Liz noted an expression of sadness flicker across the Doctor's face as the blades on the two gunships began to rotate. 'Terrifying, isn't it?' he said. 'Mankind can make even an instrument of death and destruction almost beautiful.'

CHAPTER 9

The Mi-24 helicopter gunships rose from the tarmac, then twisted across the runways like a pair of dragonflies over still water. The dark nose cannons twitched inquisitively in the cold evening sky.

The larger Mi-8s followed, adopting a diamond formation against the clouds. By the time the enormous and bulbous Mi-6s had pulled themselves cautiously away from the runways and surrounding fields the air was heavy with the pulsating cadence of numerous rotor blades. A trio of MiG-25s roared overhead from a neighbouring air base, angular silver arrows that faded swiftly and noisily from view.

The pub was called the Rat and Parrot, a lovely old rustic Tudor building with thick oak beams and real ale. Yates and Benton introduced themselves to the landlord, this time using no aliases, and found the man to be quite chatty and open. He gave them a first-hand report about what he believed to have been a comet crashing into the sea on Thursday night.

'I suppose,' said Yates as they sat down with pints of foaming beer, 'a comet is the most likely explanation.'

'Sounds reasonable,' noted Benton.

'Except that everything that Arlo character said had a ring of truth about it.'

'Surely not, sir? He was just a freak. Too many drugs and not enough baths, I'd have thought.'

'Maybe,' said Yates, sounding unconvinced.

'Mind you, I did think there was something odd about him.'

'Odd?'

'Dangerous. I can't place it exactly, but I'm pretty sure I've seen him somewhere before...' Benton's voice trailed away as his attention was drawn to the television set on the bar, and a football game in progress. 'See the World Cup highlights last night, sir?' he asked.

'What? Oh yes. Very good goal that Brazilian chap scored,' said Yates absent-mindedly.

'True,' noted Benton, 'But the defending was shocking. Now if that had been in England, the centre-half would have clattered him into the tenth row of the stand. Let's see him try and score from there! That's the trouble with your average Johnny Foreigner: give them a slap and they don't want to know...' Again Benton's concentration gave out on him and he stared intently at his beer.

'What's the matter?' asked Yates.

'It's... annoying,' said Benton, 'I know I've seen that Arlo bloke before, but I'm blowed if I can remember where.'

Yates stood and drained his glass. 'Come on, John,' he said. 'We'd better get back to HQ and get in a report about all this jiggery-pokery. Though what the Brigadier'll make of it, I shudder to think.'

The Doctor stared out of the side portals of the helicopter, a childlike excitement marbling his evident anxiety. The din inside their Mi-6 was such that Liz had spent almost the entire take-off with her hands over her ears. The Soviet soldiers, sitting impassively on benches, seemed less concerned.

The Doctor turned away from the window. There was little to see now, and their target – the alien mining complex, or whatever it was – was still some distance away.

'This really is the back of beyond,' observed Liz over the noise of the rotors.

'It's easy to forget that hundreds of square miles of the Soviet Union are well inside the Arctic Circle,' commented the Doctor. 'And that the taiga covers nearly half of the country. That's something like a quarter of the world's forests.'

'All the same, a rather remote landing point for our not-so-friendly aliens.'

The Doctor laughed. 'You can't expect them to keep coming out of the sewers next to St Paul's! London might be the invasion capital of Earth, but it hasn't got a monopoly, you know.' He paused, rubbing his chin. 'In many ways this is an ideal location. Sparsely populated, but well within one of the world's superpowers. Or perhaps there's something very specific they want here. It is supposed to be a mine, after all.'

'You're assuming that they came here by choice.'

The Doctor nodded. 'I think it unlikely that they came here by accident. But you're right: we shouldn't make any assumptions at this stage.'

Liz turned to Captain Shuskin, seated at their side. 'Do you have any idea what to expect?' she asked, almost daring her to come out with a stock response, full of pride and patriotism.

Instead, Shuskin shook her head honestly. 'No. I've been analysing and re-analysing the reports in my mind ever since I was briefed on the problem. The only thing I know is that whatever is there, it isn't human.' She glanced out of the windows. 'The gunships will be approaching the target area soon.'

Benton spent most of the journey back staring blankly out of the car window, occasionally muttering aloud. He was furious with himself that his normally so reliable memory had let him down. Yates seemed absorbed in the mixture of Radio 2 muzak and the one o'clock news, with its lead story about the still-unsolved and apparently motiveless murder of two young people close to the site of the Redborough '70 pop-music festival. Meanwhile, in America, the Beatles were preparing to play the Altmount Speedway Stadium to an expected audience of half a million. As the report segued into sports news, Yates looked across at Benton.

'Arlo's worrying you, isn't he?'

'To be frank, sir, yes.'

'Very well. When we get back to HQ, check on his background. See if you can dig up anything tangible.'

'Thank you sir,' said Benton. 'I'm sure he might be important.'

Flight Lieutenant Nikolai Pakilev stared through the bulletproof perspex and saw only dark clouds merging seamlessly into the angular pine trees of the forest. The instruments showed an empty sky, bar the tiny points of light representing the Mi-8s behind them and the other gunship to Pakilev's left.

Pakilev eased the joystick to the right, the helicopter arcing away to adopt a different line of approach. Radio silence was to be maintained until an enemy target was positively identified: for the moment, both he and Grennikov were simply following through the approach they'd agreed with their commanding officers.

Pakilev checked his wing-mounted armaments for the hundredth time, cycling through the options on the weapons display. The four pods each held thirty-two 57mm unguided rockets, and the rails carried four air-to-ground, wire-guided missiles. His orders were clear: engage with any aerial targets, and launch strikes against the construction to ascertain its ability to resist direct attack. The complex was now only a few kilometres away.

Despite the drone of the blades and the cramped conditions in the cockpit, Pakilev remained calm and detached. He was merely the mind of his machine. The sweat running down his neck, the pins and needles tingling in his legs – none of this was important. The only senses that mattered were the external ones of the gunship, the radar signals spreading out invisibly into the darkness, the laser rangefinder that would surely see use before too long.

He glanced down again at the radar screen, splashes of green luminescence dappling his face. The Mi-8s had now come closer, and the target was no more than –

Wait, the signals were wrong, too small and numerous for the supporting utility helicopters. The tiny contacts were travelling *towards* the Mi-8s, having appeared without warning some kilometres to the rear of the gunships. How could the enemy launch so many craft when the reconnaissance photographs had shown no airfields in the area?

Pakilev established radio contact with Grennikov on an open channel, hoping to warn the other helicopters if their instruments had not yet picked up the enemy craft. 'I will move to intercept the multiple enemy targets,' he stated. 'You continue on to the destination.'

Pakilev's gunship had already come to a halt, circling around as it hovered. Soon it had turned through 180 degrees, then the nose dipped, and the blades once more began to push it through the air. The craft's maximum speed was 275 kilometres per hour; even so, Pakilev knew that the enemy targets would intercept the Mi-8s long before they would come into range of the gunship's weapons.

'Blue Flight, you have multiple targets coming towards you. They are small – very small – they might even look like a flock of birds on your equipment. But be warned. Suggest that we now keep all radio channels open. Over.'

Once back at UNIT HQ, Mike Yates checked at reception and was told that neither the Brigadier nor the Doctor had yet reported in from their various destinations. However, a hastily scribbled note from the Brigadier had been left for him. It mentioned a file on higher-than-normal radiation levels in the sea, which the

Brigadier felt might have some connection with the events at the pop festival. The file, the note went on to say, had been given to the Doctor but, in his haste to leave for the Soviet Union, he'd barely glanced at it. Yates, the note concluded, should 'take appropriate action'. Whatever that meant.

'Sergeant Benton,' said Yates with irritation. 'Before you start chasing up our long-haired weirdo friend, go down to the Doctor's lab and pick up this file for me, will you?'

'Yes, sir,' said Benton, immediately turning down the corridor.

Yates watched him go, and felt like calling him back. It was a menial task and Yates was angry that he had delegated it to Benton, who was not only a friend, but also much too busy with his own work to be treated as a dogsbody. It said much for Benton's superbly developed discipline that he hadn't complained to Yates's face about being asked to do what any first-day recruit could have done. But Yates knew that the chain of command made any sort of apology inadvisable. The infallibility of rank must be seen to be maintained.

So he turned, annoyed by his own shortcomings, and headed for the Brigadier's office and the bottle of Scotch in his filing cabinet.

The Mi-6 carrying the Doctor and Liz suddenly banked to one side. Liz could tell from the Doctor's face that this was a worrying development not envisaged in the original mission plan, but he waited patiently while Shuskin ran towards the front of the helicopter.

Moments later she returned, clearly worried. She barked out orders to the soldiers, and then turned to Liz and the Doctor. 'Blue Flight have come under attack.'

'From what?' asked the Doctor.

'We can't tell from the garbled messages. But they're small and agile.'

'So what's happening?' asked Liz.

'We're making preparations to land. Plan B. We'll have to approach the target on foot.'

'A whole regiment got wiped out,' said Liz. 'And they were better armed than we are.'

'I'm aware of that,' snapped Shuskin.

'Can't we go to the aid of the others?' asked the Doctor.

Shuskin shook her head emphatically. 'No.' She smiled one of her bitter smiles. 'You forget, Doctor. This helicopter has no offensive armament whatsoever.'

John Benton would have been surprised that Captain Yates was even beginning to regret his impatiently snapped instruction. Benton had always obeyed orders without question. As a raw eighteen-year-old, then a private in the rifle brigade of the 17th & 21st Lancers, Benton had been taught harsh lessons in the military way. If it moves, salute it; if it doesn't, whitewash it.

He reached the Doctor's lab to find it in darkness. Entering, he switched on the light and looked around for the file he had been sent to get. He spotted it on the workbench next to the TARDIS and picked it up, turning for the door. He paused for a moment as he passed the police box, looking at it with a smirk on his face as wide as the Thames estuary. If he'd told any of his mates from the 17th & 21st that he worked with a man who travelled through time and space in a police box, they'd have sent for the regimental trick cyclist and a straitjacket.

Benton reached the door and switched off the light.

Something made him turn back and look around the room. There was a tiny red light, flickering under the Doctor's workbench. Benton assumed that some of the Doctor's equipment was still switched on, and he was about to leave when a part of his subconscious decided that this was the moment to free-associate, and, in a flash of inspiration, he suddenly remembered where he'd seen Arlo. It was in the newspaper last week. The article on that pop festival. A photograph of Viscount Rose, the hippie landowner who had lent his grounds to those whacked-out freaks. Of course, Arlo's picture must have been in that article. Benton paused – he could hear ticking. Great clocks filled his thoughts as a picture formed in his mind of Rose standing with the leader of the Venus People. Smiling.

'Connection…?'

Tick. Tick. Tick.

Benton shook his head. His brain seemed wrapped in cotton wool. 'Think,' he said angrily.

Tick. Tick. Tick.

'Of course!'

Then the room exploded, and Benton forgot all about the aristocrat and the hippie.

CHAPTER 10

Pakilev's Mi-24 gunship came up over a rise and hovered just above the trees. For a moment the young pilot could do little more than sit and stare.

What was left of Blue Flight was under attack, not from craft of any sort, but from swarming creatures with flapping bat-like wings. They ebbed and flowed as if controlled by a single mind, concentrating on one craft, then splitting in two to avoid the fire from the Mi-8's wing-mounted gun pods, then wheeling and arcing to attack another. From this distance Pakilev couldn't even see their weapons, although the effects were clear enough: a helicopter's engine compartment glowed brightly, then exploded in a burst of silver and red light. The smoking remains of the destroyed Mi-8 plummeted towards the ground like a hurled stone. Explosive flowers blossomed across the landscape, the trees igniting despite the cold. Each glowing beacon indicated a downed helicopter; there were more of them than craft left in the sky.

The creatures themselves were greyish, child-sized, and humanoid but barely human. Their limbs were scrawny and slender, the wings dark and angular. Occasionally a creature would come under concentrated gunfire, shuddering under the impact before falling to the ground in a rush of jumbled arms and wings. Like a dead butterfly. Or a fallen angel.

But any physical weakness was more than made up for by their number and agility. Pakilev couldn't even estimate how many there were, and it was little wonder that the radar of the Mi-8s barely picked up their attackers in time.

As unusual as the menace was, Pakilev had already begun to assess the attackers from a military perspective. Missiles were out of the question: the creatures seemed too quick, too intuitively aware of any threat of that nature. And, anyway, the gunship's missiles were designed to work only against large ground-based targets. The rockets might just be viable, but the machine gun seemed to be the best option.

The waiting was over. Time to engage.

Pakilev swept the sight over the closest group of creatures, keeping his thumb firmly pressed against the trigger. The helicopter rocked slightly, the bullets chasing across the air towards the grey figures. He caught one or two, who clattered into each other before falling. The group as a whole turned their attention towards the hovering helicopter. As they came closer Pakilev glimpsed their eyes glowing brightly, faces locked in savage sneers.

Pakilev eased the gunship backward, striving to maintain the distance between him and the creatures. All the while he kept firing. An increasing number of doll-like figures writhed under the hail of bullets and then tumbled down, but the onrushing group never seemed to dwindle in number. Pakilev could have sworn he heard them giggling like children.

A handful of the imp-like things broke off from the main mass and darted towards him, wings a blur of motion. Pakilev twisted the machine gun towards them, then released a clutch of rockets towards the others. Most missed, but some of the rockets clipped the small targets, exploding and sending limbs and wings flying in all directions.

A pair of Mi-8s had silently assumed a position behind the group that was menacing Pakilev's gunship, and moments later they opened fire with cannons and rockets. Pakilev hoped that the missiles wouldn't see him as a much larger and therefore more inviting target than the diminutive creatures. No wonder the MiGs had found it difficult: heat-seeking missiles are designed to lock on to the warmth of a jet engine, not the minute patterns of living things.

One of the monsters clattered against the gunship's cockpit, its claws scrabbling against the transparent shield as Pakilev instinctively pushed the helicopter into a downward spiral in an attempt to shake off the creature. Only then did the young pilot realise that he'd now moved away from the covering fire of the Mi-8s and into a ravine where a group of dark flapping figures seemed to be waiting for him, just above the trees. It was a trap – they barely registered on the radar. Pakilev could just perceive the arms of the creatures moving in his direction, firing something –

The world exploded: blood-red, then black.

'He's lucky to be alive,' said Dr French as he stood and brushed the dust from his trousers. 'Must be all that square-bashing, it's given him a thick skull!'

Captain Yates ignored the sarcasm and watched mutely as the stretcher on which Benton had been secured was picked up by two paramedics and carried along the rubble-strewn corridor. 'My fault,' he muttered angrily, and then turned back to the young doctor, who was absorbed in clearing away the emergency medical kit.

'I'm sorry?' inquired French.

'Nothing.' Yates walked into the laboratory. 'Hell,' he said to no one in particular. 'The Doctor's going to go ballistic when he sees this.'

Dr French nodded sympathetically. 'Who do you think is responsible?' he asked. 'Black Panthers? Red Mole? The Weathermen? Baader-Meinhof? The PLO?'

'Couldn't give a toss,' snarled Yates, sweeping concrete rubble from the bench top. 'Anyway, that's classified.'

'Of course,' whispered French conspiratorially. 'Mum's the word.'

Yates peered through the huge hole blown in the work

surface. The bomb had been meant for the Doctor, that much seemed clear. It was just blind luck that poor old Benton had been sent to fetch the file. 'Must have had a heat sensor on it,' he noted out loud. Then again, Benton's distance from the bomb implied that the thing hadn't gone off immediately. Perhaps it was just a warning, or a threat. But a potentially lethal one, all the same.

Yates turned to the door. 'If you'll excuse me, Doctor, I have to find the scum responsible for this and crucify them.'

The summer sun was just fading down towards the horizon when Mike Yates reached the Brigadier's office. He slammed the door behind him, and sat down wearily. French's speculation on which terrorist organisation had been responsible had set off a chain reaction in Yates's mind. The choices were mind-boggling – any one of those mentioned would have had good reason to strike at the heart of UNIT, but none seemed to have had any opportunity. The inescapable conclusion was that this had been an inside job. And the consequences of *that* eventuality were simply too horrible to contemplate.

A knock on the door snapped Yates from his solitary gloom. 'Come,' he said in a voice that betrayed much of the anxiety that had descended around him.

'The results of the report, sir,' said Corporal Bell, coming into the office with a grave look on her face.

'Give me the edited highlights, Carol,' said Mike, reaching out for the file.

'Inconclusive,' she said with an embarrassed sigh.

'Meaning...?'

'The technology is basic. It could have been made by anyone. But there was a UNIT serial code on the timing mechanism. It seems to be Russian in origin.'

Yates sat bolt upright. 'I see,' he said quickly.

'But that's all, sir. There's nothing else to tie it to anyone in particular. I don't think we should jump to too many conclusions just yet.'

'Thanks for the advice,' said Yates, somewhat dismissively. 'Anything else?'

'Yes,' replied Bell. 'The Brigadier made contact whilst you were in conference with the police. He's staying at the Hotel Europa in Geneva. I have his number if you want me to raise him for you.'

Yates nodded. 'Yes, I think I'd better have a word, don't you?'

'We're under attack!' yelled Shuskin as the helicopter pitched violently.

Liz glanced round to see the Doctor, his face pressed against the glass of one of the tiny windows, legs braced against the motion of the helicopter. She ran to his side, clinging on to a rail overhead. 'What's happening?'

'Alien creatures,' said the Doctor. 'Firing some sort of heat or directed-energy weapon.' He turned to Liz. 'No wonder the planes couldn't cope with them. How can you be expected to attack a target the size of a child in a jet travelling at Mach three point two?'

'So the helicopters are holding out against the aliens?' queried Liz.

The Doctor's face was downcast. 'I wouldn't really put it like that, I'm afraid.'

The Mi-6 lurched again, struggling to evade its pursuers.

'There must be something you can do,' said Liz. Even the Soviet soldiers were staring at the Doctor, as if they realised his key role in all that was taking place.

'Well,' said the Doctor. 'First things first: we need to be able to protect ourselves from those heat weapons.' He turned to Shuskin. 'I must get to the helicopter's electrics – some sort of junction box that's accessible internally.'

Captain Shuskin paused in thought, and then led the way to a point just behind the cockpit. Thick cables ran into what reminded Liz of a domestic fuse box. The Doctor smiled delightedly, and ripped off the metal cover.

Shuskin went to say something, but Liz stopped her. 'Yes, he knows it's live. And, no, he doesn't really know what he's doing.'

The Doctor spoke through gritted teeth, tugging against an inch-thick wire. 'I think you've been working with me for too long,' he said.

The helicopter pitched again, and Liz could see dark shapes flitting by the windows.

The Doctor pulled his sonic screwdriver from his pocket, and aimed the point at the cable. With a shrill noise it began to melt the plastic covering. Moments later the Doctor twisted the screwdriver around and unceremoniously shoved the blunt end into the revealed bare wires.

There was a loud crack that reminded Liz of ice breaking on a pond, and the interior lights flickered for a moment. 'Are you OK?' she asked.

'I'm fine, Liz,' said the Doctor. 'Now what I need is a small piece of metal, about an inch or two in length. A hairclip or some such.'

Liz and Shuskin exchanged glances, shrugging their shoulders. 'Not sure we can help there, Doctor,' said Liz.

'What? You're both women aren't you...? There must be something,' said the Doctor, looking around the helicopter's interior. Was it Liz's imagination, or was the temperature already beginning to rise?

One of the soldiers came running forward with a thick pin used to secure an ammunition box. 'Perfect,' enthused the Doctor. Gingerly he used the piece of metal to establish a connection between the helicopter's hull and the sonic screwdriver. 'Make sure that nobody touches the hull from now on,' snapped the Doctor. He waited for Shuskin to bark out an order, then he twisted a dial high up on the screwdriver. It began to flicker, Liz catching glimpses of the interior mechanism through the brilliant white glow.

The Doctor stood up. 'That should do it.' He turned to Shuskin. 'I suggest we land as soon as possible.'

She nodded and walked into the cockpit.

'What did you do?' asked Liz.

'I've diverted all the auxiliary electrical power to the helicopter's outer structure. Suitably modulated, of course. The sonic screwdriver is insulated against electric shock, but here I'm using it to divert the power supply from the wire to the ship's exterior, via that metal pin.'

'So?'

'So it will protect us from the weapons of those creatures.' He looked around him, then drew a Paisley handkerchief to wipe across his brow. 'Is it me, or is it getting hot in here?'

The last rays of the dying sun caught the surface of Lake Geneva, throwing off a bedazzling display of fractured light. Lethbridge-Stewart rested on the balcony rail of his hotel, looking across the lake towards Montalegre harbour on the southern side. A little inland was the Villa Diodati, where Milton had once lived, and where in 1816, at the maddest Mad Hatter's tea party of all time, Lord Byron, Percy and Mary Shelley, Claire Godwin, and John Polidori had terrified each other with ghost stories.

'"And what were thou, and earth, and stars and sea,/If to the human mind's imaginings/Silence and solitude were vacancy?"' he mumbled to himself.

The Brigadier shook his head. A childish passion for dead poets was the last thing he needed on his mind right now. And yet he couldn't help but let himself drift back to Harrow school in 1943, and an essay on the homoerotic content of 'Adonais'. Now, like Ozymandias, the king of kings, he found himself sitting amid 'the decay of that colossal wreck'. His attention turned to a minor domestic incident in the street below – an angry holiday family arguing with a gendarme over the loss of their car. So much for the most civilised country in Europe.

He left the veranda and went back into his hotel room, sitting on the bed and opening his briefcase. He took out the stock on his Colt Commando high-velocity rifle. Having screwed the barrel into place, he checked the weapon's sight, aiming at the fountain in the lake. Click. His finger touched the trigger lightly and, metaphorically, the fountain lay dead. As if in acknowledgement of the Brigadier, the water pressure seemed to dip momentarily. Lethbridge-Stewart's heart pumped faster. Join the army. Be a man. Kill someone.

The noise from the street, the babbling conversations in French, irritated him. He stood the rifle by the bed and crossed again to the window. He had put off thinking about the full consequences of his visit, but now knew that something had to be done. He still wasn't sure what that something was.

The telephone rang, startling him. He picked it up, half expecting to hear someone from HQ demanding to know what he thought he was doing sitting in a hotel room playing espionage games. Instead the hotel receptionist informed him that he had an overseas call from London, England. A knot tightened in his stomach.

'*Merci beaucoup,*' he replied quickly and waited for the line to clear. 'Lethbridge-Stewart,' he said, hoping to cover his anxiety with bluster, as usual.

'Good evening, sir.' It was Yates. 'I'm sorry to trouble you.'

'That's quite all right, Captain.' Relief flooded through the Brigadier. 'How are... things?'

'Well, sir,' said Yates, with a dip in his voice that told the Brigadier that 'things' weren't good, 'I'm rather afraid we've had a terrorist incident.'

123

The Brigadier listened intently as Yates quickly explained about the bomb, adding that apart from Benton's relatively minor injuries no one else had been hurt.

'That's a small consolation, I suppose,' said the Brigadier. 'How on Earth was security penetrated?'

'As far as we can tell, sir, it wasn't,' continued Yates. 'The most important aspect of the case seems to be the design of the bomb. Certain elements indicate that it's of Soviet origin. And there was a UNIT serial code on it.'

The Brigadier said nothing for a long time. He was thinking about what Shelley had written in 'The Mask of Anarchy':

> *Shake your chains to earth like dew*
> *Which in sleep had fallen on you –*
> *Ye are many – they are few.*

'Are you still there, sir?' asked a worried Yates.

'Yes, Captain. The Russians would not have gone to all the trouble of trying to kidnap the Doctor when they could have blown him up as easily as that. And I don't believe that Captain Shuskin would further jeopardise the future of UNIT by trying to pull a stunt such as this.'

Yates seemed to be struggling to follow Lethbridge-Stewart's logic. 'Do the Communists need an excuse to interfere with our operations?' he asked strongly.

'Of course they do,' replied the Brigadier angrily. 'Use your brain, man – this isn't comic-book international intrigue we're talking about. The future of the planet may be at stake.'

'So who do you think planted the bomb, then?' asked a chastened Yates.

The Brigadier paused. 'Give me the serial number, Captain.'

'It's 261063240268, sir.'

The Brigadier noted the number on hotel headed note paper. 'Thank you, Yates.' And with that, he put down the phone, took his

UNIT clearance documents from his luggage, and headed for the door.

The pilot landed the helicopter as close to the construction site as possible. Smoke was pouring from the turbines; perhaps that was sufficient to fool their attackers into thinking that the Mi-6 would explode on impact. Certainly the small creatures seemed to turn their attention elsewhere, and so they missed the craft's abrupt landing, splitting asunder the huge coniferous trees to create its own clearing. Just before the wheels hit the frozen soil the engine casing exploded outward, sending more thick black smoke into the air.

Liz emerged from the downed helicopter gingerly. The soldiers fanned out to the periphery of the clearing, guns trained upward into the night sky. Engineers, coughing against the smoke, were already swarming over the mountings beneath the rotor blades.

Liz looked up. The night sky was streaked with black and grey, like some grotesque modern painting. There were certainly no helicopters or planes there now. Even the goblin-like creatures seemed to be heading away in a dark swarm. She shivered at the sound of their rustling wings, fading all the while.

The Doctor joined her. 'I don't think I recognise the alien species,' he noted, 'But their intent so far has been unequivocal.'

'That was a clever trick you pulled with the modulated power supply.'

'It's always very difficult to ascertain precisely how different types of energy will interact,' the Doctor observed. He pulled his sonic screwdriver from his pocket. The casing was dark and scorched. 'Much longer and I think this would have gone pop!'

The Doctor and Liz turned as two BTR-40PB scout cars trundled down the ramp at the back of the helicopter, the gun turrets swinging from side to side. Shuskin came over to them, delighted, it seemed, to have got this far. 'So, Doctor, you still believe that subtlety might work where an entire armoured column did not?'

'It's better than the other option you presented me with.'

'The mechanics report that the helicopter needs much repair.'

'Leave the scout cars here,' said the Doctor. 'Their guns might come in useful in case the helicopter is attacked again. But for us, going in on foot means just that.'

'We'll leave behind a handful of troops,' said Shuskin. 'It would be stupid if we got back here safely, and there was no means of escape open to us.' She turned and bellowed orders to the men.

The Doctor turned to Liz, whispering urgently. 'You don't have to come, Liz, you do know that?'

Liz smiled, although she didn't feel particularly brave all of a sudden. 'Two heads are better than one, remember? Besides, I'm not sure I'd be any safer here with the chopper than out in the forest with you and Shuskin.'

Two minutes later, the group began pushing their way through the dense forest towards the alien stronghold.

They found the remains of the Soviet armoured column soon enough. The Doctor had warned against following the alien 'roads' towards the mining complex, but Shuskin had insisted. It was imperative for her that they discover what happened to the regiment.

The first vehicle had loomed suddenly out of the darkness. It was a T-55 battle tank, almost embedded in the undergrowth, as if it had turned away from the track in desperation. It was entirely burnt out. One of the access hatches in the turret had been pushed open, but only a blackened arm protruded, fingers locked in position like a claw.

Shuskin turned away. She didn't need to see anything else.

Just beyond the T-55 was the road, and scattered the length of that were burnt or overturned vehicles: tanks, APCs, assault guns.

A smattering of self-propelled anti-aircraft guns and even some field howitzers showed that the organisers had tried to cater for every eventuality with a piece of hardware. But they could never have envisaged the true nature of the aggressor.

Shuskin walked slowly across the road, glancing at the corpses that seemed to reach out towards her, imploring her to do something. She felt impotent in the face of such destruction.

The Soviet captain turned to her soldiers. They were worried, and looked to her for guidance. 'Spread out and check the surrounding area for survivors,' she ordered, trying her best to imply that even this great tragedy was part of the plan. 'We do not want to stay on this road for any longer than absolutely necessary.'

The Doctor, towards the edge of the group, glanced up from a map and nodded.

'Five minutes, and we return to the forest,' ordered Shuskin. 'Go!'

Shuskin watched as the men spread out, poking corpses with bayonets and attempting to pull open welded-shut hatches. Individual beams of torch light were lost in the darkness. She thought about crossing to the Doctor and Liz, but they seemed more concerned by the unusual substance that formed the alien road. And, anyway, just at that moment Shuskin didn't feel like sharing the grief of a Soviet soldier with Westerners.

A scream snapped Shuskin out of her reverie. Somewhere, a torch beam was flailing into the sky. She could hear brutal chuckling. There was something deadly, still, in the shadows.

There was a second scream, and then silence.

THIRD INTERLUDE:
BLACK ANGEL'S DEATH SONG

'Good day at work, darling?'

A cliché, no matter how well meant, is still a cliché.

'It was all right.' Sergeant Robert Franklin opened the door of the Triumph Stag, patting it proudly. 'Picked up the car… As you can see!' A smile played over his lips.

'Thank the Lord for that,' said Julia. 'I hate having to get the bus. It's so… common.' She giggled brightly and kissed her husband on the cheek. 'What shift are you on tomorrow?'

'I'm not,' he replied. 'Finished for the week.'

'Great,' she said. 'I don't go in till two.'

Franklin, smiling at the thought of a rare lie-in, keyed the ignition and eased the car through the huge wrought-iron gates of Redborough General. A career policeman, he had met his wife when she first joined the hospital as a junior pathologist. It was middle-income lust at first sight.

'Anything unusual going on, Bob?' Julia asked as the car sped off down Longman's Hill Road and towards the outlying villages. She clamped a hand to her head to prevent the *dernier* beret from flying off into old farmer Hislop's top meadow.

'How do you mean?'

'You remember that boy you were talking about last night?'

Franklin adjusted his sunglasses in the rear-view mirror, and changed gear for the climb up the hill. 'Which boy was that?'

'You know,' said Julia, angry at her husband's playful teasing. 'The one you said was "as high as a ruddy balloon". The one who murdered the boy and girl over Westbury way.'

'Oh, *that* boy,' said Franklin sarcastically. 'William Dyson. South London lowlife with a list of previous as long as the garden path.'

'What, violent behaviour, that sort of thing?' asked Julia, surprised.

'No, drugs mainly. Why do you ask?' The car reached the top of the hill now, levelling out next to the long barrow.

'I did the autopsy on the two victims this afternoon. Very nasty indeed.'

'Do you mind?' said Franklin tartly. 'I'm about to have my tea. I don't want the gory details of your butchery!'

'Very funny,' said Julia, changing the subject. 'What's on TV tonight?'

Franklin slowed the car on the far side of the hill as they approached their cliff-top cottage overlooking the Channel. 'Kenny Elliott was saying there's a documentary on *Man Alive* about the space mission to Neptune.'

'And it's *Thirty Minute Theatre* tonight, isn't it?'

Franklin nodded as the car slowed on the gravel driveway.

'I'll get the casserole on, darling,' Julia said, slipping out of the car.

By the time that Franklin had put the Stag in the garage, and then changed into a pure-wool polo-neck sweater and casual slacks, his wife had poured him a large glass of brandy, and left it on the dining-room table. He swallowed the smooth Napoleon in one gulp, then sank into the deeply cushioned swivel armchair.

'How's it going, love?' he called into the kitchen, and was answered with a noncommittal laugh.

'Ten minutes.'

'Make it eight.'

'Will you beat me black and blue with your truncheon if it's thirty seconds over?'

Franklin closed his eyes and smiled. 'Probably.'

For a few moments he let his thoughts drift: to the game of cricket he was due to play for the county constabulary on Sunday next; to Mrs Clark and Mrs Watson who had come into the station all of a fluster to ask if there was a killer on the loose after the 'horror' over at Westbury… Franklin's eyes snapped open.

'Julia!' he shouted, as he stood. 'The autopsy…'

'Autopsies,' she corrected. 'And I thought you didn't want to talk about "work".'

'I've changed my mind. What did you find?' He moved into the kitchen and found his wife putting down her glass of wine, about to take the beef carbonade from the oven.

'Another minute,' she said, smiling.

'Whatever. The autopsy?'

'What do you want to know?'

Franklin wasn't sure. 'I suppose I want to know if that boy Dyson did it.'

'Probably not,' said Julia, sipping her wine. 'Both of the victims had massive internal haemorrhaging, seemingly caused by extreme heat.'

'That doesn't make sense,' said Franklin. 'They'd been ripped to shreds. The girl was virtually gutted.'

'Now who's putting whom off their dinner?'

They ate in virtual silence, the sun sinking towards the horizon as they looked out from the panoramic picture window of the dining room, over the gently rolling green of their garden and the shimmering blue-grey sea.

When either of them spoke it was in short, precise bursts to which the other answered, almost telepathically. They had been married for eight years and it showed.

'I was talking to Albert Peacock about the begonias…'

'Really? Need thinning?'

'Apparently.'

Then the conversation returned to the death of the young people.

'The boy was crazed when we found him,' said Franklin. 'Absolutely out of his tree. Kept rambling on about devils and goblins.'

'Was he badly injured?'

'Lots of cuts and bruises. Best we could figure, he'd attacked the other two.'

'What with?' asked Julia suddenly.

'Sorry?'

'What weapon did he use?'

Franklin looked a little embarrassed. 'Well, we haven't found that yet, have we? Some kind of knife, I suppose.'

'No knife could have made those marks on the girl's body. They were claw marks or I'm a monkey's auntie.'

Her husband shook his head. 'Are you saying an animal did this?'

Julia shrugged. 'I'm saying a knife *didn't* do it.' She stopped. The setting sun cast dark and ominous shadows across the surface of the water. 'What was that?'

'I didn't hear anything.'

'Then shut up,' she said sharply, and moved to the window. The sky was like a Turner painting, enormous splashes of crimson and burnt orange reaching across the striated clouds.

Franklin joined her, wrapping his arms around her shoulders.

'Beautiful night,' he said.

'Is it?' Somewhere in the distance she could just make out a black mass emerging from the embers of the dying sun. She shivered.

'What's wrong, love?'

'Birds flying at night,' she said. Now Franklin understood: Julia was a West Country girl, and in those parts the old superstitions still carried some weight.

'It doesn't mean anything,' he said softly. 'Birds must fly at night all the time.'

'Not in a group like that. It's bad luck.' She stared closer. 'They look like ravens,' she said in a low voice.

Franklin laughed, but his mirth was hollow. He pulled his arms tighter around his wife and they huddled together, watching as the twilight was engulfed by the black cloud.

PART 4:
WAY OUT

CHAPTER 11

Shuskin ran forward, torch light glinting off her pistol in the darkness. She quickly found the soldier, face down in the cold soil. She flipped the body over with her boot, continually glancing back to the trees and burnt-out vehicles around her.

His pale throat had been cut in a ragged arc. Splashes of blood, ink-black in the moonlight, covered the man's uniform. His eyes were staring. He hadn't even fired a shot.

Shuskin picked up the fallen machine gun, her eyes fixed on the dark undergrowth. She could hear the other soldiers, blundering in her direction, blotting out any sounds made by the killer.

'Quiet!' she snapped. 'This thing is still close by!'

She turned away from the dead soldier, flicking the safety catch off the Kalashnikov as she scanned her surroundings again. Trees and stunted bushes grumbled in the arctic wind, the barren darkness revealing deeper shadows.

There was a sudden sound of movement to her left. She swung round, saw only the Doctor, his hands instinctively rising above his head. 'Let me have a look at the poor fellow,' he said.

Shuskin nodded, and was about to turn away when she saw something. She squeezed the trigger, letting off twenty rounds. There was a shocked look on the Doctor's face as the bullets flew around him.

Shuskin ran past the Doctor. Slumped against a fallen tree trunk lay a creature, almost ripped in two by the machine-gun fire. It was a goblin, a kobold, a legend given form in the modern world. Artificial wings, seemingly made of steel and plastic, lay under its body in tatters. Shuskin remembered tales from childhood, and how every scratch against the window pane at night could have been a creature such as this. It was sneering even now, as if it knew what she was thinking – parental threats, beasts under the bed. The mouth below the hooked nose opened, and Shuskin heard high-pitched laughter.

She smashed the butt of the gun into the creature's face, breaking teeth and bone in the process. It stared back at her through shuttered eyes, spitting out blood. And began laughing again.

Bruce stood over the Xerox 914 copier, flashes of light illuminating his face. It was like taking candy from a baby. He had been challenged only once, and the dumb grunt who'd come into the office had only wanted to check that everything was working.

'Anything else I can do for you?' the soldier had asked.

Not unless you could persuade Corporal Bell to sit on this machine with her pants around her ankles. 'No, no,' replied Bruce. 'I'll be finished here soon.'

Bruce placed the Photostats in a large envelope, returned the originals to a manila folder, and set off for the Brigadier's office. Much of the information he wanted had been kept there, stuck in a pair of filing cabinets, locked up with a key so tiny it resembled something from a Christmas cracker. Bruce had seen tighter security at a kindergarten.

Time to go. You could only put so many lies in place, and eventually somebody would find out that in reality Bruce was about as committed to UNIT as Martin Luther King had been to the Ku Klux Klan.

He closed the door on the Brigadier's office, and strolled towards the science wing. One corridor – leading to the Doctor's laboratory – was still partly cordoned off with yellow tape. The computer room that adjoined the Doctor's workshop had been slightly damaged, and much of the equipment had been moved. Bruce turned the corner, and saw a light on. Damn. He hadn't expected company.

He strolled in, smiling casually at the technician who was busy working at one of the terminals. 'Hi, I'm Davis, from the States.'

'Hello,' said the man, his eyes buried somewhere behind the thickest glasses Bruce had ever seen. 'I'm Billy Donald. I'd heard you'd joined us.'

'Yeah.' Bruce looked absently around the room, scratching his chin. 'Do you think you could give me a hand with something?'

'I'm sure I could. I'm only here to do a system backup.'

Bruce's face fell. 'So I won't be able to use the computers?'

'Luckily I've not started yet. What do you want to do?'

'Establish a link with the UNIT building in New York?'

'No problem,' said the man, swivelling his chair towards the terminal in front of him. His fingers moved swiftly over the keyboard. 'At least it's cheap at this time of night.'

'That's what I was thinking,' said Bruce. He watched the screen over the technician's shoulder, pretending to be interested.

'There,' said the man, turning back to Bruce. 'All hooked up and ready to –'

The hydrochloric acid hit him in the face. His hands flew up, scrabbling blindly. The technician screamed and fell, cracking the back of his head on the ground. The black and white floor tiles bubbled and melted as the acid streamed over it.

Bruce glanced away, returning the flask to the bench. By the time he looked down again the man was motionless. Bruce tutted. Science labs could be such dangerous places.

Night fell over Geneva as the Brigadier crossed the city to UNIT's worldwide headquarters. He walked for some of the way until, certain that he hadn't been followed from the hotel, he hailed a taxi and asked for the Rue de Montbrillant. He had purposefully spoken in an appalling French accent in an attempt to discourage dialogue. Too much to think about.

Lethbridge-Stewart pondered his position in the silent taxi. He wasn't even sure he could justify his actions to his superiors, but he was in too deep now to go back. The only option seemed to be a frontal attack, just as at Suez when he had led a division to Port Said to head off a counterattack from Colonel Nasser's crack Republican Infantry. Hit them where it hurt and make their eyes water… Metaphorically speaking.

The plaza in front of the UN building was deserted when Lethbridge-Stewart arrived. Then again, he had hardly expected cheering crowds. Approaching a lone sentry the Brigadier removed his pass and some papers bearing the UNIT emblem.

'Halt,' said the sentry in English. 'Advance and be recognised.'

The Brigadier stepped into the strong light of the building frontage and saluted the private. 'Warm night,' he said.

'Yes, it is, sir. Thank you, sir,' said the sentry, returning the salute. 'Pass in peace.'

The cool marble of the entrance hall contrasted with the sticky heat of evening. Lethbridge-Stewart acknowledged two bored-looking staff officers with further dismissive salutes.

A cry of recognition stopped him in his tracks. 'Brigadier, sir?'

He turned to find a beaming face behind him. It was Captain Munro, who had been under Lethbridge-Stewart's command during the Auton invasion. He was now on the Secretary General's staff after a short spell back in the regular army. The Brigadier groaned inwardly but gave a brief, reasonably convincing smile to indicate pleasure at having run into an old friend.

'Good evening, James,' he said, hoping to keep the conversation as brief as possible.

'I didn't know you were in town, sir,' beamed the delighted captain, seeming not to have taken the hint.

Lethbridge-Stewart thought quickly and nodded. 'Yes, precisely. Very hush-hush. Loose lips sink ships and all that.' He finished shaking hands with Munro and half turned. 'Sorry to have to cut this short, Jimmy. Urgent business, you know how it is.'

'Of course, sir,' said Munro, looking a little perplexed.

With that Lethbridge-Stewart hurried off down the corridor towards his objective. The Strategic Operations Defence Command Centre lay deep within the complex and it took the Brigadier some time to find the correct floor, despite having been in the large briefing area on many previous occasions.

The unfolding lack of activity worried the Brigadier. He hadn't expected his entry into UNIT's inner sanctum to be quite this easy, no matter what his rank was. Briefly he considered what would happen if an alien attack were announced in mainland Europe right now and three-quarters of the staff officers seemed to be otherwise engaged. Finally he approached the entry hall to the Command Centre and once again found it deserted and in near darkness.

He knew that a precise inventory of all UNIT equipment was held in the UNIT security records, which were stored in this section of the building. Having switched on his torch, the Brigadier passed banks of computer terminals until he found the large telex section and a filing cabinet marked 'Top Secret' in twelve languages.

The holy grail.

It was only as the Brigadier pulled at the cabinet and the top drawer opened that he suddenly realised he had been set up. In the split second before the klaxons began he knew that he had been given the subtlest trail of crumbs to follow. The intention seemed to be to incriminate him beyond recovery.

As the alarms blared Lethbridge-Stewart found himself a seat and waited to see what would happen next.

* * *

Liz and the Doctor watched the creature intently. It was no bigger than a child, but it spat and lashed out with surprising force whenever anyone approached. It stared with utter contempt through bruised eyelids, as if daring one of the humans to try putting it out of its misery.

'Do you recognise it?' asked Shuskin, thankful that her angry attack on the creature had gone unobserved.

The Doctor shook his head. 'No. But then it's a very big universe.' He pointed towards the wings, and the large belt that held them in place. 'The fact that these work at all indicates how light the creatures are. Which just goes to confirm their reliance on agility and sheer numbers.'

'As we saw from the air battle,' observed Liz.

The Doctor nodded. 'Earth's military forces aren't equipped to deal with them.'

'It doesn't seem to want to talk,' said Shuskin.

'Perhaps it can't,' said Liz. 'Maybe it left its English/Alien phrase book behind.'

'How many soldiers would talk when captured by the enemy?' The Doctor took a step closer to the creature, which lunged at him, hissing.

'Then there's nothing more we can gain from it,' said Shuskin, drawing her pistol.

'Put that thing away!' snapped the Doctor. 'You might not have signed a treaty with these creatures, but please don't descend to their level!'

Liz glanced back at Shuskin, and wondered for a moment if she'd start firing at the Doctor again. But instead she replaced her gun in its holster, a look of disappointed incomprehension crossing her face.

'What can you do?' Liz asked the Doctor.

'My people have a rite, a psychic ability that allows the memories of a dying Gallifreyan to be transferred to another's mind prior to assimilation.'

'Assimilation?'

'Too complex to explain. But the process – somewhat melodramatically – is known as "soul-catching". I've never tried it with an alien before.'

'Oh.'

'Actually, I'm not sure anyone has.'

'Oh.'

'And I was never very good at it anyway.'

'Oh.' Liz paused. 'Doctor, you do know what you're doing, don't you?'

Bruce had been hard at work at the terminal for some minutes, all the while hoping that the soldier wouldn't return. Finally he took the spool of magnetic tape from its spindle, and walked over to the technician's corpse. He pulled off the man's white lab coat, and then unbuttoned the shirt. The man was taller than Bruce, with a very cheap taste in fabric, but there wasn't much he could do about it now.

Bruce quickly dressed the almost faceless corpse with his own clothing – a sad waste of *haute couture*, if not of human life – and then dropped the body back on to the floor. He removed the corpse's spectacles and poured some more acid over the body, then carefully smashed the flask on the floor and overturned chairs and test-tube racks.

Bruce stood back to admire his handiwork. It wouldn't fool an expert, but there were few of those in this pox-hole, and it should be enough to get him clear.

He rummaged in the pocket of the lab coat, and found the dead man's pass and his car keys. 'Well, Mr Donald,' he said. 'I think we'd better be going, don't you?'

* * *

Major-General Hayes burst into the Command Centre, red-faced and seemingly flustered, no more than thirty seconds after the sirens had first sounded. Behind him came some twenty troops, all armed to the teeth. Even the Brigadier thought this smacked of overkill.

Lethbridge-Stewart sat calmly, arms folded, a thin smirk on his face which he knew was guaranteed to irritate Hayes. 'What kept you?' he asked casually.

'I beg your pardon, Lethbridge-Stewart? Stand to attention!'

'Yes, sir,' said the Brigadier, snapping out of the chair and saluting. His eyes were fixed on Hayes, trying to determine if someone he considered a close friend was the very person who had manoeuvred him into this predicament.

'Well?' said Hayes angrily. 'I presume you have some sort of explanation for this, Brigadier?'

Some of the troops behind Hayes shifted anxiously at the mention of Lethbridge-Stewart's rank. Shooting a man who had command of thousands of men is not usually advisable, even if he is a spy.

'Security is lax,' said the Brigadier simply. 'I noticed it the last time I was here, reporting on the Stahlman fiasco.'

'What?' screamed Hayes.

The Brigadier merely blinked impassively back at him. 'A little exercise, sir. I assumed you would approve.'

Hayes was almost purple now. A large vein throbbed at his temple. 'Lethbridge-Stewart,' he said through gritted teeth, 'you have not heard the last of this. You will return to your hotel, pack, and be on the next plane to London this evening. Am I understood?'

The Brigadier nodded mutely. He had lost.

'Furthermore, I shall be making a full report of this incident to the Security Council.' And it was then, as Hayes moved close to the Brigadier to issue his threat, that he slipped a piece of paper into Lethbridge-Stewart's hand. 'I don't know what game you're playing,' continued Hayes, 'but it stops here.' He turned and marched out of the room, most of the troops following him. 'Make sure the Brigadier is returned whence he came,' he called over his shoulder to the remaining trio of soldiers.

Lethbridge-Stewart was led to the front of the building, placed in a staff car and driven, without any conversation, to his hotel. He was then escorted to the lift and taken to the door of his room. At this point the soldiers turned away.

'Aren't you going to make sure I leave?' asked the Brigadier.

It was the sergeant of the three who answered in a strong Texan accent. 'No, sir.'

'Why ever not?'

'Orders, sir,' replied the sergeant. 'You've got your orders, I've got mine. Sir.' He saluted and turned to leave.

Inside his room the Brigadier sat heavily on the bed and opened the piece of paper that he had been given. It was a page torn from a memo pad. There was no signature, but Lethbridge-Stewart recognised Hayes's handwriting instantly. 'You are right,' it said simply. 'We have a cuckoo in the nest who is particularly ruthless. You must be equally so. Deal with him.' Beneath this there was a name, and an address, and two small doodles of a gun and a tombstone.

The meaning was clear. The Brigadier looked out across the lake at the glittering fountain, lit up like a space rocket. Then he glanced into the corner of the room at the rifle he had assembled. Ever since his arrival he'd been hoping to avoid this, but the moment had come. For the sake of UNIT, he must take a life.

CHAPTER 12

As dawn approached Liz watched soldiers pin the alien's limbs to the forest floor. It thrashed wildly, spitting and screeching.

The Doctor approached, a look of great concentration on his face. He seemed to be muttering something under his breath. He knelt down at the creature's side, stretched out a hand, rested his fingertips on its forehead. Shuskin had the unsavoury job of holding the head in position.

The moment the Doctor touched the creature it became still, its eyes glazing over. Despite the cold, the Doctor's furrowed brow was damp with perspiration.

A moment later his whole body jerked, as if he had been electrocuted. Despite this, the Doctor's hand stayed on the creature's forehead.

The Doctor twitched again, his free arm flailing. His closed eyes flicked open. They stared through Liz and the forest, focusing on something unimaginably distant. Something terrifying.

No images, no words, no memories. Just an emotion.

Rage.

It boiled and seethed, a blood-red sea of terrifying aggression, swamping everything else. Only gradually did the Doctor feel other sensations, shrouding the anger like a gently forming dew: a resolute sadness at having to leave behind the home world, the entrapped planet of savage beauty.

Moments later the Doctor glimpsed the goblin creatures clinging to a projectile, hurtling through the empty vacuum of space. It was as if their hatred was propelling them across the vast distances between the planetary arcs. The imagined roar of the propulsion unit was a shout of defiance to the rest of the universe.

Even this memory, surging through the Doctor's mind, was more emotional than visual. He felt barely restrained anger, a thirst for destruction. He knew that nothing else mattered.

There was a final backward glance at the alien world that had once been an intruder in the solar system. Countless generations ago it had been captured by the gravitational pull of the cold blue planet. It had become a moon, a mere satellite, with a thin, cloudless atmosphere.

Their world's ignominious fate was a never-ending source of disgust.

Another memory flickered: the frozen pink poles, the volcanoes of ice, the solid lakes. An incredible world, almost sculpted by hand.

The creatures rested weary limbs against the metal hull of the spacecraft, knowing that soon the killing could begin.

The cloud-covered planet approached.

Kill. Destroy. Feed.

The Doctor was swept up in the creature's lust for blood. For a moment he too wanted to stretch out his artificial wings and sever limbs and arteries and muscle. Devour all life. Devour everything. But –

Obey the plan. Wait. For the best.

What is the plan?

Obey the plan. Wait.

Tell me more about the plan.

No! You are not us! You don't belong. Don't belong in mind. Kill you!

Please tell me –

No! Kill! Kill! Kill! Waro kill. Waro kill. Waro kill Waro. For Waro. Waro Kill!

The Doctor collapsed to the floor, screaming, breaking contact with the dying goblin creature. Words flowed out of him, unintelligible at first, but the hatred, the pain, the terrible anger, was obvious. Blood trickled down his chin.

'No!' he shouted. 'No!'

The soldiers instinctively let go of the creature, but it was motionless, its eyes staring blankly.

Liz turned to the Doctor, trying to calm him. Eventually he became still, and she led him away from the catatonic creature and towards a felled tree, on which he sat clumsily. Liz and Shuskin stood at the Doctor's side. He breathed deeply for some minutes, and then opened his eyes. He flinched back at the sudden light.

'What did you see, Doctor?' asked Shuskin impatiently.

'Terrible, terrible things,' announced the Doctor in a harsh whisper. He coughed, then wiped the blood and spittle from his lips with the back of his hand. 'They're called... They're called the Waro. I saw their world. Triton. One of Neptune's moons.'

'But nothing could live there,' said Liz.

The Doctor smiled weakly. 'The universe has such a... diversity... of creatures.'

'What do they want?' asked Shuskin.

The Doctor paused, glancing across at the corpse. The colour seemed to be returning to his cheeks. 'Not much,' he replied eventually. 'The destruction of all life on Earth.'

'Why?' Liz blurted out.

'Why are some people tall and others short?' asked the Doctor. 'It's not something you consciously decide upon at birth. So, with the Waro: each individual has no choice but to feel a deep rage at... Well, at everything, really.' The Doctor got slowly to his feet. 'That creature is quite dead. It could not tolerate another intruding on its mind. It killed itself, and tried to destroy me in the process.'

Shuskin ordered the soldiers to burn the body. This time the Doctor did not contradict her. Liz watched as the spindly limbs, the bloated face, were swiftly consumed by fire.

'Before the thing died, I saw a glimpse of their facility,' announced the Doctor. 'I think they're mining cobalt. I'm not sure why. But that fact alone indicates one thing.'

'What?'

'The Waro have been coming here for a long time. "Cobalt" is derived from the old German word for "kobold", or "goblin".'

Liz found herself unable to suppress a shudder. 'So why attack now?'

'Perhaps only now is the human race strong enough to offer any sort of challenge to them. Perhaps –' The Doctor turned suddenly, clutching his head. 'I really do feel most peculiar.'

And with that he collapsed face down on the forest floor.

Mike Yates was dreaming. It was the same unfathomable dream as he had experienced so often recently. He was in a field of tall grass with a bottle of champagne in his hand. Dawn was breaking over nearby hills. Mike sipped from a glass, and then put it on the warm earth at his feet. Nearby he found a wicker basket. He knew that he had to pick it up, that it was vitally important for him to perform some task with it. Just then it began to rain. Fish. Silver fish with obscene plastic faces. Mike had to catch the falling fish in the basket. He knew this. If he didn't it would be the end of him, and of everyone. Everyone was relying on him to get it right.

The slippery, wriggling fish soon filled the basket, and Mike began to look around for another. But he couldn't find one, and there were fish everywhere. He was drowning in fish, their tails flapping pathetically, their mouths gaping –

The ringing of a telephone awoke him, but for a second he lay still, damp sheets scrunched tightly around his head. A hand lifted the receiver and passed the phone to him.

'It'll be for you.'

'Thanks, Sandra,' he said, breathing out slowly and taking the phone.

'Jill,' said the woman with a dignity that belied the circumstances.

'Sure.' Mike took the receiver and listened as the news was passed to him. He took it with little outward reaction, but inside his stomach was churning. 'I'll be there in twenty minutes,' he said at last, and dropped the telephone back on to its cradle. 'Bit of a crisis, love,' he said.

'I've got to be up for work in the morning,' said Jill. She rolled over, turning her back to him.

For God's sake, thought Mike angrily, what does she want for a meal and three bottles of wine?

'Fine,' he said. 'There's coffee in the percolator, and breakfast in the fridge. Leave the key under the mat. I'll see you next time.'

Mike dressed hurriedly, then reached under the bed for his UNIT pass and Browning 9mm. He threw a pound note from his wallet towards the woman's bare back. 'Get yourself a taxi,' he said, and left without another word.

Yates's car was cold, the sun just beginning to pull itself into the cloudless sky. As he revved the engine, Mike found himself worrying about the hollowness he felt inside. He'd always assumed that the empty sensation would go, given time – but, if anything, it had been getting worse recently.

He drove through the deserted North London streets, turning things over and over in his mind. When he reached the leafy suburb in which UNIT HQ was situated he was just beginning to recover his composure. As he entered the building it was like slipping on another uniform. One that stopped him thinking too much.

'Sorry about this, sir,' said Corporal Bell, looking a little dishevelled. 'The duty sergeant reported the death in the early hours. We couldn't raise the Brigadier, and with Major Turner in Iceland, and Major Cosworth on leave…'

It's down to me, thought Yates with a heavy heart. 'All right, what have we got?'

'Bruce Davis is dead, sir.'

'Terrific,' said Yates. 'The Americans are going to *love* that.'

Bell wisely decided not to respond to this. Instead she led Yates down the corridor towards the temporary computer room. 'I'm afraid it's rather messy in there,' she said as they reached the door.

The first thing Yates noticed was a crude chalk outline, indicating where the body had fallen. The second was the acrid stench that permeated the room. 'Where's the body now?'

'In the mortuary. Dr French is about to do an autopsy.'

'I'll bet he was pleased about getting dragged out of bed in the middle of the night,' said Yates with a slight grin. 'He's not used to dealing with human corpses, is he?' Yates crossed the room to the terminal where Lieutenant Carson, UNIT's senior computer expert, was knee deep in printouts.

'Do you *live* here, David?' asked Yates sarcastically.

'What? Oh, morning, Mike. This is a right mess-up,' said Carson, tearing another perforated page from the printer. 'If somebody had told me that Billy Donald was capable of these juvenile shenanigans, I'd have… Well, you know…'

'I'd hardly call throwing acid in some poor sod's face schoolboy antics,' said Yates sharply. But he felt a certain empathy with Carson: it was never easy finding that one of your trusted team is, in fact, an enemy. Yates had experienced similar shock after the Auton invasion. Friends and colleagues had been kidnapped and replaced by exact replicas, destroying what little trust he'd had in humanity.

'You never had cause to suspect Donald of being involved in anything?' asked Mike.

'He just did his job,' said Carson in frustration. 'You know Billy, Mike, he's a good lad. A bit of a bottom-pincher, if you know what I mean, but he knows his stuff. I've played darts with him in the Red Lion more times than you've had hot dinners.' He made another note on the sheet in front of him. 'I still can't believe it.'

Yates glanced down at the printouts. 'It looks like Greek to me,' he commented.

'Hexadecimal notation,' said Carson. 'Amounts to the same thing, I suppose.'

'Anything out of the ordinary?'

'No. If this was sabotage, I'd have expected the worst. Files messed about or deleted. There's nothing like that. Some surface damage that a six-year-old could have come up with, but nothing that can't be put right in ten minutes. I can even tell where the last message was sent to.'

'Really?' Yates raised his eyebrows.

'It's to the New Mexico office,' said Carson. 'Unfortunately, I can't tell *what* it was yet.'

'Right,' said Yates, a clear course of action opening up to him. 'We can get into the whos and whys later. The desk sergeant said that his car was seen leaving at speed?'

'Yeah, a white MG,' replied Carson. 'I've been in it loads of times. Very nippy.'

'Then the first thing to do is find the murdering animal and string him up by his goolies.' He turned sharply. 'Carol, get on your bike down to police liaison and get Green Door into operation.'

Bell nodded quickly. Green Door was the UNIT code name for an operation to track a fugitive. It was usually handled in conjunction with the local constabularies, and involved circulating photographs of the wanted person and setting up road blocks and checks at air and sea ports. 'Anything else?' she asked.

'Yes,' said Yates. 'Get me a coffee and two aspirins.'

* * *

The hotel manager had been very obliging, not only lending the Brigadier his car when Lethbridge-Stewart explained that due to certain 'operational necessities' he was unable to use official UNIT transportation, but also in giving directions to the Rue Voltaire.

After slipping out of the back entrance of the hotel, the Brigadier drove through the narrow streets of Geneva's right bank. He found himself thinking about Aden, and Private Bull who had been condemned, on the orders of then Colonel Lethbridge-Stewart (with support from the Chief of General Staff), for cowardice in the face of the enemy. And the last thing he had said to Lethbridge-Stewart before sentence had been carried out. 'War is hell, Colonel. Death can't be worse than that.'

And then they shot him.

The Brigadier rubbed a hand across his forehead, trying to massage away the pain. If the pain went then, perhaps, the doubt and the guilt would go, too.

He parked the car a street away from his target and prepared to execute his orders – unsigned, unconfirmed, worthless in international law.

When he reached number 73, he found it to be a huge old warehouse. A quick circumnavigation confirmed that the place was deserted. Puzzled, but knowing that he had little choice but to follow the trail he had been given, the Brigadier returned to the car and settled down to see if anyone would turn up. It could be a long wait.

Thomas Bruce knew he wouldn't get far in the stolen MG – even the pinheads were capable of organising roadblocks. The obvious route, south towards the Channel ports, would be swarming with cops and soldiers, so Bruce drove into Bedfordshire, keeping to the narrow country lanes. After thirty miles he passed a farmhouse. The sun was just rising over the horizon as Bruce pulled off the road and into a clump of bushes about half a mile from the farm entrance.

Quickly he changed out of the technician's clothes and into a pair of jeans and a thick navy-style woollen sweater. Even in these surroundings he looked like a walking advert for *Mainly for Men*. He shaved, using the car wing mirror, and then removed a bottle of Chanel aftershave from his toiletries bag. There was no need, he thought, even in this uncivilised part of the world, to look and smell like a barbarian.

The farmhouse appeared to be deserted. Bruce banged on the door several times but, clearly, the farmer was in the pastures tilling the land, or whatever the hell he did. He turned, about to leave, but then saw a man striding across the yard from the milking sheds.

'Morning,' said the man.

'Hi,' said Bruce in a flat New York accent. 'I'm sorry to trouble you, but I appear to be having some difficulties with my car. Can't get the darn thing to go.'

'Well,' said the farmer brightly, walking towards his Land Rover, 'Let's see if we can sort the blighter out.'

During the short trip back to the MG, the man told Bruce his life story. Bruce feigned interest in his cautionary tale of being corrupted by life in the city and finding true happiness on the farm. 'It's a wonderful life,' said the man as they approached the MG, and Bruce had a sudden vision of himself stuck in a Frank Kapra movie. Thankfully Bruce was able to curb his overwhelming urge to resort to violence as much of the man's tale was lost in an impenetrable accent.

'Ah, right,' said the farmer as they came to a halt. 'A sports car. You don't want to be driving one of them: you want to get yourself a nice Ford Escort. Very practical.'

Bruce breathed in slowly and then pointed to the car. 'I think it's the engine. Or Something.'

'Righto, soon have her back on the road for you,' said the farmer, pulling open the bonnet. 'Now, if you could just try starting her up for me, then we'll –'

Bruce smashed the bonnet down on to the farmer's head, knocking him unconscious. He stood over the man and drew his Colt .45 from inside his trousers, pointing it squarely at the man's head. Then he had second thoughts. 'No, friend,' he said to the prone figure, 'you and life deserve each other.'

He bundled the farmer into the boot of the MG, then got into the Land Rover and drove off.

Within half an hour he had reached the motorway and, almost immediately, faced a lengthy tailback at a police roadblock.

'What's the problem?' he asked in a thick Irish accent when he finally reached the front of the queue.

'Escaped prisoner, mate,' said the young policeman, checking something on a clipboard. 'Keep your eyes open for this bloke.' He turned the clipboard around, showing Bruce the photo of the technician he had killed earlier.

'B'Jesus, but he's a right evil-looking beast, and no mistake,' said Bruce. 'It's in the eyes, you know. You can always tell. What'd he do? Murder? Rape?'

'Dunno, Patrick,' said the policeman hurriedly, eager to get to the next car. 'Just don't you go offering him lifts, all right?' He waved the Land Rover through the roadblock.

'Right you are then, sir,' said Davis. As he pulled away from the roadblock he couldn't help but laugh.

Liz checked the Doctor's vital signs for the second time that minute. Still no change. It seemed that the Doctor was in a deep coma.

Of course, she had only a vague idea what was normal for the Doctor anyway. She knew that he had twin hearts, a lower-than-human body temperature, and a physiology with massive built-in redundancy. But only the faintest exhalation could be detected from the Doctor's mouth. And that was surely bad news in anyone's book.

She suddenly remembered her parents, on the day that she announced she was going to Cambridge to read medicine rather than physics. They'd been outwardly supportive, but deep down she'd known they didn't approve, that they were concerned that she was letting her romanticism get in the way of her rationality. She'd qualified – BM BCh, with a one-year BSc in physics just for good measure – but of course they'd been right. Four months as a house officer in some benighted inner-city A&E department had been enough for her. Thank God she'd made an impression on the Physics Department at St Leonard's. She was working towards her PhD within four weeks of shoving her white coat in a bin and walking out of the hospital.

But there were times – and this was one of them – when her years studying medicine were something of a comfort, although, as she tried to find the Doctor's pulse again, she wasn't sure that having qualified as a vet wouldn't have been more useful.

She felt rather than saw someone walk up behind her. She turned. It was Shuskin. If impatience was an Olympic sport, then without any doubt here was the USSR's next gold medal winner. 'Is he better yet?' she asked.

'No,' said Liz, trying not to get cross. 'You can see that, surely?'

'We cannot wait any longer. As soon as we establish radio contact with base I will be requesting a full-scale nuclear strike.'

'But... but that could be catastrophic.'

'Don't worry, we will make sure the Americans are fully aware of the situation.'

'That's not what I mean, and you know it.'

Shuskin seemed unperturbed. 'Now that we have definite proof of these creatures' aggression I do not have any other options.'

'But what makes you think that a nuclear strike will work when your other displays of military muscle have failed?'

'We only need one hit for the target to be obliterated,' replied Shuskin. 'And we will launch as many missiles as it takes.'

CHAPTER 13

Mike Yates loathed post-mortems. On a scale of most-hated things, they came right behind sandals, free-form jazz, and girls he was chatting up saying the two most dreaded words in the English language: 'my boyfriend'.

For that reason he elected to stay outside the pathology lab while Dr French dissected the corpse. Yates had tried to contact New York HQ to inform them of Davis's untimely death and request that his next of kin be informed, but thunderstorms had brought down phone lines on the east coast the previous night. He still hadn't been able to contact the Brigadier, despite having left several messages at the hotel. For the moment, Yates was on his own.

After an inordinately long period during which he engaged in pointless small talk with Claire, the medical secretary, Mike was beginning to feel fidgety and nervous. It was ridiculous: he was acting commander of UNIT, and yet he felt like a small boy waiting outside the headmaster's study after having been caught smoking behind the bike shed. A feeling that Mike Yates knew very well.

'You can go in if you want. I'm sure he'll have finished by now,' said Claire brightly.

Mike shook his head. It was hard to be all butch and manly when making excuses, but he knew it would be even harder if he was on his hands and knees vomiting at the smell of embalming fluid. 'I'm allergic to some of the chemicals they use,' he said. 'I'll just hang around here. Anyway, you were saying…'

To Yates's immense relief the double doors of the laboratory swung open and Dr French emerged with an enigmatic expression on his face. 'Captain Yates,' he said, 'How goes the hunt for our demon bomber?'

Mike growled something under his breath.

'So, I take it you want to know what killed this man, then?' French asked.

'No, actually, I was thinking of selling you tickets to the regimental dinner-dance.'

'I'm busy,' said French.

'So am I, Doctor,' replied Yates angrily. 'I've now had two incidents under my command. One fatal.'

French shrugged in seeming disinterest. 'Then you'd be better off cracking puerile one-liners with the local constabulary.' His voice was even and calm. 'Talk to them.'

'I'm talking to you!' hissed Yates through gritted teeth. 'So tell me something I want to know.'

If French was taken aback by Mike's anger, he didn't show it. 'Go and get yourself a cup of tea, Claire,' he said. 'You look knackered – you'll have been up half the night.'

The secretary left the room quickly, blushing slightly. French sat in her chair and dropped the autopsy report on the desk. 'Pull up a seat, Captain.'

Mike considered standing as a show of strength but French's apparent disinterest in continuing the fight persuaded him to opt for comfort. He sat opposite the doctor and asked the obvious question. 'So: how did he die?'

'Fractured skull, massive cerebral haemorrhage. Struck by a blunt instrument at the back of the skull. Probably the lead piping. In the laboratory.'

'By?' asked Mike.

'Who do you think I am? Dixon of Dock Green?' French glanced down at the file. 'Mind you, it's possible he just hit his head on the floor when he fell. That would be consistent with the evidence.'

'And the acid?'

'Nasty stuff. Went right through muscle and bone. Certainly it contributed to the poor chap's death. In fact, I wouldn't be surprised if getting it in the face caused him to fall over and smash his bonce. I'm not being too technical for you here, am I?' Yates ignored the man's facetiousness. 'However, the interesting thing is that most of the acid was applied after death.'

'What?'

'Thought that would surprise you. Most of the stuff on the face and all of it on the hands by the look of the tissue damage and the splash marks around the body. Now, I don't want to tell you your job, but…'

'It sounds as though the murderer didn't want the victim to be identified, either facially or by fingerprints.'

'Very good, Captain,' said French. 'Do you do this for a living?'

'Which means that the body may not be Bruce Davis.'

'That's right.'

Yates considered this for a moment. 'The man who died was wearing Bruce's clothes. That suggests to me that the corpse is either him or was killed by him.'

'Only one way to tell for sure,' agreed French. 'Dental records. I'll send Claire to fetch them when she gets back from her tea break.'

'Good man,' said Yates, standing quickly. 'It's time the Brigadier was brought up to speed.'

'And if you can't get in touch with him again?' asked French with a hint of sympathy in his voice.

'Then,' said Mike, 'I guess it's down to me. Again.'

'Don't be a fool, Captain Shuskin,' said the Doctor.

Liz and Shuskin spun round. He was still lying on the ground, his eyes closed.

'Sorry?' said Liz in surprise.

The Doctor sat bolt upright. 'I'm advising Captain Shuskin to be cautious,' he said, staring ahead unblinkingly for a moment.

155

'The fallout would be enormous. Make you very unpopular with the rest of the world.'

Shuskin snorted. 'So we sit here and do nothing?'

'Of course not,' said the Doctor, getting to his feet.

'Are you all right?' asked Liz.

'I'm very well, thank you. Just catching up on forty winks. Soul-catching can be rather tiring.'

'Well, next time, how about warning me before collapsing in a heap?'

'I'll try to bear that in mind,' said the Doctor. He turned to the Soviet captain. 'Now then, my dear, subtlety is what we require. Just a few of us, moving through the forest, have a chance of getting safely to the base. Then we can see what's there, and make a fair and balanced decision. Much better than blundering in with nuclear weapons flying all over the place, wouldn't you say?'

'I am not convinced. We will just be picked off like vermin.'

The Doctor pointed towards the blackened remains of the Waro creature. 'They are very reliant on those primitive artificial wings,' he said. 'Give me a few minutes, and I'll come up with something that jams the motors. That should make us immune from attack.'

'Very well.' Shuskin nodded. 'But I am having all nuclear missile bases put on immediate stand-by. And if we do not report back to base by dusk tonight, a massive strike will be launched against this area.'

The Doctor smiled. 'Thank you, Captain. I knew you'd see sense.' He turned to Liz. 'Would you mind giving me a hand? Time is rather of the essence.'

The stress and anxiety of the last few days finally caught up with the Brigadier and he slumped wearily in the front seat of the car, dozing intermittently.

He was woken suddenly by a tapping on the window. He

shook himself awake and looked dizzily through the glass. A red-lipped smile was the first thing he took in. Sitting upright and winding down the window, Lethbridge-Stewart found himself looking at a young woman in a very short leather skirt, fishnet stockings and a tight angora sweater.

'*Bonjour,*' she said with a charming smile.

'I beg your pardon?' said the Brigadier, still disorientated.

'*Anglais?*' the woman asked with a slight tremor in her voice. 'You are liking it, yes?'

'Young lady,' said the Brigadier, recovering his wits, 'I am not liking it. *Comprenez-vous?*'

'*Oui.* Up yours!'

Delightful, thought the Brigadier, as he closed the window. Farther down the road he could see a small knot of similarly dressed women watching each passing car with interest. Clearly he was in the middle of the local red-light district. He glanced at his watch. Ye gods, but they worked all hours on the Continent.

He eased himself back in his seat, and stared across the road at the warehouse. He was beginning to feel more than a trifle foolish.

Half an hour later, just before dawn, a lorry approached the warehouse from the far end of the street. It was a large military vehicle with a green canvas rear. A man in dark clothing jumped from the cab as it approached the building. Putting a key in the lock, he looked around furtively. The huge doors opened to admit the lorry, then slammed shut a moment later.

The Brigadier stepped from the car and watched with interest as lights began to flicker behind the warehouse's filthy windows. Thinking quickly, he withdrew his wallet and nervously approached the group of prostitutes. He coughed loudly to attract their attention.

'Look,' he began. 'Delicate matter, this, but I have a proposition to put to you…'

* * *

It was a long and boring drive to the holiday town on the south coast. The radio was full of hippie drivel and the road bent and twisted all over the place. Dammit, didn't the Brits know how to build a straight road?

Bruce changed down into second, throwing the Land Rover around a small roundabout and scaring half to death the old woman in the little blue buggy thing to his left. He wondered if she knew her car had only three wheels.

He drove slowly along the almost deserted promenade. This early in the morning the amusement arcades were just opening up, and old men bent double with age were carrying armfuls of deck chairs down to the beach.

The Land Rover came to a halt, facing the sea. Bruce flashed the headlights, then turned off the engine. He left the keys in the ignition, pushed open the door, shooing away the gulls that picked at the strewn remains of somebody's fish and chips. A stiff wind buffeted the seafront, bringing with it the tang of salt and seaweed.

'Oi, mate,' said one of the deck-chair attendants, 'You've left your lights on.'

Bruce ignored him, and vaulted over the cast-iron railings, landing smartly on the sandy beach. The tide was in, and it didn't take Bruce long to reach the water's edge. He stared out at the dark sea, the wind tugging his hair. Waiting.

A little later he heard a droning noise over the crash of the waves. A dark shape skidded towards him across the water, gliding to a halt just in front of him.

He stepped nonchalantly aboard the hovercraft, which turned and moved swiftly back over the surface of the Channel.

It was Liz who reminded the Doctor that, if he wanted to construct a device to jam the artificial wings of the Waro, then perhaps letting Shuskin torch the one specimen they had wasn't such a good idea.

'Ah,' the Doctor had said, fiddling with some equipment he'd found in one of the armoured personnel carriers, 'I hadn't thought of that. Probably the after-effects of the soul-catching. Perhaps if you could ask Shuskin to search the area thoroughly something might be found...'

And so the Soviets had inspected the area around the destroyed vehicles. One of them found a Waro corpse, and dragged it across to the Doctor.

'Good man,' he said.

In this light the creature looked more like a grotesque vampire bat, with large ears and rows of needle-sharp teeth. The corpse's eyes were blank and accusatory.

Liz examined the wings more closely. They emerged from a box held on to the creature's back like a rucksack, simple motorised limbs and joints connected by a strong rubbery material. Without saying a word the Doctor passed her a flat piece of metal that he had been using as a lever, and she began to prise off the back. 'It certainly looks primitive,' said Liz.

'That's what I'm relying on,' said the Doctor. 'The control mechanisms and software must be quite sophisticated, given the degree of agility we've witnessed, but I rather expect the motors and so on will be simple. Less to break, I suppose.'

'And easier to jam,' observed Liz.

'Let's hope so,' said the Doctor. 'Mechanical and electrical interference is such a complex phenomenon. Fiendishly complicated if you want to manipulate it, but you try watching your favourite television programme when there's a thunderstorm overhead...'

As if on cue the sky darkened.

'Odd,' said the Doctor, still using his sonic screwdriver to construct the jamming device. 'I wasn't expecting inclement weather.'

Liz glanced upwards. 'Doctor!' she screamed. 'That's no storm cloud!'

'What?'

The first alien creature swooped into the Doctor's shoulders with such force that he tumbled backward. He tried to grab the creature's artificial wings and hurl it from him but another screeching Waro crashed into him.

Liz saw yet more creatures diving down, like vultures attracted to the dying. Soon the Doctor was swamped beneath a mass of black leathery wings.

FOURTH INTERLUDE:
ELIMINATION TIME

'So, what were they actually like?' asked David Arthurs.

'Amazing,' replied Bob Decker. 'They did loads off the *White Album*. They started with "Happiness is a Warm Gun", then "Yer Blues". It was a really happening scene, you know?'

Arthurs nodded knowingly, but secretly he was fuming. He'd waited years to see the Beatles, only to miss them at Madison Square Garden because of work commitments. Decker had arrived back from leave and had been talking about it non-stop ever since. Arthurs was torn between wanting to find out more and trying to pretend the whole thing had never happened.

'No old songs, then?' he asked.

'Just "Rock and Roll Music". A girl next to me was screaming for "I Feel Fine". All the cats were laughing at her!'

'If I were you, I wouldn't mention you'd been to see them to any of the uniforms. They think they're long-haired, pinko, fag subversives on drugs.'

'Small minds, man,' said Decker with a cheeky grin.

'Yeah well, if you don't like it, go live in Russia!'

'You know,' he said wistfully, 'New York looks really beautiful at this time of year.'

'You're crazy,' said Arthurs, as he checked his computer screen. 'I hate cities, man, they freak me out. I need the space and the clean air to get my head together.'

'Oregon's OK,' said Decker quickly, 'but nothing happens here. Leastways, not that Joe Public's going to hear about.'

Arthurs laughed. 'This is UNIT, baby. If something happens here, the whole world knows about it.'

The pair were just starting a twenty-four-hour shift at UNIT's 'listening station' in the foothills of the Columbia plateau. Their work, as computer operatives, was important, if sometimes tedious. Being 'a pair of buggers', as Decker and Arthurs often dubbed themselves, was frequently boring, and they occasionally wondered if they weren't frittering away their MIT talents looking for 'space junk, little green men, and communists'. But they knew that, almost uniquely in the Western world, they were able to put their dreams into practice. When the alternative was working for NASA with a bunch of jumped-up college drop-outs, collecting bits of rock from the moon, *this* was the real thing.

But the long hours often took their toll. Several of their colleagues had burnt out during the early years of UNIT's existence, unable to face another night staring at a blank screen, waiting for a blip that might be the start of an invasion of Earth by hostile aliens. It was Decker who had been among the first to track the trajectory of the Nestene mother ship the previous summer, and Arthurs who had spotted the massive Julsaen fleet's attempted landing in Argentina.

'John read some of his poetry,' said Decker, swinging around in his chair. 'New stuff. It was wild. We all held lighters up when they did "Something". Man, you should have been there.'

'There'll be another time,' said Arthurs abruptly as he took a bottle of cola from the freeze box behind him. He hurriedly changed the subject. 'Who do you think's going to win the Republican primaries?'

Decker shook his head. 'Difficult to say. Nixon should be dead in the water by now, but he keeps coming back. I've got a funny feeling about Rockefeller.'

'What about Reagan?' asked Arthurs.

'Mad Ronnie? You crack me up sometimes,' said Decker. 'He might be OK for all those uptight geeks in California, but no country in its right mind would elect an actor.'

'None of them will take Kennedy,' noted Arthurs with a grin.

'Yeah, right.'

A silence settled over the pair while Arthurs finished his drink. Then he turned to Decker. 'You ever think about the future, Bob?'

'How'd you mean?'

'You know, what the world's going to be like in, say, twenty years? If we don't get wiped out by aliens before then!'

Decker grunted noncommittally. 'The world's a ball of confusion right *now*, baby. Things can only get better.'

'Sure,' said Arthurs, with the excited zeal of a man who has undergone a Damascus-Road-like conversion. 'See, a few weeks ago I was talking to one of the installation guys when he was fixing the mainframe crash. He told me about the latest developments. Man, it's so exciting. I can see a time when computers will be as important a household item as a television is now. Computers are the future.'

But Decker wasn't listening, he was looking intently at his secondary terminal. 'Come and have a look at this.'

'What?' asked Arthurs, propelling himself across the floor on a swivel chair.

'I was just having a random trawl through the subsystems and I hit this. It's in the New Mexico UNIT personnel log.'

'So?' Arthurs raised his eyebrows.

'It's got a restricted access code. Nothing in the personnel logs should be "eyes only", except maybe that guy in England who's got highest clearance. Certainly not some grunt in the desert.'

'Maybe it's a glitch,' said Arthurs, picking up his phone and calling their supervisor at the field office on the next level of the building.

In the minutes before the man arrived, Arthurs and Decker started to crack the access code. When the supervisor finally appeared, he was shown the file. He said he'd never seen a code like it, and immediately contacted UNIT's New York HQ, who revealed that the prefix was unknown to the Head of Personnel.

He was as perplexed by its existence as the men in Oregon. After sanctioning Decker and Arthurs to continue attempting to access the file, the supervisor left them to it.

It took them almost four hours before they got through the seven levels of security and found the final password to be 'badgeman'. Decker gave a short cry of delight as the screen went blank, then filled with a standard UNIT disclaimer and the words 'Top Secret – Eyes Only'.

'Yes!' he shouted, bringing Arthurs scurrying back from a trip to the lavatory.

'What's up?'

'We're in,' said Decker with a broad grin.

Arthurs looked over his shoulder at the message. 'Right,' he said quickly. 'I'll get Stark down to have a look at it.'

'I want to see it first,' said Decker angrily.

'But it's Top Secret. Level Seven security. We're not supposed to –'

'I don't care. I've spent the last four hours trying to get into this goddamn file, and if it's the last thing I do, I'm gonna know what it says.'

Decker began to scroll down the document. The first twenty or so pages contained detailed eye-witness statements regarding various alien incidents, from the initial setting up of the organisation in the aftermath of the robot Yeti attack, through to recent events, like the Inferno project. Only a fraction of this information was public knowledge – if this were to fall into the wrong hands...

'What the hell is *this* doing here?' asked Arthurs, reading a report from a Captain Turner on the Cyber invasion of London in the spring of 1969.

'This is amazing,' said Decker. 'I mean, you could sell this to the newspapers and make a million bucks.'

'Don't even think about it,' said Arthurs, leaning over and

scrolling down further. He stopped at an insignificant three-line message at the bottom.

THE PROPERTY OF THE CIA. AWAITING COLLECTION.

IF YOU ARE NOT AUTHORISED TO VIEW THIS MESSAGE
YOU HAVE THIRTY MINUTES TO LIVE.

'What the hell does that mean?' asked Decker, not knowing whether to laugh or take the message seriously. As he said it, airtight metal emergency doors began crashing down with resounding clangs all around the access room, entombing the pair.

'I think it means we kiss our sorry asses goodbye,' said Arthurs in resignation.

One by one the lights and the computer terminals flicked off.

PART 5
COME TOGETHER

CHAPTER 14

The Waro swarmed over the Doctor's fallen body, their talons and claws etched with red. The entire attack had taken seconds – even the soldiers hadn't had time to respond – but to Liz it was all in terrible slow motion. She watched, her body as cold as the arctic wind, as more and more of the creatures landed on the Doctor's motionless form. All the while they shrieked like grotesque children. Liz had never heard anything more chilling in her life.

Liz ran forward. She caught sight of a dark, winged figure through the corner of her eye, and ducked just in time. A Waro flew overhead in a blur of claws. Thankfully – from her point of view, at least – most of the creatures were concentrating on the Doctor, a writhing mass from which only a velvet-jacketed arm protruded.

She dived towards the Doctor's outstretched hand. It was holding something tightly, although the fingers, the arm – the whole of his body, as far as she could make out – were motionless. On her hands and knees Liz approached the mass of spitting creatures, and snatched the object from the Doctor's palm.

It was the jamming device.

Liz didn't have time to wonder if it was finished, or whether it would work – she concentrated on switching the thing on, then aimed what she hoped was the business end towards the alien creatures.

Nothing happened. What was worse, some of the creatures became aware of her presence, turning their vile, dripping faces in her direction. From all around her there came the sound of gun fire.

Fantastic, she thought. Shoot the Doctor, why don't you?

The device seemed not to have had any effect. She glanced down at it. What would the Doctor do in her position? Hit the thing, probably.

No, Liz wouldn't resort to such unscientific methods. She looked more closely at the device, based on an intercom that the Doctor had ripped from one of the tanks. He'd added all sorts of esoteric components to it, the sonic screwdriver having soldered various incompatible leads and cables together. And then she noticed that some of the wires were still trailing free. But which was supposed to be joined where? There were two slim yellow wires, a thicker green one, and a brown flex that looked not unlike a telephone cord. Logic dictated that the two yellow ones should be joined together – but she knew the Doctor too well. It would never be that simple, surely?

No, the answer was to be as obtuse as possible, to connect the yellow wires to the cables farthest from them.

A machine gun fired from somewhere behind her. She'd managed to blot out all the noise and confusion since retrieving the Doctor's gadget, but this was deafeningly close. She turned, half expecting to have to shout at a Soviet soldier '*Be a bit careful or you'll hit me* '

And the Waro that had crept up behind her toppled into her lap, spewing blood and bone. Shuskin stood a few feet back, now firing at the Waro that circled overhead. She was shouting loudly – Liz couldn't tell if she was telling Liz something, or ordering her troops into action, or simply swearing in colloquial Russian – but occasionally she stopped firing and seemed to be shaking her fist in the air in some madly theatrical gesture.

167

Liz looked down at the Doctor's jamming device. It was covered in the dead Waro's bile-coloured blood. So were her hands, her blouse, her lips, her face.

She felt nauseous, but swallowed hard, wiping her hands on her trousers. Then she set about fixing the wires together, bending and twisting them into shape, but hoping that the connections would hold. And that the machine wouldn't blow up when she came to switch it on.

'Here goes nothing,' she said lightly, flicking on the device and aiming it at the clustering Waro.

'Can things get any worse?' asked Mike Yates, throwing up his arms in anguish as yet another crisis dropped comfortably into his lap.

'Is it really our problem?' asked Corporal Bell, expecting some sort of outburst in response. She'd started to worry about Yates recently, his flashes of anger having become more frequent. He'd even developed a facial tic that she was sure hadn't been there before.

'It'll be everybody's problem if the aliens decide to invade any time during the next couple of weeks!' said Yates. He stared at the telex again. Addressed to all UNIT field officers, it described a disaster at the 'secret listening post' in America. A sudden and unexplained spike in the power supply had caused the emergency nuclear safeguards to malfunction, leading to a 'zero-99 situation'. Or, in other words, the airtight doors had come down, the oxygen supply had switched off, and two highly trained and capable computer experts had suffocated.

The file they were working on had vanished, taking with it half of the data on the mainframe. East-coast thunderstorms, now this. According to Bill Filer, the Intelligence Chief at UNIT's New York HQ, it was the 'biggest series of balls-ups since Pearl Harbour'.

Yates had spoken to Filer just minutes before on an apparently

168

unrelated matter – only now it seemed that it might not be quite so unrelated after all. Yates had finally got through to New York using one of the Home Office's IE-pirated videophones, to tell them that Bruce Davis was either dead or, probably worse, a murderous traitor.

Filer had only one question, and it wasn't the one Yates expected. 'Bruce who?'

'Davis. Your crash retrieval officer. Just arrived here.'

'Never heard of him,' came the reply.

At that moment a few things started to make sense. Then came the confirmation from Dr French that the body in the lab was, in fact, William Donald. 'I couldn't find dental records for Davis,' French had told a less-than-surprised Yates, 'but I could for poor Billy, and they're a prefect match.'

It was almost inevitable, therefore, that Corporal Bell was bearing the brunt of Yates's increasing frustration.

'What's the latest from the police?'

'No sign of the fugitive. I suppose we ought to assume that he's slipped through the cordon by now. After all, the officers were looking for Billy Donald, not Mr Davis.'

'Or whatever his real name is,' said Yates. 'I don't suppose there's been any word from the Brigadier?'

Bell shook her head.

'Do you know, they used to kill the bearers of bad news?' said Yates.

The Doctor's jamming device worked almost immediately. Artificial wings that had been motionless or gently flapping as the creatures bit and slashed at his comatose form suddenly began moving vigorously. The goblin creatures clutched at the Doctor, looking bewildered, but one by one their wings pulled them off and up into the air. Some ascended and became pinpoints circling in the crystal-blue sky; others pitched and yawed and crashed into the ground.

Shuskin came and stood next to Liz, a grim smile of satisfaction on her face. The other soldiers formed a protective ring around the Doctor, shooting at the Waro as they flew into the air and preventing any more from approaching with a constant barrage of machine-gun fire. When none of the creatures remained on the Doctor's body Liz handed the device to Shuskin and ran to his side.

He was still and very cold. His face was covered with numerous cuts and bruises, although one arm had been thrown up to protect his eyes. Deep gashes had been made into his chest and shoulders. He'd already lost a lot of blood – if, indeed, that stuff that flowed through his veins could be classified as blood.

Liz tried to move the arm that protected his face, but it was stiff, as if the Doctor's entire body had been cast in bronze. She placed her fingertips over the Doctor's pale lips. She felt the gentlest tingle of exhaled breath.

'Not again,' she said sadly.

'You really should stay in for another night or two, Mr Benton,' said the consultant neurologist. 'I can't overstress the potential dangers of treating concussion lightly.'

'So you've said,' noted Benton. Five times already. 'My mind's made up. I need to get back to work.' He glanced at himself in the mirror opposite his bed and saw his head swathed in bandages. He looked like the top half of an Egyptian mummy. Funny really. Benton smiled and returned his attention to finding his jacket.

'It's on the back of the chair,' said the consultant helpfully.

'Thank you.'

Benton slipped on his brown suede jacket. It had been in the bag of clothing brought into Challesford Royal Infirmary by Corporal Bell. She'd been chatty, as usual, and admitted that she was worried about Mike Yates's ability under pressure, but

Benton had been too out of it to take much notice.

It had been even worse when he'd first arrived. When Benton recovered consciousness in the sterile surroundings of the hospital he had been confused and groggy, unsure of anything much, including where he was or how he'd got there. Then, gradually, the pieces started to slot into place. He'd been in the Doctor's lab and…

Something important was missing, some vital piece of an enormous jigsaw. Benton struggled to remember, but still it refused to come to mind. He could remember all sorts of stupid things: that the last three winners of the European Inter City Fairs Cup were Leeds United, Newcastle United and Arsenal; that the capital of Bolivia was La Paz; that the girl with whom he'd lost his virginity was called Deborah Phelan, and that her brother played wing three-quarter for London Irish. His brain was clouded by trivia. Long-forgotten scenes from his childhood, of his early days in the service, were as fresh as daisies, and yet he couldn't remember what he'd been thinking about immediately before the explosion.

Carol Bell had told him about the bomb – that Mike suspected the Russians but that, thankfully, he'd talked to the Brigadier who had given him alternatives. Mike, she said, seemed to be heading for a breakdown. Benton nodded passively at this new bit of information, and stored it next to a memory of a scene from *Steptoe and Son*, when the old man dunked his pickled onions in his bathwater.

Mike had always been a bit panicky, especially when he was given the 'Big Chair', but Benton had always assumed that, with his public-school background and his training as an officer, it was just something that Yates would grow into.

Damn it! Why could he remember the name of the fifth Marx brother, but not this… whatever it was?

* * *

'We can't wait any longer,' said Shuskin. 'The Doctor's device clearly works. We must press on towards the base and see what is there.'

Liz had just finished using the Doctor's sonic screwdriver to solder the wires together. She looked up, about to argue.

Shuskin raised a hand. 'I understand your concern for the Doctor,' she said. 'But we must complete the mission. I will leave five men behind to move him to safety.'

'It's just a shame there isn't time to rig up another one of these jamming devices,' said Liz. 'That way –'

'In a few hours' time,' said Shuskin, glancing at her watch, 'missiles more powerful than the bombs that devastated Hiroshima and Nagasaki will be flying overhead, to a target not more than ten miles away.' She smiled, and Liz detected warmth and honesty there, perhaps for the first time. 'You seem to think it bizarre that I love my country. That is your prerogative. But if it is all the same to you, I would rather not marvel at the nuclear weaponry of the Union of Soviet Socialist Republics from this close a distance.' She snapped a fresh magazine on to the Kalashnikov. 'So, let us do what the Doctor wanted – find a more subtle solution.'

'You speak as though he's already dead.'

Shuskin stared down at the seemingly lifeless body. 'For all I know, he is.'

Despite continued protestations that he should stay in hospital, under observation, at least for one more night, Benton was adamant: he was going and that was all there was to it. The doctor threatened to call up UNIT and have them force Benton to stay; Benton promised the man a 'good chinning', and he quickly found someone else to bully.

Benton finished slipping on the last of the clothes that Bell had brought him, took a quick drink of Lucozade from the bedside

172

table, and then, with a throbbing in his head that was not a million miles away from Ringo Starr's percussion on the last Beatles LP, he walked out of the hospital, hailed a taxi, and asked for St Anthony's railway station.

On the back seat of the taxi was a discarded copy of the previous day's *Daily Mail*. Benton flicked at it idly as the taxi driver made small-talk about the World Cup, and the price of petrol, and the state of the country. Benton grunted absent-mindedly as he found himself looking at a familiar face in the pages of the newspaper.

'Arlo,' he said, wondering why life so often seemed to run on coincidences just like that.

'You what, guv?' asked the taxi driver, taking a break from his racist rant to check on his heavily bandaged passenger.

'They've gone to Wiltshire,' said Benton, scanning the page for more information.

'Who's that, then?'

'The Venus People.'

'Oh yeah, them loonies. I had one of them in the cab a few months back.'

Benton wanted to scream at the man to shut up, to stop the mayhem in his head, but he bit his tongue and looked out of the window as they approached the railway station. He had business to complete.

The dark forest was as dead as the cold soil that crackled underfoot. Liz and Shuskin made their way swiftly towards the Waro mine in unnatural and unnerving silence. No birdsong, no animal cries, barely a breath of wind. The sky overhead, a blue jewel framed by the ragged angularity of the trees, was occasionally crossed by the sinister flapping shape of a Waro on patrol. None seemed to see them, and Liz began to wonder if the Waro were preparing instead for another Soviet air attack.

The gradually thinning trees let more of the afternoon light splash down on to the ground, the gentle incline becoming steeper. Shuskin's map-reading appeared to be reliable: they had avoided the strange alien roads, along which the Waro seemed to concentrate their interest, and the summit of the hill should give them a view down on to the Waro's base.

A different image crossed Liz's mind, and it made her shudder. The roads didn't go anywhere – she'd looked at their positions plotted on Captain Shuskin's map, and they encircled the base and extended outward into the taiga, but terminated suddenly. Now it struck her that they weren't roads so much as strands of an enormous spider's web. What better reason to build roads in the middle of a forest than to tempt a military force into certain locations and along certain paths?

Liz considered mentioning this to Shuskin, but she seemed instinctively to have come to the same conclusion. 'If we avoid the roads,' she had said before they left the Doctor and the others behind, 'I think we are in with a chance.'

Moments later they came to the top of the hill, and Liz turned her thoughts away from the deadly silver pathways. The trees were sparse and stunted here, and Liz and Shuskin ducked from one piece of cover to another as they approached the edge. All the while Liz kept a tight hand on the device, remembering how silently the Waro had come up behind her. And there was no one to watch her back this time.

Liz and Shuskin crawled on their stomachs for the last few metres. The vista below gradually unfolded – a massive crater in the middle of the forest, as sensitive and subtle as any human opencast mine. Scattered around the edge were large buildings, not unlike grain silos, and deep in the artificial chasm were what seemed to be motor units and conveyor belts.

Shuskin immediately scanned the area with a pair of binoculars. 'Something's wrong,' she said, passing them to Liz.

'What do you mean?'

'I see Waro patrolling overhead, and moving between the various buildings. I see what appears to be mining equipment. But...'

'But?' Liz scanned the area intently.

'None of the machinery is moving.'

'Perhaps they're having a break,' said Liz. 'Union rules or something.'

'They are an invading military force,' said Shuskin, seeming to have missed the humour in Liz's voice. 'We no longer stop our battles to have tea, Dr Shaw.'

'Well, maybe there's just been a power failure. Or they've mined what they came for. There could be a hundred and one reasons why the machines aren't working.'

'We had better find out,' said Shuskin.

The plan was brilliant in its simplicity. Or, alternatively, it was a foolish, desperate gambit by a man who had been sent chasing from pillar to post and was, frankly, at the end of his tether.

Either way, Lethbridge-Stewart had paid his eight hundred francs to the ladies, and now he wanted to see his money's worth.

The girl who had tried to sell herself to him was called Sandrine and was from Zürich. Her father was a *bürgermeister* and her mother, recently deceased, had been a *hausfrau*. None of this really mattered, but Lethbridge-Stewart always liked to know who he was dealing with. The girl introduced several of her colleagues, and the Brigadier outlined his plans in a mixture of French and English. To his great relief, they seemed to understand him and, equally importantly, they didn't mind taking orders. You don't have to know the language to realise that money talks.

The diversion that he asked them to perform was straightforward enough. Six girls lined themselves up in front of the warehouse and began hollering at the top of their voices, taking their clothes off, and fighting with each other. The Brigadier had asked them to spare no indignity, just make as much noise as possible. He was hoping that the last thing the men in the warehouse wanted was a 'scene', and, as he hid in the shadows beside the doors, he knew that he had to make the most of the one opportunity he was likely to get.

Two minutes later the doors creaked open and three men emerged, two carrying sub-machine guns. They fanned out, looking suitably menacing. Sandrine and her friends, having valiantly performed above and beyond the call of duty, took one look at the guns and fled into the bright morning, their money well earned.

Thankfully, they had kept the men occupied long enough for Lethbridge-Stewart to slip through the doors and conceal himself alongside a lorry. The moment the huge doors closed again the tailgate came down, and the men began unloading large quantities of documents in plastic bags. Most of them were speaking in French, though the Brigadier heard other languages occasionally, including English. He distinguished few specific words, but one caught his attention. It was a name – 'Houghton' – and it sent a chill down the Brigadier's spine.

The man he had been sent to kill. Lethbridge-Stewart fished in his pocket and removed the piece of paper that Hayes had given him. In the dim light he looked at it again, puzzled. Executing Michael Houghton and escaping would not prove easy. Too many people about. He estimated there must be at least ten of the dark-clothed men in the warehouse.

Above him was an office, a dim light shining through the window. The Brigadier crouched low, and moved closer to the rickety iron steps that led up to the badly painted door. As he shuffled forward his attention was caught by the man directly above him at the office window. Lethbridge-Stewart didn't need to be told that it was Houghton.

The Brigadier removed his machine pistol and checked the magazine, clicking it into place. So this was it: war – to the death. Lethbridge-Stewart knelt, steadying his aim with his non-shooting hand, aiming the gun towards the man silhouetted in the light of the window.

Easy. So very easy.

Do it!

The metal sight crossed the man's head, moved down on to his chest.

Lethbridge-Stewart's mind erupted in a cacophony of voices.

Shoot him! End it! Now!

So very easy.

Too easy.

'No,' said Lethbridge-Stewart loudly. Loud enough that even those in the office heard him. The sound brought the men unloading the truck running towards him, their guns pointing in his direction. The Brigadier knelt and placed his gun on the floor.

'Do not move!' said a man above him. The Brigadier kept his downturned hands pressed against the damp ground.

'Who you are? Why are you here?' asked the man, whom the Brigadier took to be Houghton.

'I'm here… I *was* here to kill you,' said the Brigadier. 'I had my orders, but…' He paused. 'Things are rarely as simple as they first seem.'

Houghton looked at him curiously. 'Stand up,' he ordered.

As he got to his feet, Lethbridge-Stewart realised that he knew several of his captors by sight. Staff from UNIT HQ. What was worse, they knew him.

'It's the Brigadier,' said a Frenchman whom Lethbridge-Stewart knew to be a sergeant attached to the administration section.

'What?' exclaimed Houghton angrily.

'Now you know me,' said the Brigadier evenly, 'I would

177

appreciate the same courtesy.'

'Major Mick Houghton,' said the man, snapping to attention with a salute that, in the circumstances, was both absurd and yet performed with supreme dignity.

'Stand at ease,' said the Brigadier, with much the same quality. This was getting silly. 'What on Earth is going on?'

'Perhaps you could tell us that, sir,' said Houghton.

It seemed that they were all UNIT troops, and Lethbridge-Stewart outranked the lot of them. 'Lay down your weapons, then we'll talk.' It was a ludicrous request to make, but it made about as much sense as most of the other things Lethbridge-Stewart had said and done during the previous forty-eight hours.

The men glanced at Houghton, who nodded. The soldiers put down their guns.

'The office would seem as good a place as any,' concluded Lethbridge-Stewart, marching up the stairs.

Liz and Shuskin set off towards the mine, staying close to the trees, their feet crunching on the layer of ice and snow that lay over the dark soil. Liz risked a sideways glance at Shuskin. She was watching the sky intently, her finger on the trigger of the Kalashnikov. She indicated that they should head towards the closest of the alien towers. Even from here Liz could see that the conveyor belt that ran down into the heart of the mine was motionless.

The silo-like building, when they finally reached it, seemed to have been constructed from the same tough, blemish-free material as the roads that criss-crossed the taiga. It was surprisingly warm to the touch, reflecting back what sunlight there was. There seemed to be no windows or door in the structure; it simply sprouted from the ground like some silver toadstool.

Shuskin gestured towards the top of the conveyor belt. There was an engine of some sort – Liz could make out gears and cogs – and presumably the ore was refined in one of the buildings down in the mine, and then brought up here to be stored and –

No, she saw what Shuskin meant now. 'It's all one solid piece,' she said. 'It's not a motor at all. More like a statue.'

Shuskin nodded, her fears confirmed. 'Whatever the Waro want from here, it's not raw materials.'

'So what's going on?' asked Liz.

'It has been bothering me ever since the intelligence reports suggested that this facility was a mine,' admitted Shuskin. 'I am sure there is nothing here to extract. Believe me, we would be doing it if there were.' She paused, deep in thought. 'I once saw an American cowboy film. One group were defending a fort, but were short on manpower. So they made dummies, and placed them up on the ramparts as if they were soldiers. That film taught me that psychology is vital in warfare.'

'But why the false mine?' asked Liz. 'It's not as if the Waro are short on numbers.'

'No,' said Shuskin. 'But they wanted this location to seem more important than it really is.' She turned away from the Waro complex, her voice bitter. 'Hundreds of good Soviet soldiers have died, just to find out that there's nothing here.'

CHAPTER 15

It was a strained meeting, neither side fully trusting the other, yet Houghton and Lethbridge-Stewart were both aware that each was potentially talking to his only ally in a macabre game of chance.

The Brigadier sketched in the background of his trip to Geneva, and the convoluted and bizarre path that had led him to this location. Houghton, who revealed that he had gone through basic training with the Brigadier's old friend Jimmy Turner, seemed anxious to reassure Lethbridge-Stewart that he and his men were innocent of any duplicity. All of the men, except two who had been posted to guard duty at the warehouse door, stood behind Houghton, in more ways than one. They would have gone to hell and back for the Major.

'What are you doing here?' asked the Brigadier after a discussion about 'the security of the realm' had done little but take them round and round in circles.

'There is,' said Houghton, 'a conspiracy within UNIT. It extends to the highest level. I really don't know who to trust any more. You may be part of this, in which case I'm a dead man. But I might be already anyway. Certainly if you were sent here to kill me then they know about us.'

'*They*? Who are "they", man?' asked the Brigadier.

'The great *they* who are in charge of the eternal *whatsit*,' Houghton said with a cynical snarl. 'If I knew who "they" were I'd kill them myself and face the consequences. But how do you fight shadows?'

The Brigadier turned away from Houghton and stared out of the window and down towards the heaps of plastic bags in the centre of the warehouse. 'And those?' he asked.

'That material has been "borrowed" from UNIT HQ,' replied

Houghton. 'Personnel files, official communiqués, internal memos… Anything we could get out hands on. You're welcome to look at it. Our only wish was to try to find out who the traitors are. And what their plan is.'

'We'll worry about that later,' said the Brigadier, who suddenly realised that he and Houghton shared the same goals. Almost despite himself, he trusted this capable young soldier who was placing his career and probably his life on the line. 'I'm prepared,' said the Brigadier at length, 'to take over responsibility for this operation. As the senior officer here it will therefore be under my orders that these investigations are carried out.' It was an astonishing offer, and Lethbridge-Stewart was amazed to hear himself make it. He was giving the men a lifeline they thought they would never have, a simple reply to the questions they would be asked if captured. An opportunity to say that they were just following orders. The Brigadier was, in effect, taking the pressure of a firing squad away from the men and, in doing so, placing a noose around his own neck.

'I can't let you do that, sir,' said Houghton, both relieved and horrified to hear the Brigadier's proposal.

'It wasn't a request, Houghton, it was an order. You do still remember how to follow orders, don't you?'

'Yes,' said Houghton. 'But I think you're being a complete pillock. Sir.'

Lethbridge-Stewart grinned. 'I'll be the judge of that,' he said. 'Now, if "they" led me here, it's imperative that we leave this location and secure another base for ourselves.'

Houghton immediately saw what the Brigadier was driving at. 'Who sent you here?'

'Major-General Hayes.'

The look on Houghton's face was pitched somewhere between shock and outright horror. 'I had no idea…' he began, but let his sentence fade away.

'That the conspiracy went so high?' finished Lethbridge-Stewart. 'No, Major, neither did I. Until now.'

Liz and Shuskin ascended the hill in silence. As they approached the top the sky began to fill with Waro, and Liz wondered how much longer their luck would hold. Suddenly a dark figure flew towards them through the dark trees, claws outstretched.

Shuskin fired a rapid burst at the creature, the bullets scything into it as it hung momentarily in the air. Then it collapsed on to the ground, torn in two, its innards steaming in the sharp arctic air.

'They know we are here,' said Shuskin, somewhat pointlessly. 'Operate the Doctor's device.'

Liz scrabbled in her pocket and found the gadget. Some wires had come free.

'Hurry!' shouted Shuskin, firing the machine gun in seemingly random directions in the sky.

'But it's broken!' cried Liz. 'I'm not sure if I can repair it!'

Shuskin took her handgun from its holster and passed it across. 'Then take this.'

'But I've never –'

'Take it!' snapped Shuskin. 'And keep one bullet for yourself, just in case.' She swivelled, releasing a barrage of fire up into the sky, and then both women rushed headlong for the forest.

Liz gripped the gun in her hand as if it was her last link with sanity. 'There's no place like home,' she found herself muttering under her breath, a mantra to stop her screaming in terror. 'There's no place like home.'

Another Waro came down through the branches of the trees, shaking its head from side to side, spitting.

Liz shot the thing in the shoulder, ran over its crumpled body, ignoring the green blood that bubbled from the wound.

Before she could think about what she had done, Shuskin pushed Liz forcefully to the ground. Liz tasted snow and soil – felt the rush of wings as another goblin creature swept over her, shrieking in annoyance. Shuskin dragged her to her feet. The woman suddenly looked capable of carrying Liz all the way back to Moscow, single-handed.

Liz ran until her heart seemed swollen in her chest, concentrating on nothing but Shuskin's hand at her shoulder, the pistol still clenched in her fist.

'Come on!' shouted Shuskin.

'I'm trying,' screamed Liz. But all around she could hear the sounds of Waro landing gently on the crisp ground. Braying like animals who scented a kill.

The preparations to leave were made quickly and with a minimum of fuss. This was a military operation after all, and everything would be executed with precision. The Brigadier prided himself that, even if those UNIT forces loyal to the conspiracy were to burst in now and shoot them all as insurgents, they would die as soldiers.

Small consolation.

The documents were loaded back into the lorry and the Brigadier briefed each man about what they were to look for once they had the chance to examine them. Houghton had dual Swiss and English nationality, and had pulled some strings with a relative of his mother's in order to arrange the use of a disused chateau on the outskirts of Berne. He assured the Brigadier that it would make an ideal safe house for the group. Within an hour they had stripped the warehouse of everything incriminating and were ready to move.

'I'm surprised that they haven't raided us yet,' said Houghton as he climbed into the lorry. 'I expected that hours ago.'

The Brigadier shook his head. 'That wouldn't be cricket, would it?' he said. 'Why catch us at it when they can just as easily shoot us in the back while trying to escape?'

'You don't mean –?'

'I'm afraid so. Prepare your men for action, Major. I think we might have a situation on our hands.'

Houghton turned. 'Take a man around the rear, Sergeant. Make sure we're not surrounded.'

When the all-clear was received, the massive doors swung open and the lorry inched out into the deserted street.

'Looking good so far,' Houghton called over his shoulder from the driver's seat. Lethbridge-Stewart sat hunched at the back of the vehicle, looking pensively through the canvas cover for any sign of movement. The lorry went through a ninety-degree turn with agonising slowness, and then started to pull away from the warehouse. 'Home and bloody dry,' said Houghton with a cheery dismissal of their predicament that put a smile of the faces of most of his men.

'Any sign that we were followed, sir?' asked one of the soldiers closest to the Brigadier.

'No,' he replied. 'It's as quiet as –'

But he never finished the sentence. The wailing sirens of a large number of Swiss police cars shattered the quiet of midday. UNIT jeeps followed close behind.

'They've got us trapped,' shouted Houghton angrily. Lethbridge-Stewart moved to the front of the lorry to see three police cars blocking the far end of the street.

'Drive through them. Fire a few warning shots,' the Brigadier said and returned his attention to the pursuing cars at his rear. 'Hold on tight, you men,' he continued. 'This might get a little rough.'

Taking two snipers with him, Lethbridge-Stewart lay flat against the drop-board at the back of the lorry, and fired off three quick shots above the leading police car. 'Aim for the tyres,' he said, as he noticed a familiar face sitting in the passenger seat of the first police car. Hayes.

They wouldn't get very far if Hayes had the authorities in his pocket. The first shot from the pursuing UNIT troops fizzed past his head and buried itself in the torso of a young soldier crouching behind him, loading his rifle. The Brigadier glanced around and sensed the same futility he always felt when one of those in his command died a pointless death. Another letter to write to another distraught mother, to be delivered with another coffin: 'Find enclosed the remains of your son, together with a medal and a note to say 'we won''. 'Damn,' he muttered. 'What's the point?'

'Sorry, sir?' asked one of the marksmen next to him.

'Rhetorical question, Private,' replied the Brigadier.

'Poor old Innes,' said the soldier. 'I did three tours with him. He was a good lad.'

'Yes,' said the Brigadier. Then he decided what the point was: survival. 'Fire at will!' he ordered. 'If it moves, shoot it. If it doesn't move, shoot it until it does!'

The lorry ploughed through the flimsy barricade next to the police cars and careered off into the city with a fleet of armed vehicles in pursuit.

Liz and Shuskin stood back to back as the ring of goblin creatures closed in on them. While the Soviet soldier fired at the advancing creatures, Liz struggled with the anti-Waro device.

'I'm running out of ammunition,' said Shuskin through gritted teeth.

'That's not all we're running out of,' said Liz, trying desperately not to glance up at the approaching, snarling creatures. She couldn't afford to let them fluster her. She just had to concentrate on the wiring, on breathing life back into the Doctor's contraption.

'They've got weapons,' observed Shuskin. 'I can't understand why they're not just shooting us.'

'Probably not macho enough for them. They want to tear us

limb from limb with their bare hands, or they're not interested.'

'More fool them,' spat Shuskin, lobbing a grenade in the direction of the closest group of Waro. Liz felt the blast sweep past her back, followed by a downward hail of soil and ice and... No, she really didn't want to know what was now falling from the sky.

'Really, ladies,' came a voice they both recognised. 'There's no need to go to quite these lengths to attract my attention.'

Liz glanced up, relief flooding over her. Coming through the trees towards them was the Doctor, his clothes torn, his face still scratched and bruised, but with a steely determination in his eyes that shone through the shadows. Best of all was the fact that, in his hands, he carried another converted intercom.

He pointed it at the nearest Waro and pressed a switch. Immediately the creature rocketed into the air, squealing.

'Retreat might be advisable, Captain,' said the Doctor.

The two women ran through the gap in the cordon created by the Doctor's intervention, while the Doctor calmly moved his device in an arc against the remaining Waro.

'I'll catch you up in a moment,' urged the Doctor as they ran past him and deeper into the forest.

Liz risked a glance behind, and saw that the Doctor's device was becoming increasingly ineffective against the Waro. Perhaps they were reprogramming the software that controlled the wings to override the effects of the Doctor's interference. 'Come on, Doctor!' she shouted.

The Doctor had clearly come to a similar conclusion. He made a final adjustment to the jamming device, then threw it at the onrushing Waro before turning to run. Soon he was alongside Liz and Shuskin. 'I'm not sure we'll be able to use that trick again,' he said. His limbs were a blur, but he wasn't out of breath.

'They're... not... stupid,' agreed Liz, panting.

'No,' said the Doctor. 'They're evil, egotistical and depraved.

But they're certainly not stupid.'

Suddenly there was an explosion, just to their left. A fir tree flowered into a ball of flame that threatened to knock them off their feet. The Waro had started to use their hand weapons.

'We must have riled them,' said the Doctor brightly.

'I'm so glad,' said Liz.

'Well, if they're concentrating on three small targets on the ground,' said the Doctor, 'it means they're slightly more likely to miss a whacking great thing like that.' He pointed upward, at the enormous green helicopter that was descending towards them out of the dull grey sky.

'They got it going again!' exclaimed Shuskin in delight.

'With a little help,' added the Doctor. 'I can honestly say that it's twice the helicopter it was.'

With surprising grace the craft landed on the snowy soil, the rear door already open to receive them. A number of Soviet soldiers jumped down to give covering fire.

'Really?' said Liz, still running fit to burst. If the Waro didn't get her, heart failure was sure to.

'I've improved the shielding against the Waro's energy weapons,' said the Doctor proudly. 'There's every chance we shall escape from here in one piece.'

'Excellent,' said Shuskin, without a trace of irony as she clambered on board. 'I must report to my superiors.' She ran towards the cockpit without a backward glance at the creatures that had pursued them.

When the helicopter was safely in the air, and the Doctor was watching the Waro flit around the craft with unnerving detachment, he finally asked Liz what they had seen at the mining centre.

'There's nothing there,' said Liz, her heart still pounding. 'It's all a sham. It looks like a mine from the air, but it's nothing of the sort. You could put two hundred and forty volts through those "motors" and you wouldn't get a dicky bird in response.'

'That must be what the Waro was hiding from me when I performed the soul-catching,' said the Doctor.

'But I still don't understand.'

'You're not thinking of these things in military terms,' said the Doctor. 'Standard invasion procedure: establish a false bridgehead in order to divert attention.'

'So all of this... all the destruction...'

'Was just to distract us, yes. Perhaps they wanted us to go halfway around the world on a wild-goose chase.' The Doctor turned to look at Liz for the first time, his voice now sombre. 'So the question we now need to ask ourselves is: where is the *real* invasion?'

If Hayes had hoped that the Brigadier would hand himself over without a fight, then he'd underestimated Lethbridge-Stewart for perhaps the last time. The Major-General must have pulled all sorts of strings to get the local police force involved, thought the Brigadier. The last thing his friends would have wanted was an undignified chase through the shopping centre.

Which is exactly what Houghton and Lethbridge-Stewart had just given them. Now they were clear of the city, heading towards the Alps. All the while their pursuers drew closer.

The Brigadier knew their plight was still hopeless, but the fighter in him wouldn't countenance surrender. The men, buffeted and bruised in the cramped conditions of the back of the lorry, accepted their situation with the kind of barrack-room humour that Lethbridge-Stewart understood and excelled in.

'We've got them worried now, sir,' said Sergeant Hutton, a tough Yorkshireman who had served with the Brigadier in the Scots Guards. 'They don't know whether to ram us or shoot us!'

The Brigadier laughed as much as the rest of the men. It was just what the situation needed, having the whole thing brought down to earth. 'How's the wife, Harry?' he asked, kneeling beside the man and checking his Browning.

'Just fine, sir,' said Hutton as he aimed another shot at the leading APC. 'Damn,' he said, as the shot pulled to the right. 'The driver's that German git from relief watch. I owe him one.' He looked at Lethbridge-Stewart with a gleam in his eye. 'Just like old times, eh?' he said.

For a moment there was nothing that the Brigadier could say. He had, almost certainly, condemned these men to at best dishonourable discharge and at worst traitors' graves. 'Who's got the radio?' he asked, and was told that young Laverre was the man in charge. 'Can you raise HQ?' he asked.

'Yes, sir,' said the terrified youth.

'Right. Get me somebody, anybody, who outranks Hayes. And a bit sharpish.' He turned back to Hutton with a wry grin. 'Aden was never like this, was it?'

'No, sir,' replied Hutton. 'You saved my life there, sir. You and Johnny Benton and that coloured lad we used to have with us, remember?'

The Brigadier fired another shot at Hayes's car, but it missed, the lorry rounding another sharp corner. 'Yes, Harry. You've never let me forget it.'

'What was that lad's name?'

'Hartfield,' said the Brigadier.

'Aye, that was him. Jacob Hartfield. Jamaican, wasn't he? Quiet lad. I remember Johnny Benton and some of the others getting him drunk in Al Mukalla and trying to have him tattooed. He fought like a lion that night, I can tell you!'

Lethbridge-Stewart heard someone calling for him and turned to find Laverre holding out the radio handset towards him.

'I've reached someone, sir. Called him out of a meeting.'

'Good man,' said the Brigadier. He grabbed the handset. The risk, of course, was that the officer was also tainted by the conspiracy.

But it was their only hope. 'Sorry to interrupt you, sir –'

Suddenly the lorry swerved violently to the left, lurching out of control.

'They've hit the tyres!' cried Houghton as the lorry pitched over on to its side.

FIFTH INTERLUDE:
THE FOUR SYMBOLS OF THE SAUCER PEOPLE

They had camped on the ridge of Knighton Down, with Salisbury Plain sprawled out before them. At sunset the previous night they had knelt and prayed to Jesus-from-Venus to come in a halo of light and groove with them. Big Tye from Glastonbury had even produced a battered old Philips tape recorder and stuck on his cherished fourth-generation copy of Cosmic Sounds' 'The Zodiac' to usher in the second coming of the age of Aquarius, or Scorpio, or something.

Nothing happened, other than that the sun died awesomely on the far horizon over Stonehenge, and Mad Paula, who'd been on a concentrated diet of cheap blotter-acid and Tizer in the van ever since they'd left the south coast, had experienced a divine visitation or (more likely) a bad trip.

It was four days to the summer solstice, and in Wiltshire that meant pilgrimage time. Just like Chaucer's ragamuffin army of everymen, so the Venus People found themselves with strange bedfellows. There was the Wicca crowd (mostly a bunch of reformed football hooligans from the North who said they were into peace, but were really looking for love). Then there were the itinerant Christian mystics, who were pleasant enough, but seemed absorbed in their own private trip. And the Anarchists kept themselves to themselves, seemingly incapable of trusting anyone outside their group.

And there were others. Thousands of lost individuals, seeking kindred spirits, all gathering around the outskirts of the plain. Waiting.

One of the Venus People had become tired of 'The Zodiac', so he'd gone into his van and fished out something by Atomic

Rooster instead. When that caused a rumpus, most of the Venus People had gone back to their campfire, singing Negro spirituals long into the night, while the pagans heralded the sunrise with interminable drumming. Scouse, Saddest Moon and Starchild declared this 'uncool', and moved back to the ridge.

They were very different people, but they shared one thing. An overwhelming hatred of 'Kumbyar'.

Now the cold of early morning had given way to a beautiful, cloudless day, the sky painted a blue that seemed possible only in the Technicolor musicals of the 1940s.

'Nice day for the end of the world,' said Scouse laconically.

'Maybe tomorrow!' countered Saddest Moon. They laughed, but Starchild looked astonished that they could find levity in such a serious event.

'I don't dig this,' she said quickly. 'It's a serious happening, all right?'

'Cool your boots, babe,' replied Scouse. 'No need to act like a mong. We're just getting into the scene.' He kissed her, savagely, on the lips, and her frown melted away.

'What is it with you two?' asked Saddest Moon.

'It's a love thing, la,' replied Scouse simply.

Starchild stood up, easing the cramp from her legs, and walked to the edge of the ridge.

'It's like the top of the world,' she said. And turned around quickly. 'Hey, wouldn't it be like, amazing, if they came now?'

'The Saucer People you mean?'

'Right.'

Saddest Moon nodded sagely. 'We've got to wait. This is the gathering of the tribes. The global village. Cats have got to get here from, like, everywhere.'

Scouse snorted. 'Are you gonna be there for the love-in?' he asked cynically. 'I'll tell you what, though, it's all rubbish, isn't it?'

'No. It's psychedelic,' replied Starchild, sad and hurt that her friends couldn't understand her enthusiasm. 'You ought to clean your head, babe. The ancient writings, the prophecies, it's all coming down. Arlo says so.'

'Yeah?' asked Scouse with a sarcastic grin. But even he had felt the power of Arlo. He had answered the call when the Venus People marched down Lime Street to taunts and ridicule from a motley crew of Everton fans. He'd joined the People there and then, ignoring the prickling embarrassment. 'You are chosen,' Arlo had said, and he was.

'The signs have been witnessed,' added Saddest Moon, a young farmer's boy from the Fens who had met the group on the road near his home, and gone with them after leaving his mother a note to say that 'Jesus has called me'.

'Exactly,' added Starchild, who came from the North but never talked about her past life. 'The symbols. The sky bled at the festival, false religion is being cast down into the bottomless pit, Babylon is falling. The Four Horsemen – it's the Beatles, it *has* to be.'

Scouse grinned. 'There's five of 'em now, doll.'

'George is God,' she said dismissively. 'Everybody knows that.'

The sound of a car coming up the bridle path caused her to stop. She turned towards the oncoming Mercedes, crawling along the dirt road. It slowed to a stop beside them and the driver's window opened, revealing a man in his early forties with dark, stylish hair and a drooping moustache.

'Where might I find Arlo?' asked the driver.

Starchild felt the hatred he had for them, felt it burn her skin. She sat on her haunches and said nothing.

'Over there, in the van, man,' replied Saddest Moon, before adding 'Peace' and raising his hand.

'Yes. Of course,' said the driver. The car swished past them.

'Nice motor,' said Scouse, following the progress of the car. 'That was Lord Rose, or whatever his name is.'

'Names is for tombstones, baby,' said Scouse.

Rose was getting out of the car next to Arlo's caravan. In his immaculate Savile Row suit and leather driving gloves, he looked completely out of place in this environment.

'I don't trust that cat,' said Starchild as Rose entered the van.

'You what?' asked Scouse.

'I don't know what his game is, babe, but his vibes are all wrong.'

'Don't be so suspicious,' countered Scouse. 'He's all right is old Hippie Pete. He's no breadhead.'

'That's right,' said Saddest Moon. 'He's used his dough to help Shelter, Release, *Oz*, all the alternative scene. He isn't a trendy swinger, babe, he's one of us.'

Starchild said nothing, but every time she looked at the Mercedes, she found herself shivering.

In the caravan, Arlo was lying on a battered old mattress in a haze of nicotine and marijuana. Rose's arrival, without ceremony, didn't cause him much surprise. It was just like the cat to enter without knocking.

'Nice to see you, dad,' said Arlo sarcastically. 'Cool threads. They having a sale at Jackson the Tailor or what?'

Rose crossed the caravan without a word and slapped Arlo across the face with the back of his hand.

'Insolent cur,' he spat, and repeated the dose, before kicking the terrified hippie on the seat of his loon pants. 'Get up, sharpish, laddie,' barked the viscount.

Arlo struggled to his feet, holding up his hands in a gesture of submission. 'Cool it, man,' he kept repeating as Rose hit him again and again.

'I warned you about the UNIT men,' exclaimed Rose. 'And what do I discover? You've only gone and told them about the end of the world, you ignoramus!'

PART 6:
SUBTLE ENERGIES COMMISSION

CHAPTER 16

Bruce stepped out of the hovercraft and into the plain black car. Its engine was idling quietly, the only noise in the deserted cove. The driver stubbed out his cigarette and, avoiding eye contact, settled into his seat.

The sedan moved smoothly across the beach of rough shingle, the deep grinding of the wheels sounding like the wash of the tide from within the vehicle. Bruce stared at the back of the driver's head, noticing a band of pink scar tissue around the thick, tanned neck. It was as if the man had been clumsily garrotted – or had been the unfortunate recipient of Baron Frankenstein's spare-part surgery. Either way, he was an ugly brute, stuffed into a cheap suit that stank of garlic.

Bruce imagined a gun sight moving across that blubbery neck and up his cropped black hair. Pulling the trigger. Blood and bone and brain spraying everywhere. From this range, and even against that thick skull, it would make one hell of a mess.

He stared out of the window, bored. England had been a bit of a buzz. But now he only felt empty disappointment. The drug-like rush from every mission was fading more quickly, the spaces between jobs beginning to feel like an eternity. If things carried on like this, even killing might lose its appeal.

Joke.

The road hugged the coastline, gently ascending the cliffs. Eventually it turned its back on the azure sea, moving inland. Some minutes later the car passed through a broken gate covered with warning notices and on to a track. The ground became artificially flat, a ruler-straight, rusted railway line stretching into the distance. The car followed the track for about half a mile, and then turned on to a concourse of broken asphalt and stopped.

The driver stepped out of the car, leaving the engine running. Bruce pushed open the door, and followed the man past the disused railway platform. Numerous weeds sprouted between the old wooden sleepers. The adverts for Orangina and the local hypermarket on the wall of the former ticket office had almost faded beyond recognition.

The station was deserted but for the freight train standing on the one clean-looking track. The big driver approached, pulled open one of the sliding doors, and immediately walked away. Bruce didn't board the train until he'd heard the dark sedan leave.

Rusted steps led into a boxcar that smelled of straw and animals. There was a connecting door at the far end, with light visible through a small glass window. Bruce strode into the next carriage.

It was a computer room, its bright silver walls windowless and claustrophobic. White-coated technicians moved between the banks of equipment, checking readings and swapping spools of computer tape. Only one of them seemed to notice Bruce's arrival, and he came over, arm outstretched, as if to shake the man's hand.

Bruce gave him the data reel he'd stolen from UNIT HQ, and the man immediately turned away, satisfied. Bruce moved through the next carriage, full of leather armchairs and crew-cut men in tight-fitting suits, and towards a red door. He knocked once, and pushed it open.

The room beyond was dark save for a single table lamp on top of a mahogany desk. The pool of light illuminated a pair of hands, leafing through a document.

Bruce strode smartly up to the man. 'I believe this is the

information you require, Mr President,' he stated, placing the manila envelope on the table.

The hands came into the pool of light again, and pulled out a few sheets. There was a grunt, made ambiguous by the darkness. 'Geneva,' said the man. 'We have another job for you.'

Benton took the train to Salisbury, sitting next to a young man who said he was a member of the Lowlife Brotherhood Republican Movement. He tried to indoctrinate Benton, then gave up, talking about football instead.

Five years from now, thought Benton, you'll be selling insurance. He lapsed into sleep just as the kid was giving twenty reasons why Leicester City would *never* be champions.

Benton snapped back into wakefulness just as the train pulled into the station. The young man had gone. Benton stuffed the newspaper he'd bought at the kiosk into his holdall, and jumped to his feet.

A succession of local buses, all of which seemed to run on the principle that the fastest way from A to B was via X, Y, and Z, took Benton to the edge of Salisbury Plain. He'd been on manoeuvres there many times before, and had a vague idea where the hippies were likely to be found. Even so, it took him a number of hours to track down the Venus People.

As he approached the site – some fields that bordered MoD land – Benton felt that he was buzzing and alive, his mind full of the electricity of new thoughts and ideas. It was *years* since he had felt like this.

Benton hid in some bushes as a trio of hippies shuffled past, talking animatedly about 'the big gig' where 'it's all coming down'. The two lads were trying their best to sound calm and relaxed, but even Benton could detect the excitement in their voices. The girl had absolutely no time for their cynicism. Her zeal blazed like a torch.

They were young and stupid, Benton could tell that. Their minds had been poisoned by the evil guru who was feeding them a diet of lies and letting the drugs do the rest. Benton felt sorry for them, but a good bath, a haircut and a dose of national service would sort them out. Never did him any harm.

He shook his head. His mind was wandering again. It was happening more frequently now. Perhaps the doctor at that hospital had been right about the delayed effects of concussion.

He turned as an engine started, first time. Not one of the charabancs. A Mercedes he'd not noticed before was pulling away from the camp. Although he didn't get a decent look at the driver, Benton *knew* that it was Viscount Rose. He also knew who Rose was visiting, and he knew why. They were hatching plots. Fiendish schemes.

It was time to strike at the heart of the action. Benton removed his jacket and left it in the bushes with his holdall. He undid a few buttons on his shirt, rubbed some soil on to his hands and face, and then backtracked a couple of hundred yards parallel to the dirt road. He breathed deeply, and waited for his whirling thoughts to gather themselves. Here we go.

He stepped on to the road in full view of the Venus People. A new convert to their cause.

Quizzical eyes looked at him as he reached the edge of the camp and smiled a bewildered, lost smile.

'Peace,' he said, doing the gesture as he came within earshot.

'Love,' replied the girl, beaming a smile that wasn't shared by her two friends.

'I've come down from the Smoke,' explained Benton. 'I want to know when the saucers are showing up.'

It was dark and something was pressing against Alistair's chest. Ignore it. Must be night-time. Get some sleep.

The sensation refused to go away. Alistair found breathing

difficult. And the darkness wasn't right, either.

Lethbridge-Stewart moved his head, and it hurt. But he realised that it had been dark only because his eyes had been half shut, his face pressed against something cold and glassy.

Windscreen, and rough tarmac beneath. And the pressure on his chest had been caused by his falling on to his front against the truck's door. The truck.

The memories came back like objects viewed through fog. Houghton. The bullet meant for him. Hayes. The chase.

The entire truck had rolled over on to its side, somehow throwing the Brigadier right into the cabin. Behind him he detected moans from the men in the back. Houghton was just coming to. The young lad with the radio seemed to be out cold.

The driver, bleeding from a wound across his forehead, pushed open the other door, and began pulling himself upwards, on to the side of the truck, which was now effectively on its roof. Houghton and the Brigadier followed suit, leaving the rest of the men to untangle themselves.

The police cars, lights still flashing, and UNIT jeeps had formed a circle around the downed truck. Rifles pointed in their direction. The Brigadier jumped down on to the concrete.

For the first time in years he suddenly remembered his encounter with an Italian border checkpoint, soon after he had joined the army. Lethbridge-Stewart had tagged along with a group of young soldiers who had decided to use some leave to explore the beaches of the Med. They were only interested in cheap booze and foreign crumpet, but they'd taken a wrong turn, and had ended up heading towards the border. When Private Partridge had seen passport control he'd had a rush of blood to the head, and had decided to do a handbrake turn to try to go back the way they'd come.

Within seconds they'd been surrounded by Italian police with machine guns. Partridge had just laughed. Their CO had been much less amused when he'd got to hear of the incident.

'Sorry, sir,' said the driver, interrupting the Brigadier's reverie. 'I should have been able to -'

'Perfectly all right, old chap,' said Lethbridge-Stewart. 'Nothing more you could have done.'

The Brigadier noticed Hayes, standing to the side of one of the UN jeeps. He looked extraordinarily pleased with himself as he raised a loudhailer to his lips. 'You men,' he ordered through the howling feedback of the device, 'put your weapons down. Place your hands above your heads.'

'Damn,' said the Brigadier under his breath.

'Sorry, sir?' queried the driver.

'I said, I suppose we'd better do what he wants.' Lethbridge-Stewart turned to Houghton. 'Don't worry, I'll take full responsibility for this.'

'Like hell you will, sir,' said Houghton. He was raising his hands above his head, but there was a nervous tension in his voice. 'I'm not about to play dead for this lot.'

Before the Brigadier could say anything Major Houghton drew his pistol and threw himself on to the road, clearly hoping to make a fight of it.

He was dead before he hit the ground.

The Brigadier ran to Houghton's side as the noise of the machine-gun fire faded, and stared at the body and the blood that flowed on to the tarmac.

He pushed the man's eyes shut, and turned round as Hayes walked over towards him.

'That was stupid,' said the Major-General. 'In any event, it would have been so much easier if my friends in the police force had found you with a warm gun in your hand,' he said, with barely a hint of sympathy. 'This escapade should have ended back in the warehouse.'

'Every drop of blood is on your hands, Hayes, not mine,'

spat the Brigadier.

'Lethbridge-Stewart, is that any way to talk to –'

'You've made an enemy of me, *Hayes*,' said the Brigadier angrily. 'Whatever happens, I'm going to make sure you damn well pay for what you've done.'

John Benton's acting career had ended in junior school when his cameo as Third Shepherd in the nativity play was critically panned after he forgot his one line.

But he had just put in a performance that Humphrey Bogart would have been proud of.

The Venus People had recognised him, of course. He had expected that. Arlo came out to see him, and looked at Benton as though he were something that had just crawled out from under a stone. Benton's reaction was to play it cool, and act dazed.

And it worked. The Venus People took pity on him.

He told them he had thought about what they'd said, and that they were right. The world was doomed and it needed the power of the aliens to get it sorted out.

Scouse looked at him quizzically. 'I don't dig this,' he said flatly. 'He's a square.'

'So were you when I found you,' said Arlo. He turned to Benton. 'OK, soldier boy, suppose we believe you?'

'What's to suppose?' asked Benton reasonably.

'You could be a spy.'

'So could he,' said Benton pointing to Scouse. 'Or any of them.'

'This is heavy,' said Scouse angrily. 'He's turning us on each other.'

Arlo stopped and squatted down beside the camp fire, warming his hands. 'Why should we believe anything you say, soldier boy? You're never happy unless you've got a war on your hands.'

Benton didn't answer. Instead he threw his unloaded Walther P38 handgun into the fire.

'It's time to decide whose side you're on. Isn't that what you lot are always saying? Well, I'm on the side of the Saucer People. And the reverse vampires. And anybody else who's up for a bit of destruction.'

Arlo nodded. 'You'll do for me, soldier boy.' He turned to the Venus People and smiled, the sort of smile sharks make before biting people in two. 'Get him ready for the Treatment.'

The Brigadier found himself immediately separated from the rest of the men, and bundled into one of the UNIT vehicles. After a short ride they came to a small airport. As the Brigadier was hauled out on to the tarmac he noticed a US Air Force B-52 that had just landed, taxiing in their direction. He clamped his hands over his ears as he and the group of accompanying soldiers moved in the direction of the bomber. Lethbridge-Stewart glanced backward to see Hayes watching the scene intently from the passenger seat of the Jeep.

Inside the aircraft a man whom the Brigadier recognised strode over towards him, a sickly smile on his lips. 'Ah, Brigadier. Delighted you could join us.'

'Mr Davis,' said the Brigadier, with as much civility as he could muster. 'Or whatever your real name is.'

'Bruce,' said the man matter-of-factly.

'I haven't been in touch with Captain Yates recently,' said the Brigadier, 'but, seeing you here, I wouldn't have to be a genius to put two and two together, would I?'

'And your conclusion is?'

'From what I saw back in the warehouse, I'd imagine you were working for the CIA.'

'That's very astute of you,' observed Bruce. 'I'm not sure what you saw in the material that Houghton's men had borrowed, but you may as well know that we have a long-standing interest in ALFs and UFOs.' Bruce snorted. 'I'll admit, I was sceptical at first, but the evidence I've seen...'

'Evidence?' queried the Brigadier. 'You should be aware that any material regarding possible encounters with alien life forms should be handed to –'

'I'll let my friend explain,' interrupted Bruce, moving towards the door of the B-52. A grey-suited man strode into the light, looking the Brigadier up and down.

'I'm heading out on a different plane,' said Bruce, his back still turned. 'I don't suppose we'll meet again. It's not been a pleasure.'

Once the doors had clanged shut again, Lethbridge-Stewart turned to the other man. 'And you are?'

'Names are not important,' said the man. 'What is important is that you recognise that UNIT are the new kids on the block. We've gotten quite used to getting to the alien life forms first. And we've never handed over a damn thing.'

'How long has this been going on?' asked the Brigadier.

'You mean contact with aliens? For us, it all began back in the 1940s.' The man paused as the plane manoeuvred for take-off. 'I'm a fair man, Lethbridge-Stewart. If you really want to know the truth about the extraterrestrials then I'll show you – everything.'

'Could you give us the layman's tour of Neptune?' asked the BBC's Space Correspondent, to the relief of the assembled pressmen. Most of the first ten minutes of Professor Trainor's press conference had been depressingly technical, and filled with impenetrable jargon. The boys from the tabloids were looking bored and restless, and even the journalist from the *New Scientist* had a faraway look in his eyes.

As far away as the nearest boozer, at least.

'Certainly,' said the professor, with a slightly irritated sigh that seemed to ask what was wrong with the explanations he had previously given. 'Perhaps Mark can field this one.'

'What? Oh, yeah, right…' Mark Wilson sat up from a slumped position in the seat next to Trainor. He had hoped to get away without saying anything during the event and had been delighted with his lack of involvement so far. Now, sadly, he was going to have to sing for his supper.

'Well, Neptune's a blue planet, the eighth in our solar system, midway between Uranus and Pluto,' he said. Even the man from the *Sun* was finally scribbling something in his notebook. 'It was discovered in the 1840s, and is the smallest of the four "gas giants". It has a very eccentric orbit, at times being the furthest planet from the sun. We know very little about the planet, but we can tell from observations carried out in this country, and in America, that the atmosphere is made up largely of hydrogen and helium, that the surface temperature is minus four hundred degrees Fahrenheit, with wind speeds exceeding one thousand miles per hour.'

'Not, perhaps, the most hospitable of places to visit,' said Trainor with a quick chuckle that most of the press sycophantically joined in with.

'So, is there any chance of life on Neptune?' the man from the *Daily Mirror* asked.

'In a word, no,' stated Trainor. 'Mind you, we said the same about Mars…' He turned to Wilson with a wicked grin. 'Sorry to interrupt, Mark. Please continue.'

'Thanks,' said Mark. 'Neptune has two moons that we know of – Triton and Nereid – and possibly several more. Our most recent probe has confirmed a faint series of rings, similar to those around Saturn. We're very interested in Triton, the larger of the moons, which is pink and almost planet-sized. Preliminary results suggest that it may have a nitrogen-based atmosphere.'

'Any chance of life there?' asked the disgruntled man from the *Mirror*.

'None whatsoever,' said Trainor. 'I can guarantee there are no little green men on, or near, Neptune!'

* * *

At the back of the conference hall, Viscount Rose showed his security pass to one of the many UNIT guards checking entry. He found himself a seat just as Trainor cracked his glib joke. Rose joined in with the laughter around the room. And he continued to snigger long after the subject had changed.

Benton was taken to one of the caravans by several of the Venus People. He was given a white smock to put on and had his other clothes taken away.

'If you wanna *be* one of us, you got to *look* like one of us,' said Scouse with a snarl that suggested he still wasn't convinced by Benton's story.

After a while, Arlo appeared at the caravan door.

'Is he ready to rock, or what?' he asked, and Benton was brought to the fireside, where all of the Venus People sat in a large circle. 'This is the appointed place,' said Arlo solemnly, as Benton was forced to kneel before him.

'What's all this in aid of?' asked Benton.

'The Treatment,' said Arlo. 'This is where you enlist again, soldier boy. You've got to go through the ceremony, or, like, it's no deal. Dig?'

'Dug,' said Benton, and swallowed as Arlo pulled a large dagger from his voluminous kaftan.

'Where those of the former age turned to violence and the spilling of blood, we turn away from such things,' announced Arlo to the hushed Venus People. He hurled the knife into the fire, where it landed on the remains of Benton's handgun.

'Where those of the former age lived by words, we live by deeds,' said Arlo, pulling pages from what seemed to be an old leather-bound Bible. He threw these into the fire.

'Where those of the former age looked to a new heaven and a new earth, we look beyond this planet for our deliverance.' He took something from his pocket. 'This is our body,' said Arlo to

Benton in a whisper.

Benton looked at Arlo's outstretched hand, and saw a flying-saucer-shaped sherbet sweet.

'Eat,' said Arlo.

Benton took the sweet and slipped it into his mouth. He felt the rice paper exterior crumble on his tongue, and tasted the bitter sherbet within. He grimaced as his mouth went momentarily numb.

'Come in,' said Arlo. 'Come in. The ceremony is about to begin.'

'What the hell was...?' Benton managed to mumble.

'The sacrificial wafer. With a mescaline coating. Time to fly, soldier boy.'

'I feel... I feel odd,' said Benton, his voice sounding muffled and slurred.

'Take it as it comes,' said Saddest Moon. 'It's the weirdest trip, baby. But good, you know?'

'Just let yourself float downstream,' continued Starchild. 'Relax.'

'Can't,' said Benton, struggling to hold his fragmenting mind together. 'It's too much...'

He screamed as his senses flooded with information: everything was expanding, becoming more intense. Colours were brighter, sounds sharper. He felt as though his eyeballs were on stalks and he was seeing everything from a new, strange perspective.

Around him, people's faces were melting, coagulating into new shapes.

'He can't handle it,' he heard someone say, but Arlo's voice cut through everything like a hot knife through butter.

'It's cool,' said Arlo strongly.

Benton looked towards the sky. It was the bluest sky he had ever seen in his life. Bluer than blue.

'I'm up there,' he suddenly said.

'Sure man, sure,' soothed Arlo.

Then the sky began to darken.

Benton began to panic. 'They're coming,' he shouted, his hands shaking in front of his face as he tried to cover his eyes to shut out the overwhelming sensations.

'What a mong,' said Scouse with a sarcastic sneer. 'He can't take it!'

But others were looking to the skies and gasping. The sky was black with countless twittering raven-like shapes, flocking over them.

'Oh Jesus,' said Arlo, without any apparent irony. Behind him, the goblins began to swoop down on to their prey.

CHAPTER 17

Mike Yates stared back at the reflection of himself in the mirror, his face covered with shaving cream. 'And another thing,' he said, waving his Wilkinson Sword razor for emphasis. 'This Valentina Whatsherbloodyname. Now, I'm no chauvinist, but I don't see why she should be placed in charge of UNIT in the Brigadier's absence.'

Sounds like chauvinism to me.

'No, absolutely not,' said Yates, finally beginning to shave. 'Women have many noble and varied qualities. But they're simply not as strong as men in a physical situation. A biological fact. End of story.' He paused. 'People always get me wrong about this: I actually *believe* in women's lib. But you've got to draw the line somewhere, haven't you? I mean, that women's football team that wants to get into the league ... It's just stupid. They've got Chelsea – what more do they want?'

Satisfied, Yates worked at the bristles on his upper lip for a moment.

Perhaps their brains make up for the lack of brawn.

'Look, this thing with the Russian woman isn't really about feminism,' he stated firmly. 'It's a matter of national sovereignty. We're both captains. She's coming to the UK. So *I* should be in charge.'

Before the inner voice could say another word there was a knock at the door. 'It's Corporal Bell, sir. Come to drive you to Brize Norton.'

'Come in, Carol,' said Yates. 'I won't be a jiffy.'

There was a pause. 'Are you alone?'

Mike was surprised. 'Yeah. Why do you ask?'

'I thought I heard voices.'

'Oh,' said Mike, his face flushing beneath the shaving foam.

'Oh, I was… I was just doing the crossword.'

In the bathroom? You berk!

Bell paused. 'I'll just wait out here, if you don't mind,' she said.

Yates arrived at Brize Norton just as the VC10 touched down. He stepped from the car, pulling on his peaked cap, and strode across to the plane.

The Doctor, Liz and Shuskin came down the steps and on to the runway. All seemed tired, and Yates was shocked to see that the Doctor's face was covered with tiny cuts. 'Welcome back,' he said brightly.

'Hello, Mike,' said the Doctor.

'How's Benton?' asked Liz.

'He *was* OK, but he released himself from hospital, and no one's seen hide nor hair of him since.'

'You have received our preliminary report?' asked Shuskin, cutting through the small talk.

'Yes, sir. You must be relieved that the number of aliens at the Siberian bridgehead is diminishing rapidly.'

'We now have wider concerns, Captain,' said Shuskin. 'We need to find their site in Great Britain.'

'Not that we can be entirely convinced that they mean to attack here, either,' said the Doctor. 'The Waro have devastated entire worlds. They will almost certainly strike where we least expect them.'

Liz shook her head. 'No,' she said firmly. 'I was thinking about that on the plane. You said you don't believe in coincidences. Well, what can be more coincidental than us finding out that the Waro come from one of Neptune's moons just as British Rocket Group are announcing the results of their latest probes to the planet?'

'You think there's a connection?' asked Yates.

'Liz has a point,' said the Doctor. 'What if one of the BRG

probes went to Triton?'

'So Professor Trainor has been working for the Waro?'

'Possibly,' said the Doctor, his eyes downcast. 'Or perhaps they're forcing him to cooperate. No one in England knows more about Neptune and its satellites than Trainor.'

'Which means at the very least he is a target,' said Yates.

'How was the press conference?' asked the Doctor.

'Went without a hitch yesterday.' Yates smiled, seeing what the Doctor was getting at. 'But then, anyone with designs on the professor would hardly want to kidnap him from under the eyes of UNIT.'

'Whereas today?'

'He's unguarded.'

'I'll go up and see him,' said Liz.

'No,' said Yates. 'I don't want you putting your life at risk when we have no idea –'

'But we don't want to alarm him – or those who are watching him – either,' interrupted Liz. 'I have a legitimate reason to be there.'

'This sounds sensible,' said Shuskin.

She'd been silent for so long Yates was starting to think she wasn't even listening. He glared at her, when her face was turned away, but said nothing.

'I'll take that as agreement,' said Liz.

The Doctor was about to say something when Yates's radio crackled into life. Even over the hissing static Yates could tell it was Benton. And he was screaming.

'They've come up out of the stones! The goblins are here!'

Viscount Rose sat in the drawing room of his father's stately home. He looked up from *The Times*, casting a jaundiced eye around the room. The Rossettis and Hunts and the other early works of the Pre-Raphaelite Brotherhood would be the next to go, exquisite works of art and priceless family heirlooms sacrificed to the greater good. But so be it. Rose's reward lay in heaven, or at least somewhere far beyond these rooms of dust and decay that stank of mothballs.

He laughed out loud. Perhaps he would sell the Bronzino in the hall. That had always been his father's particular favourite.

An almost inaudible rap on the door was followed by the entrance of his butler.

'What is it, Miller?' Rose asked, angry at the interruption.

'My apologies, sir, but the young gentleman is here to see you.'

'What?' Rose sat upright. 'That scruffy, good-for-nothing vagabond has dragged his stinking carcass here?'

'Indeed, sir,' said Miller gravely. 'He's in the great hall. Somewhat agitated.'

'I'll give him something to be agitated about. Take my riding crop and see him off the premises!'

'He was most insistent that he be allowed to see you, sir,' noted Miller.

'Very well,' said Rose with a long-suffering sigh. 'Show him in.'

Miller returned a moment later with Arlo. He was looking even more dishevelled than normal, and began babbling the moment he saw Rose.

'It's crazy, man, just –'

'Be quiet!' snapped Rose angrily. 'That will be all, Miller.'

'Will sir require anything further?'

'Yes,' Rose noted. 'A pot of tea. For one.'

As Miller closed the door Rose turned to Arlo, who was standing fidgeting beside the fireplace.

'Cool pad you've got here, man,' said Arlo nervously. He seemed terrified.

'You came here to tell me that?'

'No, man…' Arlo seemed to be having trouble speaking his mind. Rose decided to help him.

He strode across the room, grabbed the hippie by his scrawny neck and slapped him viciously across the face. 'You have something to tell me?' said Rose, releasing his grip.

'They've been killed!' blurted Arlo, slumping down to his knees. 'They're dead. All of them.' On and on he raved until Rose brought him to a halt with a swift kick in the ribs.

'Who has killed whom?' Rose asked.

'The goblins, dad. They ripped us to pieces.'

'You seem unhurt,' said Rose.

'Jesus, man, I just got in the van and I drove like it was the end of the world, you dig?'

Rose paused for a moment. This was, he was forced to admit, an unexpected development. 'You cannot expect an alien intelligence to conform to your patterns of reasonable behaviour,' he reasoned.

'But they went ape, man. They slaughtered all my friends.'

'I believe the Venus People were looking for a new life beyond this awful planet. Maybe they've found it.' Rose seemed satisfied with this, moving away from Arlo and towards the French windows.

Arlo stood, anger surging through him. 'They call us freaks, man, but you're evil.'

'I beg your pardon?' Rose turned calmly, a slim revolver drawn just as Arlo threw himself at the viscount. A single shot hurled the young man backward. He found himself clutching his shoulder, eyes screwed up in pain as Rose towered over him.

'If you want the animals to perform tricks for you, you must be prepared to feed them,' said Rose. 'Get up!'

Arlo struggled to his feet. He felt sick, his body racked with pain.

'Now, get out,' said Rose, pushing Arlo through the French windows.

'I'll tell them, man. I'll tell them it was all your idea!'

212

'No you won't,' said Rose, returning to his seat and his newspaper. He rang the bell for Miller. Where was his blasted tea?

Arlo ran blindly from the Earl of Norton's stately home towards the woods a hundred yards from the house, still clutching his injured arm. He glanced behind him, expecting to see Rose following him.

Instead, through eyes stinging with tears, Arlo saw what appeared to be one of the carved gargoyles on the building flap gently into the air. He screamed as it swooped down towards him.

CHAPTER 18

The Doctor picked his way through the corpses, his face ashen. A patch of mist stretched from the monoliths of Stonehenge, just visible over the rise, towards the Venus People's camp site. Had the situation been different the Doctor would have pondered aloud mankind's eternal yearning for the stars, progressing from megaliths to gaudy caravans. But whatever the Venus People were searching for, it shouldn't have ended here, like this.

He watched as Shuskin and some UNIT troops turned over the bodies, searching for signs of life. They worked slowly and methodically, their faces masks of concentration and emotional detachment. 'This one's got a pulse,' exclaimed one soldier, waving for the medic.

The Doctor turned away in disgust. A massacre, then, as he'd feared. Benton's screams were still fresh in his mind. It had taken them some minutes to calm him down, his words coming in sobbing bursts through the background interference. Apparently he'd travelled to Stonehenge in search of the Venus People, but could only remember the subsequent attack in nightmarish flashes. He'd survived the night, but the carnage revealed by the morning sun had scared him out of his wits. Without thinking, he had used his UNIT radio to call for help, and somehow they had picked up the signal at Brize Norton.

Yates stood at the Doctor's side. 'We've found a couple of survivors,' he said. 'The rest have been torn to ribbons and...' His words trailed away.

'Eaten?' queried the Doctor. 'It's easy to forget that humans can be part of the food chain.'

'Why did the aliens attack these people?' asked Yates.

'Physical hunger, in part.' The Doctor paused, suppressing a shudder at the memory of the soul-catching. 'But that's not the whole story. It's rare in nature for a creature to attack another when it is not hungry. But many of these poor people were killed for the sake of killing. That's still hunger, but of a different kind. The Waro can only control their aggression for so long. Occasionally the bloodlust becomes irresistible, do you see?'

'Why the Venus People and all the other hippies?'

'Drifters in society,' said the Doctor. 'If Benton hadn't radioed in the attack might have gone unreported for a number of days.'

'Then the Waro have done their homework,' said Mike.

'Well, *somebody* is guiding them,' said the Doctor. 'Benton might have some idea. Have you found him yet?'

Yates shook his head. 'We'll find him soon enough.' His voice wavered slightly, betraying his true uncertainty.

'Of course,' said the Doctor. 'Have you discovered anything else?'

'The boffins are reporting higher-than-normal radiation levels,' stated Yates, pointing across the field to a white tent, surrounded by plastic-suited figures who were taking samples from the soil and overseeing the removal of the bodies from the site.

'You don't need to be a rocket scientist to work out that it's not the radiation that killed these poor people,' remarked the Doctor. Then a thought struck him. 'Before I left,' he said, 'didn't Lethbridge-Stewart want me to investigate unusually high radiation levels in the Solent?'

Yates nodded, remembering the Brigadier's note and the file that he'd sent Benton to collect.

'I glanced at the report just before we departed for the Soviet Union,' continued the Doctor. 'South-east of the Earl of Norton's land. Something *did* come down in the sea during the pop concert.'

'When Benton and I interviewed the Venus People a few days back,' said Yates, 'we came to the conclusion that they'd seen something land in the water. It wasn't just their overactive imaginations.'

The Doctor nodded. 'Time for a swim, Mike. Do you think you can arrange –'

Without warning a figure lunged at the Doctor from the hedgerow, arms flailing. 'You've got to do something!' screeched the man.

'Sergeant Benton?' asked the Doctor, holding the man's arms tightly until he sank to his knees. 'John?'

He wore some sort of kaftan or smock, his legs blue with cold. It looked like he'd been sleeping rough for a week, not a single night. His eyes were distant dull-grey circles, the rest of his face covered with dirt and dark bruises.

'Doctor?' said Benton. 'You've got to do something.'

The Doctor crouched down in front of Benton. 'All right, old chap, don't worry. We'll sort everything out.'

'Goblins!' screamed Benton suddenly, his eyes looking through the Doctor, no doubt towards the events of the previous night. 'They came out of the stones, out of the sky.' He began to sob uncontrollably. 'And the screaming…' He twisted his head quickly from side to side, as if pinpointing a noise. 'There! Someone's still screaming. They need our help.' He tried to get up.

Yates laid a comforting hand on the man's shoulder. 'Easy, John. There's nothing more you can do.' He turned away bitterly. 'Nobody here needs our help.'

A horn blared into Liz Shaw's slumber and she woke with a start, swerving the car away from the oncoming truck. She swore under her breath, her heart beating rapidly. The lorry driver appeared to be gesticulating in her direction, but Liz ignored the man, and concentrated on the road.

Maybe this wasn't such a good idea after all, she thought. Corporal Bell had offered to drive her up to Cambridge, but Liz was determined to do something without UNIT mollycoddling her. And, anyway, her Mini Cooper hadn't been out of the garage in weeks.

Liz had assured Bell that she wasn't feeling tired, despite the long flight back from Siberia, and that she knew the route well. She'd be there in no time, she had said.

Or in the morgue, if you're not careful, she thought as she wound down the window and pushed the slider on the heater towards cold. A few minutes later she turned the car in the direction of St Leonard's, thankful that the roads from here were much less monotonous. The melancholy she felt, passing the landmarks that she knew so well, was even greater than that she'd experienced during her earlier visit. It was a lovely day, but it was frightening how people were moving around without, it seemed, a care in the world. For one mad moment Liz wanted to stop the car, get out and shout, 'The aliens are coming! Stay in your homes!' But that would be rank hypocrisy: she was as implicated in the wall of official denial as the military and the police. At least she had something practical to do, a role to play in the defeat of the invisible menace. But occasionally she envied the people with mundane jobs, the women pushing children around the shops.

You're getting old, she told herself.

Soon she was driving through the campus, a mass of green on the edge of the city. Young people, seemingly barely out of school, walked by in blazers and chatted on stationary bikes. One lecturer seemed to have taken his students out towards the river that ran through the grounds of the university college, and was holding forth, his arms flapping in excitement. Liz was sure she recognised him from Sunday night's party, before he'd rushed off to throw up.

Liz's recollection was rudely interrupted by a gleaming Mercedes that bore down on her at great speed, its wheels a blur of smoking rubber.

217

'What the –' she exclaimed, wrenching the wheel to one side.

She hadn't counted on the ditch that edged the driveway being quite so deep. The car tipped on to its side, forward momentum pushing Liz towards the windscreen, and then rolled over.

With a shattering crash Liz finally succumbed to unconsciousness.

Mike Yates drove with the Doctor in Bessie to the south coast and the site of the Redborough '70 festival. This time the Doctor hadn't bothered to try to contact Viscount Rose. It didn't seem to be worth the effort.

'Radiation may indeed hold the key,' said the Doctor as the car reached the seafront. The area was still covered in the litter of the festival and the Doctor shook his head at the mess that surrounded them. 'They claim to love the planet, but they defile it,' he said sadly, stepping out of the car to pick up a discarded lemonade bottle. 'I'm not unsympathetic to their aims. I believe in peace and freedom as much as the next man. But quite what that has to do with making such a mess is beyond me.'

Mike shrugged. 'More important things to worry about?' he suggested.

The Doctor hauled a large oxygen tank from the back seat of Bessie. 'I must say,' he said, removing his cloak, 'I was surprised that Captain Shuskin agreed to my coming down here quite so readily. Not the sort of thing the Brigadier would have gone for, I'm sure.'

Yates snorted. 'I expect she had her reasons.'

'Well, whatever they were,' said the Doctor, 'I'm grateful to her. Now, as I say, if I can get similar radiation readings to those we found at Stonehenge then I'll be able to predict where the Waro are likely to strike next.'

'How?' asked Mike, reasonably.

'Ways and means, Captain,' replied the Doctor as, completely without embarrassment, he removed most of his clothing and poured himself into a bright orange wet suit.

'You sure you'll be all right down there?'

'Captain Yates,' said the Doctor as he strapped the oxygen tank on to his back, 'I'll have you know that I taught Jacques Cousteau everything he knows.' He paused and adjusted his goggles. 'How's Benton by the way?'

'Recovering. Tough as old boots is the sergeant.'

'Good,' said the Doctor. 'I'll be back up in twenty minutes at most.'

'I'll be here,' said Yates as the Doctor waded into the English Channel.

The Doctor chuckled as he began to swim through the water. Jacques Cousteau! Jacques Brel, more like. Humans, so gullible to someone with the storyteller's knack. Mind you, there was that time during his first incarnation when he had fished the coral reefs off the Santa Cruz islands...

He dived deeper, his eyes gradually becoming accustomed to the gloom. He followed the seabed for some time, all the while pausing to check the Geiger counter secured to the belt of his wet suit. He began to make out a great dark object in front of him. From a distance it was like an underwater television picture of a sunken wreck. But, as he got closer, a clearer shape emerged. It was cylindrical.

The propulsion unit.

The Doctor gave a small cry of delight that didn't get much beyond the mouthpiece covering the lower part of his face.

The Geiger counter clicked alarmingly, and the Doctor had to remind himself that, even with his metabolism, prolonged exposure to radiation was best avoided. He checked his watch. Five minutes before Mike would expect him back at the surface. Just enough time for a better look at the alien craft.

As the Doctor came closer to it, something moved to his left. He half turned in surprise, and found his face covered by a Waro that had come skittering towards him. The Doctor clawed away the goblin creature as another attacked him from behind. Then another.

They were all over him, ten or more, obviously left behind by the main force to prevent investigation of their landing site. The Doctor cursed himself that he had thought the Waro so stupid as to leave the propulsion unit unguarded.

He was forcing himself higher in the water but the little creatures clung to him, sharp teeth and claws cutting into his wet suit and then his skin. The Doctor thrashed with his arms and legs, knocking another two of the creatures away from him, but there were too many of them and he was being dragged back down again by their weight and ferocity. With the last of his failing strength, he unhooked the oxygen tank from his back. Taking a final gulp of air from the mouthpiece the Doctor aimed the top of the tank away from him and twisted at the valve. The pressure within the cylinder was released, and the Doctor found himself flying upward through the water. The burst of oxygen from the tank was just enough to fling the Waro aside.

The Doctor held his breath, his eyes stinging as he shot through the water. Then, suddenly, he broke through the surface and gulped in fresh air. A helicopter hovered above him, lowering a line in his direction.

'What kept you?' he managed to say as he grabbed on to the steel cable with the last of his strength. He looked up to see Mike Yates's beaming face sticking out of the helicopter door.

'You look like you need a hand, Doctor,' shouted Yates above the roar of the blades.

'I was getting on quite nicely, thank you,' replied the Doctor drily.

Once aboard it took the Doctor some minutes to fully recover his senses and then struggle out of the wet suit. He was aware that Yates was asking him something but his ears were ringing loudly. 'Sorry, Captain?'

'Did you find what you were looking for?' repeated Yates.

'More than I bargained for,' said the Doctor. 'Why the helicopter?'

'It was sent down by Shuskin,' said Yates sourly. 'To let us know our presence is required urgently.'

'Why?' asked the Doctor.

'Professor Trainor has been kidnapped. Liz didn't quite make it in time. But she saw Viscount Rose's car leaving the professor's chambers at great speed. Oh, and Benton's awake again. Gave us a very good description of someone who left the hippie site just before the attack.'

'Rose?' asked the Doctor.

'Rose,' came the reply.

By the time the helicopter landed on the shore a large number of UNIT vehicles were already in place. Teams of divers, armed with dart guns, were disappearing beneath the cold water of the Channel. The Doctor and Yates climbed out of the helicopter, and walked over to the communications truck that was functioning as a temporary command centre. Shuskin stood impassively, listening to a UNIT sergeant. She dismissed him as she saw Yates and the Doctor approach.

'Is Liz all right?' asked the Doctor.

'Dr Shaw is unharmed,' stated Shuskin. 'I have arranged transport for her. And local police have been alerted to the abduction of Professor Trainor.'

'So it seems the professor is innocent of duplicity,' said the Doctor, relieved.

'But Rose is in it up to his neck,' said Yates.

'He left this morning,' said Shuskin, gesturing towards old

Norton's stately home. 'A search of the grounds has revealed only another victim of the alien creatures. All ports, terminals, and stations have been alerted to watch for Rose.'

'Viscount Rose is probably rich enough to charter his own plane,' said the Doctor sadly. 'We might well not see him again.' He turned, looking out over the English Channel. 'Have the divers found the propulsion unit?'

Shuskin turned towards the water's edge. 'Let us see.'

As the Doctor and the two soldiers stood and watched a number of divers broke the surface. One of them swam over, pulling off his mask, while the rest struggled with plastic bags full of metallic objects.

The leading diver saluted as he approached Shuskin. 'It's gone, sir. No creatures, no space rocket. We've picked up what they left.'

The Doctor immediately took the bags from the other men, and emptied their contents out on the ground. There were various thick cables, what appeared to be junction boxes, a number of empty cylinders, and all sorts of brass-coloured components. 'They did a very thorough job if this is all that you found,' said the Doctor. 'They've stripped the entire propulsion unit in a matter of minutes, probably moved everything further out into the Channel.'

He pulled a jeweller's eyepiece from the pocket of his smoking jacket, and stared intently at a number of circuit boards. 'It's all primitive enough,' he said. 'But...' His voice trailed away. 'Oh dear.'

'What's the matter?' asked Yates.

The Doctor examined another alien module before continuing. 'These components didn't survive the journey from Triton.' He dropped the eyepiece into his pocket. 'They look like the remains of a bomb primer.'

'What sort of bomb?' asked Yates.

'I don't think I'd surprise you by saying nuclear, would I?' said the Doctor gravely. 'Which explains the radiation levels.' The Doctor paused, scratching his chin. 'If these fragments are a reliable guide, I'd say that the nuclear device or devices brought to the Earth by the Waro actually lack much of the necessary fissile material.' He closed his eyes for a moment, muttering. Yates glanced across at Shuskin, but she seemed unperturbed by the Doctor's behaviour.

'Cobalt-60,' said the Doctor at last, opening his eyes. 'There's no cobalt on Triton, but the Waro knew that there would be some on Earth. Rose must have told them all they needed to know.'

'What does Rose hope to achieve?' asked Yates.

'I'm not sure,' said the Doctor. 'I don't think he's realised quite how dangerous the Waro are. But the important thing for the moment is cobalt-60. We can't let the Waro get their hands on any, or they'll render the Earth uninhabitable.'

Some time later, Yates sat back in Bessie's passenger seat and reflected on the Brigadier's dealings with authority. He had often listened to the Brigadier's arguments with the 'bureaucratic buffoons' of Westminster, but never before had Yates been forced to grapple with the tortuous logic that represented common sense in the corridors of power. Over the last few hours he and Shuskin had endured telephone conversations with a seemingly endless procession of jobsworths, pedants, and self-interested civil servants: forty-five minutes had elapsed before anyone had admitted that the United Kingdom even possessed a significant amount of cobalt-60. At length, Yates had been told that, while most of the Earth's reserves of cobalt-60 were in military establishments in the US, Britain did have a 'reasonable quantity' of the material. It was kept, with minimal security as far as Yates could ascertain, in a nuclear power station on the Northumberland coast. He and Shuskin then spent many fruitless minutes trying to persuade the authorities to move the fissile material to a top secret MoD base some miles away. There had been objections to bringing the cobalt out on to the roads, but eventually the civil and military commanders had agreed to the UNIT proposal. Once the cobalt was safely stored in the MoD facility it would, it was hoped, be safe from Waro attack.

The ensuing convoy of vehicles – with Bessie at the centre, like a surreal yellow bull's-eye – reminded Yates of footage he'd seen of Soviet May Day parades. He'd rarely seen so many military vehicles in one place before.

Yates turned to the Doctor. 'If the Waro are going to attack, they'll do it soon.'

The Doctor nodded. 'It's certainly their best chance to take the cobalt.'

Yates scanned the sky, but saw nothing. Dusk was falling, grey clouds trailing across the dark sun. 'No word yet on Rose,' he said.

'He's long gone,' said the Doctor. 'Wealth can buy so many things. It can influence, persuade, cajole. You know, Karl Marx once told me that –'

Without warning something flew over the convoy. Yates had been told to expect flapping goblin creatures, not aircraft. He quickly reached for the binoculars resting on the back seat.

'What was that?' exclaimed the Doctor, keeping his eyes on the road.

'A plane of some sort?' said Yates, trying to find the craft in the binoculars. 'Very fast. I didn't recognise it.' Even the faint glow of the engines had faded from sight, so he turned his attention in the other direction, trying to see if there were any more of them.

'What can you see?' asked the Doctor.

'Nothing,' said Yates. 'Perhaps it was one of ours...'

'Captain Yates,' said the Doctor with a smile, 'I never thought I'd find you clutching at straws.'

'Well,' said Yates, 'I don't think we –' He stopped, catching sight of something in the binoculars. 'No, there they are. An attack formation!' He reached for his radio. 'What are those things?' he asked rhetorically.

'Alien craft,' said the Doctor quietly. 'I've been analysing the sound of the engines since the first one flew over. They aren't using jet turbines.'

'All units!' snapped Yates into his radio. 'Prepare for attack from the west. Deploy anti-aircraft batteries now. Other vehicles...' He paused, a light smile passing across his lips. 'Don't spare the horses.'

The convoy began to pick up speed just as the alien craft shot overhead. Yates saw a number of matt-black dart-shaped craft, still maintaining a tight formation. He estimated their speed to be at least Mach 2, but somehow they made little more noise than a group of light aircraft puttering through the skies.

Then the craft *stopped* – no hint of slowing, just a sudden absence of forward motion, as if they'd hit an invisible wall – then rotated back towards the convoy, and started firing. Crackling bolts of green light stabbed out from the alien planes, hitting the trucks at the heart of the convoy. In an instant the cargoes seemed to wink out of existence, leaving the lorries virtually unscathed.

The first salvo of heat-seeking missiles flew from the ground towards the vessels, but they darted off at dizzying speed, twisting and turning around each other like fireflies. The green bolts stabbed out towards the missiles, vaporising them in eerie silence.

The Doctor was shouting something, but Yates couldn't hear it above the noise of more anti-aircraft missiles streaking into the air.

A stray beam from one of the alien aircraft snaked out towards the vehicle in front of Bessie, hitting the truck's cabin rather than its cargo. The entire vehicle exploded in a black-and-orange ball of smoke.

'Watch out!' shouted Yates as Bessie flew towards the fireball.

SIXTH INTERLUDE: DREAMTIME

'You seem unusually pensive tonight,' said David Boyd, pushing a stick into the embers of the fire. The shimmering heat sent tiny sparks spiralling up into the air.

Maurice Fisher smiled. 'And you're not normally up this early,' he said, pointing towards the faint glow that seemed to come from within the pale, ghostly gumtrees and the deep-red earth. It was *rakarra-rakarra* – 'dawn-dawn' – that mysterious period just before sunrise. The old Aborigine brushed dirt from his Jeans, and stared at the white man. 'What is bothering you, Boyd?'

Boyd observed the man closely. In the fitful, spitting light of the fire he seemed young again, the fissures and caverns that wrinkled his skin becoming less visible. Boyd had been with the Kukatja people for two years, and from the outset the old man had been able to read him like a book. But for all Boyd's seeming sophistication, his knowledge of cutting-edge principles of anthropology and interpersonal communication, he had never been able to read Fisher in the same way.

'I had a dream – a nightmare, I suppose,' said Boyd. 'You know how well I normally sleep.'

Fisher nodded. 'I hear you snoring,' he said, with a gleam in his eyes. 'What happened in your dream? You know how important they are to us.'

'When I was younger,' said Boyd, 'I had a recurring dream. The situations were different, but one character remained the same: a small man, almost a dwarf. Pure evil. A hooked nose, eyes deep in shadow. He would often fool my family, appearing in some sort of disguise, but I always saw through him. I tried to warn them, but – you know what it's like in dreams – you try to cry out, but you can't. And this man – this creature – used to turn towards me. And then he'd smile. And that smile was terrifying. I always woke up at that point.' Boyd found himself staring deep into the fire, watching the writhing orange and yellow tongues of flame. 'I don't suppose I've dreamed about him since I was eight or nine.'

'And yet you started seeing him in your dreams six or seven nights ago.'

Boyd smiled, barely surprised. 'Yes. Every night since.'

Fisher pushed his hands deep into the pockets of his jacket, his breath a white mist against the dark sky. 'Do you remember the lights in the sky that night? The shooting stars? They were like dreams painted across the sky,' he said with a grand gesture.

'Comets and meteorites are portents of doom in a lot of cultures,' said Boyd.

Fisher nodded, getting to his feet. 'What we saw that night went beyond superstition. There is someone I must see.' He looked down at the researcher. 'You have more Dreaming than most *kartiya*,' he said, affectionately using the word for a white outsider. 'And you've always been much more open with me than I have with you.'

'Oh, I don't know –' said Boyd immediately.

'Perhaps you had better come with me,' interrupted Fisher. 'But promise me that you will not speak of this to anyone.'

'Of course,' said Boyd. 'Who are we going to see?'

'Nedenah,' said Fisher after a pause. He walked slowly down the shanty town's one street, and out into the desert. Boyd followed a few steps behind, somehow sensing that the old man wanted to wrestle with his own thoughts without interruption.

They headed out towards the rose-red canyon to the west of the town, at length coming to a cave, its dark maw partly hidden by stunted bushes and tall grass. Boyd stood for a moment in the entrance, admiring the art scrawled all over the walls. There were snakes, roos and human faces, painted in shades of brown and yellow, and then more realistic and intricate snapshots of everyday life: children playing with spears, marriage ceremonies, funerals. Suddenly he noticed a round shape, studded with portholes, painted right at the apex of the stone tunnel. Around the saucer were white crosses, which seemed to represent the stars, and a crowd of human figures.

And then he looked more closely, straining his neck. What he'd taken to be children were, in fact, small humanoid figures, their faces abnormally large, their eyes pale green and elliptical.

The old man was already some distance into the system of caves, having switched on his torch. Boyd hurried after Fisher, knowing that explanations would come only if and when the Aborigine felt them to be appropriate.

The tunnel began to twist downwards, seemingly into the guts of the Earth. It was like descending into some great creature, and, in a moment of improbable fancy, Boyd thought he could hear an enormous heart beating sonorously in the distance. He slipped on the damp floor, cracking his knee on a protruding rock, and Fisher stopped, although he didn't turn to look at him or offer assistance. The moment Boyd got to his feet Fisher pressed on, leading the white man through a seemingly endless sequence of dark chambers where water fell like a thousand whispers.

And then, at last, they emerged into an enormous cavern. The oppressive silence within, and the way the darkness swallowed up the torch light, hinted at the size of this cave.

Fisher stood, his eyes downcast, deep in thought. Then he looked forward, cupped his hands around his mouth, and let out a deep cry, a shout that echoed around the chamber like a rumbling explosion in a quarry.

At length a figure appeared at the edge of the arc of light. Boyd caught a glimpse of slender arms and a domed head before Fisher respectfully lowered the torch. Fisher began talking at great speed, in a dialect that Boyd was completely unfamiliar with. The only word he caught was 'Nedenah', and it punctuated conversation in the same way that a person's name might. At length, the child-sized creature nodded, and replied in an equally rapid whisper.

Eventually Fisher bowed low, and then turned away from the figure. When Boyd glanced over his shoulder the little cave-dweller had already disappeared back into the shadows. Fisher took his arm, and propelled him at speed through the caverns.

Just as they were approaching the entrance to the cave system, the Aborigine spoke. 'Bet you're wondering how anything can live down there,' he said.

'I do have one or two questions for you,' said Boyd with great understatement.

'I don't know the answers. Nedenah is a shy but wise traveller. Nedenah is on Walkabout, singing the songs of the Ancestors. Like I am when I dream, Nedenah *is*.'

'Is Nedenah its name or its species?'

'Yes,' said Fisher, to Boyd's great irritation. He paused as they emerged, blinking, into the light of dawn. 'Nedenah know the lights, Nedenah know the skies. And the Earth. The lights were seen right across the world by those that *understand*.'

'And?'

'You know the Earth, Boyd. You know it trembles. It quakes. The Earth is scared. The Earth is screaming.' Fisher began to climb down towards the town. 'I have been coming to Nedenah for decades,' he said. 'My father first brought me to the cave when I was a young man – soon after I was shown the Law. In all that time, I have never seen Nedenah frightened – of anything.' He sighed. 'Today, like the Earth, Nedenah is afraid.'

PART 7:
THE HAPPENING

CHAPTER 19

Bernard Trainor settled back in his seat. He didn't like flying, the legacy of an extremely turbulent trip in an old Dakota to observe one of the first experimental rockets BRG had been responsible for. Buffeted around in the interior of the plane, Trainor had experienced fear unlike anything he had ever known. If God had meant us to fly, he had told himself, he would have given us internal combustion engines.

Trainor had not been in a plane since, having sworn never to travel by air again – a somewhat incongruous vow for one of the world's premier rocket scientists.

'Are you comfortable, sir?' asked a BEA stewardess.

Trainor mumbled that he was, and asked for a vodka.

'Sounds like a positively ripping idea,' came a muffled voice to his side.

The professor turned to find that Viscount Rose had woken up. A hand appeared from beneath the copy of *The Times* covering his face, and drew the paper away. Rose was bleary-eyed and glanced quickly at his fob watch. 'I do wish this blasted thing would get a move on,' he said angrily. 'Some of us have more important things to do. Where *is* that girl with my drink?'

'She's coming,' said Trainor.

'So is Christmas,' responded Rose.

'You've never had to wait for anything, have you?' queried Trainor, feeling that even an argument with Rose was preferable to further contemplation of the dangers of flying. 'You're a classic only child. Spoilt rotten, and wealthy as sin.'

'You're absolutely right,' said Rose happily. 'But where would you be without that money? Never forget, Professor, that we need each other.'

Trainor glanced up as the stewardess returned with a tray of drinks, and eagerly gulped down the proffered vodka.

The Doctor stood watching Bessie as she was winched on to the back of a lorry.

'Is she mendable?' asked Yates, casting a worried glance at the twisted rear axle.

'Of course she's mendable,' snapped the Doctor. 'Anything is mendable, given time and resources.' He rubbed his chin. 'Though it does beg the question,' he said, more evenly, 'if you replace every component, does the original cease to exist?'

'Good driving, though,' remarked Yates. 'I thought we were toast for sure.'

'Toast?' exclaimed the Doctor in exasperation. 'The longer you stay in the army, Captain Yates, the further you drift from your fine education.'

Yates decided to change the subject. 'Doctor, I don't understand why the aliens just vaporised the cobalt. I thought you said the goblin creatures wanted it to prime their bombs.'

'I can't imagine the Waro piloting craft like that,' the Doctor replied. 'They're not interested if they're not exposed to the elements.'

'So what's going on?'

'I wish I knew,' said the Doctor, turning away. 'Perhaps Captain Shuskin can tell us. She seems to have been on the phone for an interminable length of time.' He ignored the look of contempt that crossed Mike's face, and strode over to one of the communication trucks. With all the cobalt destroyed, the convoy had come to an undignified halt in the middle of the road.

Apparently the head of the Northumbria police force's traffic division was having kittens, the road having already been closed for an hour, but UNIT were staying put until they had a reason to do otherwise. Soldiers sat on the tanks and jeeps, smoking and laughing. It was the strangest exercise they'd ever known.

Shuskin saw the Doctor approach, and barked a few last orders into the radio. The Doctor was sure that she was lapsing into Russian more frequently as her frustration increased.

'News from a UNIT operative in the United States,' she announced. 'A large amount of cobalt has just been moved to Groom Lake Air Force Base in Nevada.'

'That's interesting,' said the Doctor. 'They must know what the Waro are after.'

'And the aircraft that attacked our convoy did not register on any radar in the UK...'

'Really?'

'Except a station in Sussex that was using your modified equipment.'

The Doctor beamed in delight. 'I knew those improvements would be worth the trouble,' he said. 'Where did the craft come from?'

'They travelled across the Atlantic from America. And they were last reported to be heading back the same way.'

The Doctor nodded. 'The technology might be extraterrestrial, Captain Yates, but I'll wager that the pilots are no more alien than you are.'

'Thanks. I think.'

'I do not understand,' said Shuskin.

'Let me put it this way,' replied the Doctor mysteriously. 'If you wanted to catch a mouse with a trap and some cheese, you wouldn't leave the pantry door open, would you?' He smiled at the baffled faces of Yates and Shuskin. 'And at least we can now guess where the Waro are going.'

* * *

Rose folded away his newspaper. He didn't often miss his butler, but he did on occasions pine for a fresh *Times*, the pages gently smoothed with a warm iron. At the airport he'd had to make do with an early edition purchased in the departure lounge, all the while trying to steer Trainor away from the tabloids with their garish HIPPIE BLOOD BATH! headlines. It simply wouldn't do to get the old boy all hot and bothered. After all, in their own ways, they had been working towards this conclusion for several years now. It wasn't the time for a sudden attack of conscience. Rose's policy with regard to Trainor was always to tell him as little as possible. The viscount had used the professor, just as he had used so many others while bringing his Great Plan to fruition. Still, Trainor should be grateful: at least he was alive.

Poor Arlo, thought Rose.

'I'm pleased something's amusing you,' observed Trainor, noting the viscount's smile. He'd now downed more vodkas than Rose cared to count.

'Oh, come, Professor, you must share my excitement.'

'I can't pretend I don't,' he admitted. 'To be able to meet…' He paused, aware that their conversation may be overheard. 'To meet our friends after all this time. To begin to process the technology-sharing.'

'Of course, old man, of course,' said Rose with a thin smile.

Meanwhile, on another aeroplane, hundreds of miles away, Brigadier Lethbridge-Stewart was thinking about how he had defeated the Cybermen. It had been so easy. So uncomplicated. 'Do this, Captain Turner.' 'Do that, Corporal Benton.' Or, better still, 'Just do whatever the Doctor says, everybody…'

Ah, now *that* was the key. Damn the man, gallivanting off to Russia when the world, when the *Brigadier*, most needed him.

Lethbridge-Stewart shook his head, sadly. They had all been hoodwinked this time. Led in every direction but 'home' by clever, unscrupulous men who knew their business. The Brigadier almost approved. Almost.

The man they called Control took the seat beside him without seeking permission and smiled.

'Your first time over the water, General?'

'Sadly not,' said the Brigadier, his words dripping with sarcasm.

'Been to Nevada before?'

'I have to admit I haven't had *that* pleasure.'

'Bit of a hole, really. All desert.' Control looked at the whiskey glass in his hand. 'Hey, where are my manners? A drink?'

'Thank you, no,' said Lethbridge-Stewart.

'Suit yourself. Ah, look down there…'

The Brigadier glanced out of the window of the B-52 bomber, and saw a collection of anonymous white buildings surrounding a large airfield. Even from this altitude he could see the concentric circles of wire fence and guard posts that surrounded the complex.

'Fort Knox?' he asked, twitching his moustache into a smile.

'Not nearly so famous. Welcome to Ranch 51,' said Control. 'Now, come and meet some *real* aliens.'

Bruce watched the dart-like aircraft through a pair of binoculars. He'd heard that the experimental planes were fast, manoeuvrable and quiet, but nothing had quite prepared him for the show they'd just put on over Groom Lake AFB. The Phantoms and Tigers that buzzed around the periphery of the base were slow-flying dinosaurs in comparison.

The experimental planes landed smoothly, and immediately disappeared into a well-protected hangar. Bruce made his way down from the observation tower and towards the runway. He waited for the squadron leader in the hastily assembled debriefing room, and began questioning the man the moment he entered.

'How was it?' he asked.

'A breeze,' the man replied. 'We were there in next to no time.'

'The cobalt?'

'Every last chunk of it was vaporised. It was being moved by road, in a well-protected convoy, but that just made our job easier.'

'Collateral damage? Not that I give a damn, you understand.'

'Two trucks were destroyed. We had to take out a couple of AA batteries as well, but I don't think they'd have posed any threat.'

Bruce smiled. 'You guys put on quite a show up there.'

'We like to impress,' said the smiling, fresh-faced pilot. He handed over some photographs of the destroyed convoy.

'And how are the aircraft handling?' asked Bruce.

The airman laughed. 'Like nothing on Earth.'

Once on the ground, the Brigadier was taken by jeep to the closest of the buildings. Control remained with him, accompanied by three armed men in dark suits and sunglasses.

'Threw these bases up in the forties,' explained Control. 'USAF originally. Test flights in the war against the commies. Weapons technology, breaking the sound barrier, early space flights, that kind of thing.'

'Is this where you keep your alien technology?' asked the Brigadier. He had read files about the mysterious Area 51 in Nevada, a supposed UFO 'hotspot'.

'I'm sorry,' said Control. 'That's classified.' He paused for a moment, then exploded with laughter. 'I'm sorry, Ally, I just couldn't resist it! You guys are so goddamn serious all the time. Yeah, this is where we keep the bugs. Everyone knows that. Nobody's got any *proof* of it, of course, but knowing that people think they know is all part of the game, isn't it?'

'Is it?' asked the Brigadier.

'Hell, yes. We've had aliens here since the forties. They'd been coming for thousands of years, of course –'

'You have captured aliens?' asked a horrified Lethbridge-Stewart.

'Yep,' said Control matter-of-factly. 'They're called Nedenah,' he continued, as he steered the Brigadier through the maze of corridors inside the complex. They passed science labs and operating theatres, eventually reaching a huge metal door guarded by two bored-looking soldiers. 'We first got hold of three in 1947 at Roswell. One died immediately.' He grimaced. 'You should have seen the autopsy.' He took a security pass from his pocket. 'Codeword: Starlight,' he said as the doors were opened.

Inside was an enormous room the size of an aircraft hangar. A number of glass-fronted isolation chambers were positioned against the walls. In the centre of the room was, quite obviously, a flying saucer.

'It's comforting to know that all of the bozos who claimed to've seen stuff like this were actually telling the truth,' said Control, pointing towards the spacecraft. 'You want to see what's inside this baby? It'll freak you out.'

The Brigadier nodded, and followed Control about thirty feet up a ramp and into the craft.

It was dark inside, though there was some illumination from a flickering panel directly in front of the entrance. There didn't appear to be any windows.

'How do they navigate?' asked the Brigadier.

'Good question. It took us fifteen years to work that out. Watch this.' Control placed his left palm on the flashing panel. The light illuminated his face, first green, then red. 'They seem to perceive colour in much the same way that we do,' explained Control. 'In many ways we're very similar. They even speak pretty good English.' He had his eyes tightly closed. After a moment light filled the interior of the craft, sharpening to blinding brilliance within seconds. The Brigadier covered his eyes with his hands, shutting out the sudden sunburst.

'Sorry about that. Should have warned you – it's a hell of a surprise the first time.'

Not quite as much a surprise as what had happened to the craft. The walls had completely disappeared. The Brigadier and Control were suspended thirty feet off the ground. White-coated technicians continued their work, oblivious to the miracle taking place above them. To the Brigadier it seemed as thought they were in a glass bubble suspended above the floor of the hangar. He stood in silence for a moment, his jaw dropping by degrees.

'Bit of a trip, huh?' asked Control. 'They fly through space like this at thirty times the speed of sound. We still haven't quite worked out the mathematics of it, but it's a great party trick!'

'How's it done?' asked the Brigadier.

'Exterior images are fed directly to the brain of the occupants by sensors in the fuselage. The craft doesn't *literally* disappear: it just seems to from our perspective. Pretty clever, huh?'

'Ingenious,' agreed the Brigadier.

'Well, it sure beats having a sunroof,' said Control, removing his hand from the panel. The solid walls and floors formed around them again.

'When may I see these creatures?' asked the Brigadier.

'Right away if you want to, but I warn you, they're a big disappointment.'

Rose and Trainor finally arrived in Las Vegas after three changes of aeroplane, several hours late. The professor had taken the misfortunes they had encountered with a stoic acceptance. Rose, on the other hand, was furious, his temper threatening to boil over as he strode through the terminal.

'Incompetent, bungling morons,' muttered the viscount.

'I'm sure they didn't deliberately set out to delay us,' said Trainor, reasonably.

'Fortunately, I have no such doubts,' snarled Rose. 'This heap of junk is ours, I take it?' he continued as they came to a halt beside a gleaming black chauffeur-driven Cadillac.

'I've never been in a car with air-conditioning before,' said Trainor, grateful to be out of the early-afternoon sun. Rose snorted in contempt.

They sat in virtual silence as the car took them deep into the Nevada desert north-west of Las Vegas. Mile after mile of nothing but sand and red rock, broken only by an occasional clump of sorry-looking vegetation.

Finally, Trainor could stand the tension no longer. 'Just where are we going?' he asked.

'We have been given a final task to perform,' said Rose enigmatically. 'Your technical expertise is needed to – how can I put this? – complete the job. Then we can go and meet our grateful friends.'

Trainor nodded. 'I see. And the job is…?'

Rose was silent for a moment, sipping a glass of champagne from the car's well-stocked ice box. 'It's quite straightforward,' he said at length. 'You've heard, I assume, of "the final solution"?'

In some ways, thought the Brigadier, Control was correct: the Nedenah *were* disappointing – at least, if you'd been raised on bug-eyed-monster movies and science-fiction television. Lethbridge-Stewart, however, found them fascinating.

There were five of the creatures, each kept in their own isolation chamber. They were about the size of children, with grey, wrinkled skin and large green eyes. They were slender and hairless, barrel-chested, with slightly protruding mouths.

The Brigadier couldn't help but think of the Second World War concentration camps, and Control seemed to pick up on his unease. 'We have to keep them like this,' he explained. 'They're stubborn little critters, and they don't easily volunteer information.'

'Why don't their own kind come and rescue them?' asked the Brigadier, feeling a wave of sympathy for the creatures.

'Oh, they've tried that. The first contact was in forty-seven. Another craft turned up a year later. The little one in the middle is a survivor from that fiasco. By the third attack, we were ready for them. Shot the sucker right out of the sky. They haven't been back since. Perhaps they're wary of letting any more technology fall into our hands. Which is a pity, because they die so easily. We had nine of them at one point.'

The Brigadier turned his face away from the creatures, angry at Control's callous disregard for life.

'But if they do come back, we'll be ready for them,' continued Control. 'We're building up an arsenal of anti-BEM technology and we're quite capable of using it against them. And others.'

'Others?'

'Oh yeah. Cybermen, Nestenes – we know all about your minor-league run-ins. The Daleks – you know about those guys?'

'I am aware of them,' said the Brigadier stiffly.

'Course you are, thanks to that shape-changer boy of yours. Well, lemme tell you, Ally, the Waro are something else again. They're mean little mothers, and we're going to wipe them from the skies.' Control chuckled. 'This ain't no game of cricket, and it won't be won on points. This is war. Don't ever forget that.'

Control steered the Brigadier away from the impassive aliens, and towards a series of laboratories that adjoined the main hangar. 'We've got Nedenah technology, masses of it. We're talking serious merchandise here. You know, for a peaceful race, they sure make a boatload of lethal weapons!' He pointed towards one room, where an almost invisible green beam was being fired at a series of sensors. 'Much of it is based on the emission of high-powered laser beams. We're bolting these weapons to the experimental aircraft we're testing here and at Groom Lake AFB.'

'To what end?' asked the Brigadier.

'Isn't it obvious? We're going to deal with the Waro ourselves. We knew all about the false bridgehead, and we also know about the Waro's need for cobalt-60.'

The Brigadier shook his head, scarcely able to believe what he was hearing. 'You've been two steps ahead of us all along.'

'Two steps ahead of the Waro, Ally. About fifteen ahead of you boys!'

'I'll try not to be too upset about that.'

'That's good, Ally. I knew you and I would get along. You see, the Waro will come to us, and they'll be obliterated. Completely.'

'Then our aims are the same,' said the Brigadier.

'Never!' replied Control angrily. His face was flushed at the very suggestion. 'You *play* at saving the world, but with that alien freak in your ranks, do you even know what your real agenda is? Do you?' He paused, trying to calm himself. 'We've been subverting UNIT ever since it was formed. And victory here will be another successful operation in our ongoing strategy to discredit you. UNIT will be destroyed, revealed as the false prophets you are. Mark my words.'

The Brigadier reacted passively. 'I'd like to speak with the Nedenah, if I may,' he said.

'Not on your life, boy,' replied Control. He turned, and led the Brigadier deeper into the complex. Lethbridge-Stewart became aware of the dark-suited men following close behind.

Control came to a halt in a corridor of cells. 'Sorry, buddy,' he said sarcastically, 'but you know how it is. We're going to have to lock you away for a while now.'

The Brigadier nodded grimly. 'You're going to kill me, aren't you?'

'Eventually,' said Control, leaving Lethbridge-Stewart in the sealed room.

* * *

Rose and Trainor climbed out of the car in what seemed to be the middle of nowhere. The professor watched sadly as the car turned back to Las Vegas, but Viscount Rose was already heading off across the desert, following a map.

'I'm told a man dies of heat exhaustion out here every four weeks,' said Trainor, shielding his eyes from the blazing sun.

'Then he should start selling tickets,' said Rose. 'That's quite a trick.'

Trainor hurried to keep up. The rucksack seemed inordinately heavy, but he knew that Rose would never agree to carry it. 'You don't seem to be taking this very seriously,' he observed.

'Oh, I am,' said the viscount with a brief smile. 'And we'll be there soon enough. Now, do shut up, there's a good fellow.'

Breaking out of his cell was possibly the easiest thing that the Brigadier had ever done. The moulded plastic door had clearly never been intended to house anyone with the strength of Lethbridge-Stewart and, after five or six hefty kicks with his army-regulation boots, the entire window unit collapsed outward. The Brigadier dived through the hole, and straight into the midriff of the guard standing outside the door. His rifle clattered down the corridor.

They rolled around for a moment on the concrete floor, grappling for a stranglehold on each other. Eventually the Brigadier got a grip of the man's shoulders, and powered his forehead downwards on to the bridge of the guard's nose. The man fell away, moaning.

The entire scrap was more Stretford End than Sandhurst, but the pragmatism of the Lethbridge-Stewarts was well known. The Brigadier scanned the empty corridor, briefly considering what he would have done as commanding officer if an important prisoner had escaped from a room with only a single guard stationed outside. Shouted a lot, probably.

For the first time in many hours, the Brigadier found himself in a position where no one was holding a gun on him, or pushing him around, or making veiled threats. It felt marvellous. He sprinted to the end of the corridor and then back along the route he had taken with Control.

Remarkably most of the corridors seemed deserted. The legacy of having kept intruders out for so long was that no one thought about a threat that appeared from within.

The Brigadier approached the section of the central complex in which he had been shown the Nedenah. The cavernous room was now in semi-darkness, and deserted but for a single bored-looking USAF cadet who sat on a low bench in front of the observation cells, completely engrossed in the dog-eared Harold Robbins novel in his hands. The Brigadier crept up behind the man, then delivered a heavy chop on the back of his neck. He fell to the floor noiselessly. The Brigadier made a mental note that, should he ever get home again, he would have to oversee UNIT's internal security procedures personally.

He looked up, and saw the Nedenah watching him closely from their glass-fronted cubicles. It was impossible to read anything into the bland expressions, but the green eyes seemed a fraction wider than usual.

'Good day,' said the Brigadier, briefly aware of how ridiculous he probably sounded. 'My name is Alistair Lethbridge-Stewart, I am a brigadier with the United Nations Intelligence Task Force, a multinational, quasi-autonomous military collective whose aim is to protect Earth...' He paused. He was uncertain whether his words were being understood by the aliens, although Control had indicated that the Nedenah could communicate with humans. 'The people of Earth are in grave danger,' he continued, but again his voice trailed away. The childlike aliens appeared to be ignoring him completely.

The secret base had finally come into view through the heat haze after a two-hour trek through the desert. Rose and Trainor had navigated completely by compass, there being no features to speak of in the broiling desert. Trainor remembered a joke he knew involving a map of the desert and a sheet of sandpaper, but decided against sharing it with the viscount.

They had used some equipment from the rucksack to plot a path through the only camera and sensor blind spot, and then followed the perimeter fence until they now stood at an unmanned secondary entrance, an electronic sentry box guarding a heavy metal gate.

'The proverbial tradesmen's entrance,' announced Rose.

Trainor rummaged in the rucksack, having studied the electronic schematics on the flight over. 'It works by looking for certain retinal prints,' he announced. 'Probably based on alien technology – it's way ahead of anything I've seen before.'

'But can you break in?'

Trainor looked hurt. 'Of course. It's just a lock.' He attached a small computerised device to the retina-scanner. 'All you need to do is come up with enough combinations – in this case, eye patterns, not numbers.' He smiled. 'The real trick is not setting off the security protocols before we come up with a valid "key".' Trainor's device hummed and buzzed for a few moments, and finally the gate swung upward.

Rose smiled. 'A tribute to the enterprise of your best researchers.'

'A tribute to what your money can buy you,' said Trainor sadly.

'But I've never used a parachute in my life,' said Liz nervously.

'I'm afraid it's the only way,' replied Mike Yates. 'We haven't got a ladder long enough!'

Oh great, thought Liz. Now everyone's a comedian.

'You will be fine,' said Shuskin impatiently. 'I will show you.' And she gave Liz a crash course in landing techniques as the Lockheed C-130 Hercules circled in the Nevada sky. It was all about bending your knees, apparently. Shuskin made it all sound straightforward enough, but Liz still couldn't help but wish she'd had longer to prepare for this mission. Like a year or two, at least.

'Do you know what we're going to do when we get there?' Yates asked the Doctor.

'Not really,' said the Doctor with a smile. 'It's possible that this might be just another wild-goose chase. I've experienced these multilayered plots before. Nothing they do surprises me.'

'The US Air Force?' asked Mike. 'The Waro?'

'No,' said the Doctor angrily. 'The CIA.'

They jumped at thirty thousand feet. The Doctor, still managing to look dignified in a pilot's overalls and helmet, was first out of the doors. In his hand he clutched a portable version of the advanced radar system he had created for UNIT's tracking stations. Before they left England he had told Liz that the device had been optimised to detect the mechanical wings of the Waro.

Liz jumped next, with Shuskin and Yates close behind her. She was swamped by the sickening feeling of hurtling descent, her stomach seeming to relocate to somewhere just below her throat. Then the adrenaline rush hit her and she shouted in terror and exhilaration. This was like nothing she had ever experienced before. She was flying like a bird.

'Yeeeeeeessssssss!' she screamed, and then almost passed out as Mike bumped into her from behind.

'Pull your ripcord,' came a muffled shout, 'or you'll be dead before you can say "Jack Robinson"!'

Liz tugged at the release mechanism and was immediately jerked upwards as the parachute opened. It was like hitting a wall, but her descent was checked and she found herself floating gently towards the sand-yellow desert below.

Now all she had to do was land without breaking her legs.

'How's your leg?' asked the Doctor.

'I'll live,' said Liz, putting her weight on her sprained right ankle for the first time. 'Owwww!'

'Take it easy,' said Mike Yates, helping her to sit again. 'They always say the last ten feet is the killer.'

The Doctor knelt beside Liz and gently massaged her swollen ankle. 'Give it five minutes.'

Shuskin returned, having scouted their surroundings. She gave Liz a look of sorry contempt before turning her attention to the rest of the group. 'I have surveyed the area,' she said loudly. 'The base is two miles in that direction. We will leave immediately.'

'Just give Liz a few moments, will you?' asked Mike.

'Not possible.'

'Listen, *Captain*,' spat Yates. 'She needs to rest, OK?'

The Doctor got to his feet and walked over to the two UNIT officers, who seemed to be on the verge of exchanging blows. This was no time for a duel by handbags at ten paces.

'Will you two stop behaving like a pair of hurt children?' snapped the Doctor. 'We're all working for the same outcome. Hopefully.'

Shuskin seemed to accept the wisdom of the Doctor's intervention, and turned away. Mike stood his ground for several seconds, before he too backed down.

'That's better,' continued that Doctor. 'Liz should be all right to travel soon. I would suggest that as we approach the base our priority is to stick to what little cover there is.'

'Why?' asked Shuskin.

'Because I scanned our surroundings with this,' said the Doctor, holding up the portable radar. 'And it's picking up thousands of small signals.'

'The Waro?' asked Mike.

'Precisely. They'll be drawn to the cobalt-60 like iron filings to a magnet. We've seen what carnage even a small number of Waro can cause, and I estimate this group is ten times as large as that in the Soviet Union.'

Shuskin's face visibly paled. 'Ten times…?'

'Maybe fifteen,' said the Doctor with a wry grin. 'The combined forced of the US Air Force and the CIA – even if they're using alien technology – might not be a match for the Waro. If our experiences so far have proved anything, it's that you can't attack small and numerous creatures like the Waro in jet fighter aircraft.'

'So, we're defenceless?' asked Mike, anxiously.

Before the Doctor could reply, Liz hobbled over to them, with the aid of Private Harrison. 'That's not like you, Doctor,' she said.

'I'm sorry, my dear?'

'You've always got a plan.'

'Well,' said the Doctor, with quick smile. 'As it happens…'

The Brigadier had spent some minutes trying to converse with the aliens, but they remained impassive. He reasoned that if he could find a way to break into the cubicles, he could show the Nedenah that he meant no harm, and thus gain their trust. He was so engrossed in the electronic keypad to the side of the door that he didn't hear footfalls behind him until it was too late.

'Place your hands on your head!' Surprisingly, the man was English, and well-spoken, but the threat in his voice was clear. 'Now, turn around. Slowly.'

The Brigadier did as he was told, and gasped in surprise as he recognised the shorter of the two men who faced him. 'Professor Trainor,' said the Brigadier. He turned towards the man with the gun. 'I don't believe I've had the pleasure…?'

The taller man ignored the Brigadier's query, motioning to the side of the room with the automatic firearm. 'Stand over there. And shut up.'

The Brigadier, hands still on his head, walked to the wall, and watched as Trainor nervously approached the cubicles. He was dirty and tired, having clearly come some distance through the desert. So, Trainor and the tall man were intruders in the base.

The professor's eyes lit up the moment he saw the aliens. 'Such beautiful creatures,' he enthused. 'Such intelligence, such grace of form and function. What are we going to do?'

'We kill them.'

The professor was shocked, and momentarily rendered incapable of speech.

'Don't look so surprised,' continued the tall man. 'We've made our allegiances. The enemy of my friend is my enemy, is that not true?'

'What are you talking about?' stammered Trainor.

'We must obey our orders.'

'Orders?'

'You don't understand, do you, Professor? These aren't the creatures your probe established contact with. You see, your staff were kind enough to make sure that all information about the creatures from Triton – the Waro – came to me first. I do, after all, pay their wages.' He paused, regarding the alien creatures in the cubicles. Something like regret flickered over his features, but in a moment it was gone. 'The Waro augmented the sensors on your probe and turned part of it into a neural amplifier. When I transmitted my own electrocorticogram they were able to place their pictures and images directly into my mind. A painful process, but they can't communicate verbally. I've been in constant contact with the Waro ever since.'

Trainor closed his eyes and shook his head as Rose continued.

'One thing has been clear since they approached the Earth – the Waro know these spineless Nedenah are here, and they want them destroyed.'

'Why?'

'They're old enemies. The Nedenah might be tempted to interfere in our plans.'

'Our plans?' Trainor laughed. 'Just listen to yourself, Peter! The Waro have been using you.'

'Nonsense. They respect my contribution. They know that this bunker might prove beyond even their abilities. And time is of the essence.' Rose smiled, his eyes now as cold and dark as the empty void of space. 'Soon they will wipe the Earth clean. Just as I always wanted.'

'I won't participate in this slaughter!' exclaimed Trainor.

Rose pointed his gun at the professor. 'Open those cells, or I'll shoot you, too.'

The Brigadier coughed, not used to being on the sidelines. 'Gentlemen, I congratulate you on getting this far. But the moment you open one of those cubicles, you'll have a hundred well-armed CIA agents to contend with. You'll never escape.'

'I didn't ask for your input,' snapped Rose angrily.

'My men have this base surrounded,' bluffed the Brigadier. 'Soon the entire complex will be under the UN's jurisdiction.'

'I don't believe you,' said Rose. 'Your pathetic UNIT thugs were reasonable flunkies at the professor's press luncheon. But this...' He indicated the vast room with the wave of a manicured hand. 'This is beyond you.'

'Maybe so,' said the Brigadier. 'But unaccountable projects such as –'

'For the last time,' said Rose, 'shut up, or I'll shoot you. Now, Professor, open the cells.'

Although the gun remained trained on the Brigadier, Trainor clearly didn't want to provoke Rose further. He worked at the keypad with a small boxlike device that he had pulled from a dusty rucksack. Eventually the door to the first isolation chamber opened with a hiss of compressed air.

Rose, mindful of the Brigadier, swung his gun quickly in the direction of the alien inside, and fired a rapid burst of fire. The alien's head exploded, showering the cubicle with brown and yellow blood.

Immediately Rose turned the gun back on the Brigadier, and

indicated that Trainor should open the next cell.

The professor was motionless, tears streaming down his face.

'Come on, man,' snapped Rose.

Trainor opened his mouth to say something, but had seen enough evidence to realise that further argument was pointless. When Rose wasn't looking, he shot a quick glance at the Brigadier. The meaning was clear enough: I'm going to try something. Be ready.

The Brigadier nodded slowly.

'Ah, slight problem,' said Trainor. 'This cell works on a different principle. The correct number needs to be entered into both keypads simultaneously. Rose, you'll have to stand over there, and enter in the numbers just as I say them.'

Rose seemed so high on destruction that he didn't recognise the professor's desperate bluff. As Rose turned to the keypad closest to him, the Brigadier began to inch forward. The moment the gun dipped slightly, Lethbridge-Stewart launched himself at the man. Rose turned, instinctively swung the gun upward – but too high, as if shooting grouse or clay pigeons. The bullets skimmed the Brigadier's head, impacting into the thick concrete ceiling, by which time the Brigadier was on him. A swift rabbit punch laid Rose out cold. The Brigadier snorted. An in-bred Old Etonian, no doubt.

'I seem to be showing an alarming aptitude for strong-arm exploits, Professor,' said the Brigadier with a smile, picking up Rose's gun. 'Now, I suggest that you open the rest of the cells. We need the help of these aliens. I can assure you that the CIA are no more interested in the well-being of the Nedenah than this fellow was.'

The sky over Groom Lake Air Force Base turned black. Wave after wave of Waro swooped into position as with every passing moment the dark, shimmering cloud grew in size. Several

250

individuals, crazed by the maddening craving to rip the flesh from the feeble humans, circled away from the main group and began attacking each other in a terrible parody of a childish game.

Still more Waro arrived. There were millions of them, filling the sky from horizon to horizon like a black shroud. They obscured the sun until the entire desert was in pitch darkness.

The first planes to meet them were F-4 Phantom fighters, scrambled from the base at the first sign of a potential attack. Four of them flew into the heart of the Waro, firing missiles and countless machine gun rounds. Two planes were swallowed by the amorphous mass of Waro, then plummeted downward, belching smoke and fire.

The Doctor and his friends had found themselves a small gully, overshadowed by towering rocks, in which to watch the battle.

'There are so many of them,' said Shuskin, stating the obvious. 'And there is nothing we can do.' She pulled out a pair of binoculars, and saw the second pair of planes punch a hole through the dark cloud, sunlight flooding through the jagged rip in the sky. It was like watching the end of the world.

'That is better,' said Shuskin eagerly, as one of the fighters turned and rammed back through the Waro curtain, scattering thousands of the creatures in its wake, peppered by shot and crushed by the hammer blow of the aircraft's impact. The second fighter crashed through, creating another burst of sunlight in the dark sky.

'They're winning,' said Liz, but even before the words had left her mouth one of the planes was engulfed by the Waro. Already they were filling the gaps in their canopy.

'There are too many of them,' said Shuskin again. 'They're using their heat weapons. And landing on the planes to plant bombs.'

All the while the Doctor said nothing, continuing to work on a complex circuit as the sky filled with the trails of plummeting fighter planes.

'Can we do nothing?' asked Shuskin angrily.

'Perhaps,' he muttered.

At last Professor Trainor managed to open the rest of the cells containing the stony-faced Nedenah. His cry of delight was lost beneath the alarm klaxons.

'Oh dear,' said Trainor. 'I hadn't counted on that.'

The Brigadier strode into the nearest cell, knowing that he had to take control of this situation. 'Now, listen here,' he said. 'I know that you can hear me. I have proved that I do not want to see you destroyed, but if you don't help me, we'll all end up dead.'

The creature angled its head to look up at the Brigadier – the unexpected movement shocked him – and smiled. It was a warm smile, beguiling and alien, but it was impossible to resist. Somehow it told the Brigadier that *Everything will be all right* and that *There is no need to panic*. In an instant the Brigadier felt that he could trust the creatures – and that he would travel to the ends of the Earth to see that smile again.

'It is time,' said the creature, in what sounded to the Brigadier to be perfect English, 'for us to leave this place.'

There were different craft in the sky now. Along with numerous F-4s, F-5s, and F-111s were oddly styled machines, triangular and disc-shaped craft that seemed to take off vertically and fly at lightning speed towards the creatures.

'What in the name of God are they?' asked Mike, venturing to the very edge of their crevasse for a closer look.

'Hmmm?' The Doctor looked up briefly, his sonic screwdriver in his mouth as he worked on a clump of complex wiring. 'Experimental aircraft, based on some of the alien designs the Americans have gained access to,' he said with a degree of professional curiosity. 'That long triangular one is very like a Dalek warship I once saw on Aridius. It's beautiful, don't you think?'

'Beautiful?' said Shuskin angrily. 'It is obscene!'

'That too,' noted the Doctor, and returned his attention to the device he was constructing.

'While the rest of the world have been trying to defend themselves against the alien threat,' continued Shuskin, 'the Americans have been collaborating.'

'Stealing,' said the Doctor absent-mindedly. 'It's not quite the same thing.'

'We should be fighting together,' said Yates, finding himself, much to his own surprise, in agreement with Shuskin.

'We pirate technology from aliens all the time. Look at all of the IE stuff we have,' said Liz defensively.

'There's a difference between a videophone and one of those... things,' said Mike angrily as a saucer-like craft skimmed above their position almost silently, hovered, banked, and then turned, firing a steady stream of laser fire at the Waro.

'Agreed,' said the Doctor, looking up from the device he was working on. 'Unfortunately, some of our friends in the United States do not believe in collective security. They want the glory of saving the world all to themselves. I would suggest there are like-minded individuals in every country, Mike.'

'Can they?'

'What, save the world?' The Doctor looked across the desert to the blazing remains of numerous aircraft. 'The alien-derived planes are more manoeuvrable than anything the US military has come up with for itself,' the Doctor said. 'But I tend to agree with Captain Shuskin. The Waro are too numerous. Now, if you'd be a good chap and shut up for a few minutes and let me finish this,' he continued, pointing at the machine, 'then maybe we can help them. They probably don't want our help, but I think they could use it, don't you?'

The Nedenah turned away from the spacecraft, and walked

deeper into the bunker. They seemed peaceful and unhurried, but what little calm the Brigadier had disappeared the moment the CIA security personnel came into the room and started firing.

'Run!' he said, as he used Rose's weapon to return fire. The black-clad guards ducked behind equipment, but kept advancing.

Somehow they managed to reach another spaceship. The Brigadier couldn't tell how long it had taken them to get to the deepest bunker, or whether the Nedenah had ever accelerated their unhurried pace at any stage. It seemed that the creatures emanated an aura of dignified calm that was difficult to ignore, even when the bullets were flying.

The spacecraft was shaped like a symmetrical egg, its surface as smooth and polished as a mirror. It was larger than any of the ships the Brigadier had been shown, and it seemed totally untouched. He had a feeling that Control didn't want to admit to having been outwitted by the bug-eyed monsters.

Trainor lowered the steel doors around the chamber while the Nedenah busied themselves with gaining entry to their ship. 'The heuristic security devices resisted all attempts to gain access,' said one of the Nedenah. It wasn't a statement of pride or jingoism, but of simple fact.

Moments later a doorlike slit appeared in the base of the vehicle, and a ramp extended down to the floor. The four aliens walked up into their craft just as the metal bunker doors rolled open again. Trainor and the Brigadier ran after the aliens.

Once they were inside, the ramp flowed back into place, moving like animated mercury, sealing the hull. The material that the ship was constructed from felt like warm metal, and it glowed when the 'door' closed, providing illumination.

The first thing the Brigadier noticed was a large chamber that adjoined what seemed to be the cockpit. Within were tanks containing more Nedenah. They were curled up like foetuses, looking more childlike than ever.

'I don't understand,' said the Brigadier.

'After all this time,' said one of the aliens reasonably, 'the food supplies were approaching exhaustion. They elected to wait in suspended animation for our return.'

'No, but...' The Brigadier paused, collecting his thoughts. 'They've been here all this time, locked in this spaceship, and they didn't try to rescue you?'

'We have higher priorities than merely the comfort of the individual,' replied the alien. 'Nedenah are committed to cultural and technological purity. Our visits to your planet are purely observational.' The creature's face fell. 'Unfortunately, we have polluted your race. You have had glimpses of our technology, but you seem incapable of using it wisely.'

'I'm sorry,' stammered the Brigadier, realising how feeble this must sound, as if one man could apologise for humanity's evil. 'But, rest assured, if we get out of here, I'll do my best to ensure that the research programmes are halted. No one country or vested interest is greater than the UN.'

'We shall be leaving in a moment,' said the Nedenah, turning briefly to watch the others powering up the spacecraft.

'Thank you,' said the Brigadier.

'You do not understand,' said the creature. 'You now face a danger much more grave than your own selfishness.'

Viscount Rose came back to reality with the sickening lurch of a man in a free-falling lift. It took him a moment to realise that the bells he heard weren't just in his mind. A klaxon was sounding nearby. Rose could hear shouting, too.

Then someone kicked him in the ribs, and he groaned and tried to turn over and go back to sleep. 'Go away,' he muttered with the simple arrogance of a man used to getting his own way.

'Who the hell are you?' asked an American voice.

Rose didn't reply, and found himself being dragged to his feet by two burly men in dark suits.

'I asked you a question!' said the American man, standing impatiently to his left.

'So you did, old man,' replied Rose. Suddenly he became aware of the enormity of the situation. This was, indeed, a fine old kettle of fish he'd found himself in. 'I … I don't suppose you have an aspirin by any chance, do you? My head is splitting.'

'You're English?' asked the man. 'You with UNIT, boy?'

'Err… No. I'm Viscount Rose. I'm thirty-seventh in line to the throne of the United Kingdom of Great Britain and Northern Ireland.' He gave a charming smile.

What happened next surprised the guards almost as much as it surprised Rose.

'Would you like a cigarette?' asked the leading American.

'Oh, I say, that's frightfully decent of you,' said Rose.

Control had Rose thrown into an interrogation cell, and left him there to sweat. After that, Rose proved to be very cooperative, describing Professor Trainor as the maddest of Britain's mad scientists, a man without a shred of moral decency and courage. 'Roger Cook's going to do a special on him,' added Rose helpfully. 'They call him "the most evil man in the world". Seems he's in bed with UNIT. That Brigadier chappy, he's in on it. And the government.'

'Roger who?' asked Control, feeling he'd lost the plot somewhere.

'Trainor duped me into coming here,' continued Rose breathlessly, not hearing Control's question. 'I had no idea what this place was, or what - who - it contained. It wasn't until we got into this room that I realised he had plans to kill those aliens.' Rose sobbed momentarily. 'I managed to stop him from killing the others.' Rose pointed to the cells, one of which was being scrubbed clean by white-coated technicians. 'But he knocked me out and ran off.'

'Oh well, no harm done then,' said Control, smiling. He pulled a Colt .45 from his pocket and shot Viscount Rose, thirty-seventh in line to the throne, in the head. 'No harm at all.'

CHAPTER 20

The Doctor continued to work on the jamming device. Every time he glanced up at the sky, there seemed to be fewer and fewer aircraft flying. The Waro were winning.

'It's looking pretty hopeless,' said Yates, as if he'd been reading his thoughts.

'Never say die, Mike,' said the Doctor. 'I'm almost there.'

Suddenly there was a hissing, droning noise from above them. Another, much larger vessel had joined the battle. It was less manoeuvrable than the USAF craft, but appeared to be resistant to the Waro's weapons. Arcs of blue light crackled around the egg-shaped object, and thicker beams of brightness stabbed into the smothering blanket of Waro.

'What's going on?' asked the Doctor.

'It is difficult to tell,' said Shuskin. 'But this plane seems much stronger.'

'So the CIA did have a trump up their sleeve after all,' said Yates.

'I'm not so sure,' said the Doctor. 'That looks like a twenty-four-carat alien spaceship to me. So the question is: who's flying it, and why?'

It had taken the Brigadier some time to become used to the idea of flying through the air on a transparent magic carpet, still less one that was travelling at Mach 4.

Trainor, on the other hand, had rolled into a ball on the invisible floor of the alien spacecraft, his arms over his head and his eyes closed. One of the Nedenah had been particularly concerned by the professor's plight, and had tried to reassure the man. 'It is a purely optical rather than a physical process. You are in no danger.'

The professor merely whimpered.

Now, in the height of battle, even the Brigadier could empathise with Trainor. The ship was surrounded by a dark swarm of grotesque goblin creatures, and the Brigadier felt unusually vulnerable. It was difficult to remind oneself that they *couldn't* see inside the ship, and that there was a barrier between the saliva-flecked faces and the ship's occupants. Whenever a creature landed on the invisible hull, some metres away, there was a spark of what looked like static electricity, and the goblin fell away.

The Brigadier stared down at his feet, watching the devilish creatures spiralling away to the desert floor, and then felt nauseous with vertigo. 'So, these are the Waro?' he said, never afraid to ask the obvious question.

'Yes,' said one of the Nedenah, turning away from a bank of only partly visible controls.

The Brigadier pointed to a dark and smoking shape on the desert floor. 'And that's the air force base where the cobalt-60 is stored?'

'Yes.'

'Which the Waro need to prime their larger bombs?'

'Yes. The bombs destroy entire ecosystems, rendering Earth uninhabitable to all but their own kind.' The Nedenah spoke in a singsong voice that made the words all the more horrifying.

'Thank you,' said the Brigadier, suppressing a shudder as a Waro seemed to career in his direction before vanishing in a flash of static. 'I like to know what's going on, that's all.'

The larger weapons of the Nedenah craft fired again, arcing outwards in myriad directions.

'It's all right, Professor, I think we're winning,' stated Lethbridge-Stewart.

Trainor groaned, and pulled his arms tighter over his head.

When Lethbridge-Stewart looked up again, he felt a hard lump form in his throat. Two of the hideous Waro creatures were flying straight for the ship in close formation. Even from this distance, the Brigadier could see their red eyes, dark with murderous hatred.

Lethbridge-Stewart was about to warn a nearby Nedenah when his attention was caught by the bulky black object that the Waro carried between them. 'That looks suspiciously like…' The Brigadier paused, aware of Trainor's fragile grip on sanity. 'What do you think?' he asked the Nedenah.

'It is an explosive device,' replied the alien, matter-of-factly. 'The Waro are known for such crude weaponry.'

The Waro were now mere feet from the ship's seemingly transparent hull. 'They're going to hit!' the Brigadier said, aghast, as the creatures, using the last of their strength, threw themselves towards him.

'Nearly there,' said the Doctor, loudly enough for the UNIT soldiers towards the front of the narrow crevasse to hear.

'Good,' said Shuskin. 'I am not used to sitting still while people around me are dying.'

There was a massive explosion from somewhere above them.

Shuskin immediately raised her binoculars skyward, although it was obvious that the large alien craft had been hit.

'It seems one of the Waro got through, planting explosives that the ship could not destroy,' announced Shuskin.

The silver egg began to list to one side. A few moments later there was another, even larger explosion, a plume of orange smoke burning briefly on the hull.

It began to fall from the sky.

'I suggest you go and investigate,' said the Doctor, returning his attention to the device just as the ship thumped into the desert. The explosion was bright enough to briefly negate the influence of the Waro blanket over the sun. 'I'll be quite safe here, but whoever is in that ship seems to have some idea of how we go about defeating the Waro.'

Shuskin nodded, and she, Yates, and the UNIT troops began to move in the direction of the towering pillar of acrid smoke some mile or so distant. Liz gave the Doctor a last, sad smile, and hobbled after the soldiers.

'It looks like it's all over,' sighed the Doctor, once they were out of earshot. The last of the USAF experimental craft had long since been destroyed.

Now the Waro, moving as one amorphous creature, began to sweep down towards the air force base.

There had been a strange calm within the Nedenah craft as it plummeted to the ground.

The flames on the outside of the ship had seemed close enough to feel, the Brigadier almost putting out a hand towards them, then flinching back as if terrified that touching the walls of the ship would puncture the illusion and send them all to the ground that much more quickly. But, beneath his feet, the desert had been rushing up pretty fast anyway.

'We're in free fall,' he had said, shaking his head. 'What do we do?' The first response he had was from the professor, still hunched in a ball but animatedly shouting that they were all going to die, and that it was all his fault. Lethbridge-Stewart had turned wearily to the Nedenah.

One of the creatures – its hands were still clamped on the guidance sensors – had turned towards the Brigadier. 'Do not worry,' it said in a childlike voice. 'You will be...' The creature paused, as if searching for the correct word. 'Unharmed,' it said at length. 'Safe' was clearly not a word the Nedenah had had much call for during the previous twenty years.

Then the Brigadier had blacked out.

Once he was conscious again, he looked around with amazement. The invisible bubble of the ship was still intact, keeping the flames at bay. It seemed to have landed on the desert floor.

'What's burning?' Lethbridge-Stewart asked through clenched teeth, his head still throbbing.

'We are discarding one layer of the hull,' replied one of the Nedenah while working calmly at a near-visible console. 'It can be replaced, in time. The Waro will think that we have been destroyed.'

'Ah.' The Brigadier smiled. 'Good plan.'

The Nedenah pressed a sensor, and the walls sprang back into focus, a burnished silver blocking out the angry red of the desert. The door appeared in the bottom of the craft, falling downward to create a ramp.

'Please,' said the alien. 'There is much to be done, and this craft is now inoperative. We must evacuate it immediately.'

The Brigadier nodded, then patted the groaning professor on the shoulder. 'Come on, old chap,' he said gently. 'Let's not get in the way.'

The Nedenah craft had landed on a small ridge behind the air base. From here, Lethbridge-Stewart could see that the horrific war in the air was over. The desert floor was strewn with the bodies of thousands of dead and dying Waro, and yet their numbers in the air – now diving down towards the base – seemed undiminished.

Numerous craft lay wrecked on the sand. The Waro crawled over the debris, searching for survivors.

'Carnage,' said the Brigadier.

Trainor didn't reply. He just stared coldly at the killing grounds, a blank expression of utter incomprehension on his face. 'Rose told me they wanted to be our friends,' he said at last.

'I imagine that's what they told him, too.'

'Oh, no,' continued the professor. 'Rose knew what he was doing. Power corrupts, Brigadier. And absolute power corrupts absolutely.'

There was a noise behind them, and they turned to find several of the Nedenah emerging from their craft, bringing with them a bulky cylindrical container.

'We have revived a number of our kind from suspended animation,' explained the leading Nedenah.

'With all due respect,' said the Brigadier, 'I think we have more important things to worry about than waking up your comrades.'

All the Nedenah made simultaneous sideways movements of their heads, as if to disagree. 'This chemical,' said one of them, pointing with a sticklike finger to the cylinder, 'was developed recently. It will interfere with the Waro's genetic enhancements and turn their violence against themselves.'

'You worked on that in the CIA bunker?' asked Trainor.

'Those of us trapped within the craft detected the approach of the Waro.'

'What exactly will this chemical do?' asked the Brigadier.

'In the short term, it will inhibit the creatures' group mentality.' The Nedenah paused for a moment before continuing. 'The Waro are very angry and aggressive. For decades their planet was plagued by destruction, conflict and infighting. Empires rose and fell. There was little technology, no exchange of ideas.'

'So what happened?'

'They genetically and chemically limited their anger. They were still creatures of hatred, but now that hatred was directed against "not-Waro". This substance will reverse that "progress", turn the Waro against each other once again.'

'And in the longer term?'

'The tempo of aggression will increase exponentially. Eventually the aggressive feelings will overload their nervous systems.'

'So they will literally die of anger?' asked Trainor. 'Fascinating.'

The Brigadier understood. 'It's a kind of mental laxative, then,' he said with a suppressed grin.

The Nedenah looked at him blankly.

'Never mind. What must we do with it?'

The alien looked towards the air base. 'Flood the skies,' it said simply. 'A tiny amount of the fluid will destroy hundreds of Waro.'

'I'm glad you've got a vat the size of Bedfordshire,' said the Brigadier, remembering how many Waro he'd seen. 'Now, how to get it up there?'

As he mused on this problem, a familiar voice echoed up from beneath the ridge.

'Sir?'

'Captain Yates?'

'Yes, sir,' came the distant reply. 'I don't believe it, sir. I thought you were in Europe.'

'Evidently not, Captain,' said the Brigadier. 'Get up here. We've got a job to do.'

It took Yates, Shuskin, Liz and the other soldiers a few minutes to fully comprehend that standing before them were a group of aliens who *weren't* interested in taking over the world.

'Something unique in my experience,' observed Liz. As she listened to the Brigadier's story, it had become clear to Liz that Bernard Trainor, a man who had been like a father to her, was implicated in the conspiracy up to his neck, and possibly beyond. She found herself unable to look at him as the Brigadier, Shuskin, and Yates discussed tactics.

'I suppose you had your reasons,' she said eventually.

'Of course, Elizabeth. Reasons are important. I taught you that much, surely?'

'Why?' she asked.

'Why? Why is the sky blue? Why is grass green? Some things simply "are", my dear.'

'That's no answer, and you know it!' she said, rounding on him with an anger that surprised her. 'You once told me truth was the only part of science that mattered.'

'I lied,' he said, shamefaced. 'The only science that matters is the search for truth.'

Liz turned away as the Brigadier, Shuskin, and Yates walked over with several of the Nedenah. 'The repercussions can wait,' said the Brigadier, seeming to have overheard the stormy conclusion to their argument. 'For UNIT, for the CIA, for all of us. We must concentrate on stopping the Waro.' He turned to Shuskin. 'Now, Captain, you say the Doctor is still out there' – he indicated the wide expanse of desert before them – 'building some form of jamming contraption.'

'Yes, sir.'

'I trust you left a radio with him?'

'Of course, sir,' said Shuskin, seemingly astonished that the Brigadier could think for a second that she would have neglected to do so. She produced the hand-held UNIT walkie-talkie. 'Channel five, sir,' she said.

'I am aware of the standard frequency, Captain,' noted the Brigadier, and operated the radio, which crackled into life.

'Hello?' said a distant voice. 'Is anybody there?'

'Doctor?'

'Well, it's hardly going to be *Round the Horne*, is it?' joked the Doctor. 'Lethbridge-Stewart? I thought you were in Europe.'

'Where are you?' asked the Brigadier.

'Close to the air base. I've got the jamming device working but its range is a bit limited. What I really need is a power-boosted, open-ended frequency modulator.'

'I have something better than that for you,' said the Brigadier enigmatically. 'We'll meet you inside the compound in fifteen minutes.'

The Doctor approached the US Air Force base with trepidation, the bulky jamming device tucked under his arm. There had been a certain grotesque symmetry about recent events, the destruction of the armoured column in the snowy wastes of the Soviet Union now reflected in the devastation of the American aircraft in the Nevada desert. The smoking remains of the planes littered the surrounding area like the carcasses of electrocuted animals. Thankfully most of the Waro seemed to have retreated, drawn towards the stored cobalt. Only vultures picked at the human corpses.

Groom Lake AFB had not escaped the slaughter. A couple of planes had crashed into the complex, shattering buildings and covering the runways with debris. The grounds were littered with the bodies of the individuals who had tried to flee.

The Doctor crept in through the remains of the main gate, keeping to the comparative safety of the walls. The sky was still dark with swarming Waro, but hundreds of them were descending gently towards the building that seemed to contain the precious cobalt-60. From a distance the Waro resembled a stationary tornado, the tip of the vortex just touching the ground. 'Come on, Brigadier,' he breathed, 'I don't like being kept in suspense.'

Suddenly a tiny creature clattered into the Doctor, shrieking in delight. The Doctor tumbled on to the rough tarmac, but kept a tight grip on his jamming machine. The moment he hit the ground he switched it on, pointing the machine in the direction of the attacking Waro. With a comic squawk, the Waro flew backwards, before being dashed down on to one of outlying runways. The Doctor saw the creature try to pull itself to its feet, its wings still flapping uncontrollably, and then slump into death. One down, two and a half million to go, he thought.

He turned quickly, expecting more Waro, but they seemed occupied with looting the cobalt-60 stores. As if on cue, the Brigadier, Liz, Trainor, and the two UNIT captains came cautiously through the air force base entrance, followed by a handful of accompanying soldiers. Even the Brigadier could not conceal his delight. 'Ah, good to see you, Doctor.'

'There you are, Lethbridge-Stewart. I'm afraid you've just missed the first demonstration of my new jamming machine.'

'Does it work?' asked the Brigadier.

'Of course it does,' said the Doctor, sounding hurt. 'Now, what have you got to show me?'

A group of aliens crept through the shattered gateway, dragging a canister on what seemed to be an antigravity device.

'Allow me to introduce the Nedenah,' said the Brigadier. 'They're aliens.'

'I think the Doctor can see that,' said Liz.

'They want to help us defeat the Waro,' continued Lethbridge-Stewart. 'The cylinder contains a substance that...' He paused. 'Well, it will kill the Waro. That's all we need to know.'

The Doctor walked over to the aliens. 'I'm delighted to meet you.'

The Nedenah looked him up and down quizzically. 'You appear to be human, but are not.'

'No, indeed,' said the Doctor. 'I'm a Time L-' He stopped, remembering his trial. 'I'm an exile.'

The Nedenah seemed satisfied with this.

'Now then,' said Professor Trainor, glancing at the Doctor with an uneasy smile. 'We need a plane of some sort.'

The Doctor noticed Trainor shudder. 'Are you all right, old chap?'

The professor nodded. 'I was just getting used to terra firma again.'

'Well, it's good to see you,' said the Doctor. It didn't occur to him to ask what the professor was doing in the middle of the Nevada desert. 'Now, that hangar looks largely undamaged,' the Doctor said, pointing across the airfield.

'Permission to take some men across to scout the area, sir?' Yates was as impatient for involvement as usual.

The Doctor shook his head. 'No, Mike. I've only got the one jamming device. Let's all go, very carefully.'

The group proceeded across the rubble-strewn runway and towards the undamaged hangar. The UNIT soldiers scanned the sky, weapons drawn, a protective ring around the others. The Doctor kept his finger on the switch of the jamming device. He knew that they would be noticed in time.

Suddenly a group of some thirty Waro came towards them, flying low over the airfield. The goblins tumbled over each other in their enthusiasm to reach their targets.

The soldiers began firing, automatic weapons spraying bullets that caught a few of the goblin creatures and tugged them harshly down towards the ground. One flipped on to the tarmac just in front of Shuskin, still twitching. A bayonet appeared in her hand, and flashed down into the creature's face.

The Doctor switched on his device, and pointed it upwards as the next wave of Waro wheeled in their direction. In an instant the formation became chaotic, Waro crashing into each other, skidding off in different directions. 'The power output of this device is much higher than the Heath Robinson contraption I came up with in Siberia, Liz,' explained the Doctor calmly, as if giving a lecture. 'But I'm sure the Waro will become resistant to it as time passes.'

'Fascinating,' said Trainor. 'How does the device work?'

The Doctor opened his mouth to respond, but thought better of it. 'I think it would be easier to tell you later, Professor.'

'Oh, of course,' said Trainor, as if comprehending their situation for the first time. 'Sorry.'

Yates shouted a warning. Another group were spinning towards them from the rear. A handful survived the withering machine gun fire, flying into the UNIT soldiers before the Doctor could turn his device in their direction. Three of the soldiers and one of the Nedenah – its bland eyes still wide with passive acceptance – collapsed under the ferocious attack and lay still.

Then the Doctor's device took effect, and the wings flapped randomly, pulling the Waro away.

'Almost there,' breathed the professor between pants of terror.

Liz screamed suddenly. A lone Waro had skidded unnoticed over their heads, and had reached down towards her with its massive claws. The talons were buried in her hair and scalp, and her feet were losing contact with the ground, the Waro beginning to flap upward. A trickle of blood ran down the bridge of her nose.

Yates swivelled and fired, ripping the creature in two. Liz crumpled to the ground, falling awkwardly on her weak ankle. In an instant Yates and Shuskin were at her side, dragging her to her feet, and then supporting her between them, her arms around their shoulders, as they trudged forward.

'When we're back home,' said Yates through gritted teeth, 'I'll treat you to a weekend in a health farm. Sort your ankle out, get a nice haircut.' He glanced at her scalp, wet with blood and perspiration.

Liz went to say something, but lapsed into semiconsciousness, her head lolling.

They reached the hangar and pulled open the vast metal doors. The Doctor stood in the entrance, pointing his device in the direction of the pursuing Waro. It was already becoming clear that the software controlling the Waro's wings was learning and developing. Each time the Doctor used the device the effects became less pronounced.

'Hurry!' he shouted, twisting his head to see the others running towards a seemingly undamaged C-133 Cargomaster. Without warning, gunfire sounded, as the Brigadier and the remaining pair of soldiers shot at a group of Waro who were spilling through a hole in the roof.

'All right, Doctor,' shouted the Brigadier. 'Let's get going.'

The Doctor turned and ran towards the plane. The Brigadier gave some covering fire, but even so the Doctor ducked instinctively just as a Waro flew overhead, screeching. He collapsed gratefully into the comparative safety of the transport plane, the Brigadier slamming shut the door just as another group of Waro came flapping in their direction.

Then he turned, a worried look crossing his face. 'I don't suppose anyone can fly this thing?'

'But surely that controls the ailerons?'

'My dear Professor, I have flown more aircraft than you've had hot dinners. It's obviously the tail rudder. Anyway, I didn't think you liked flying.'

'That's not the point, and –'

'Now, look here, those controls are clearly labelled "flaps". I may not have a thousand and one university degrees, but surely –'

'Shut up, all of you!' exploded Liz. She didn't know what was more painful, her throbbing ankle and gashed head, or watching Trainor, the Doctor, and the Brigadier squabbling over the controls of the plane. 'Can we *please* leave it to the Nedenah? They seem to know what they're doing.'

Silently the Nedenah had moved around the arguing people, flicking switches, correcting their mistakes, and, as far as Liz could see, basically preparing the plane for take-off. Now they were ready.

The Brigadier looked shamefaced. 'Yes, of course, Dr Shaw. You're quite right. I think I'd be more useful back there with you.'

'Thank you, Brigadier. And, Doctor, hadn't you better protect this plane against the Waro's heat weapons? It would be unfortunate to have come all this way, only to fall at the last hurdle.'

'I was just about to attend to that,' said the Doctor quietly, moving to busy himself with the aircraft's hull. 'Professor? Can you use my machine, just as I was showing you a moment ago?'

'Of course,' said Trainor, smiling eagerly. 'Ah, here we go.' A Waro landed on the glass of the cockpit, a bomb in one hand. The professor switched on the Doctor's machine, waved it in the general direction of the Waro, and immediately it flew off into the distance, exploding with a muffled bang. 'Let's just hope this gadget doesn't interfere with the controls of the plane, eh, Doctor?'

'My dear fellow...' began the Doctor, but Liz glared at him, and he lapsed into silence.

Trainor flicked a few switches on the case containing the Doctor's jamming device, which threw a protective blanket around the entire aircraft. Meanwhile the Nedenah expertly steered the Cargomaster through the hangar doors, and towards the main runway.

'Looks a trifle damaged,' observed Yates.

'Maybe so, Captain,' said the Brigadier, helping Liz and Shuskin with the Nedenah canister, 'but landing will be a bonus. Let's just get up there in one piece, and deal with these Waro things.'

'There,' said Liz at last. 'The cylinder is in place. Give me a few minutes, and this plane will be the biggest crop sprayer in the history of aviation.'

Trainor cried out in terror as the Cargomaster bounced along the runway, the Nedenah swerving it from side to side to avoid the larger craters.

'You all right, old chap?' queried the Doctor.

Trainor smiled weakly. 'I suppose I ought to be grateful. At least this plane isn't invisible.' He turned as a group of Waro pitched on to the nose of the Cargomaster, then flew off again just as quickly.

The aeroplane lurched into the air at a steep angle, and Liz had to push against the cylinder to stop it rolling around in the hold.

Then the plane levelled, and she returned to rigging up the tubes needed to spray the chemical over the Waro.

'How are you doing?' said the Doctor, having again used his sonic screwdriver to protect them from the Waro's heat weapons.

'We're just about ready.'

'Perhaps the Brigadier would like to do the honours?' The Doctor pointed to the valve at the end of the canister of genetic material.

'With pleasure,' said Lethbridge-Stewart.

The C-133 pulled higher into the sky, reaching the top of the cloud of flapping Waro. A fine spray fell from the plane, and its effect on the goblin creatures was almost instantaneous. Well-ordered ranks fell into squabbling and screaming chaos, and tens, then hundreds, of Waro tumbled from the skies, torn to shreds by their fellows.

The Waro screamed with delight as their old, unfettered bloodlust returned.

'The substance is taking effect,' noted Liz.

'It's like a plague,' observed the Brigadier, his face impassive as he stared out of one of the plane's windows. The chaos was visibly spreading through the ranks of flying Waro.

'The second stage of the process will begin soon,' said one of the Nedenah. 'The metabolism of the Waro will increase. Their pulse rates will double, then triple.'

The Doctor turned away from the window. 'I don't enjoy being a witness to Armageddon, Brigadier. But the Waro have only themselves to blame. They found a way of controlling their self-destructiveness, but only used that to externalise their rage.'

Liz was surprised. 'In Siberia you said that the Waro were born violent – that they could no more change their behaviour than I could change the number of arms I have.'

The Doctor looked down sadly. 'Perhaps I was being simplistic. Perhaps we all have our choices to make – and enough bad choices become ingrained as character. But a bad character is much more difficult to redeem than a single bad decision.'

Liz couldn't help but glance at Trainor, still breathing heavily from all the excitement, wrapped up in his own thoughts.

'Whatever, I must say the destruction of the Waro force here on Earth brings me little satisfaction,' the Doctor continued.

'But the Earth *is* safe,' said Yates.

The Doctor nodded. 'Of course, and I'm –'

There was a loud explosion towards the rear of the Cargomaster, and the plane began to nose-dive. As the Doctor, Liz, and the others clung on as well as they could, a Nedenah made its way carefully out of the cockpit. 'One of the Waro penetrated the Doctor's shielding.' The voice carried no hint of panic. 'A suicide mission. It carried a large bomb. Most of the tail section is gone.'

'Then we're done for!' moaned Trainor.

'Perhaps,' said the Nedenah, smiling.

The C-133 came down steeply, belching fire from the tail section. The undercarriage was jammed, and the blunted nose took the brunt of the impact, thudding into sand and then rock.

The plane skidded across the desert for some seconds, burrowing its fuselage deeper and deeper until eventually it could no longer withstand the pressure, and the entire craft split in two. There was another explosion, a flower of brightness in the desert, as one of the fuel tanks ruptured.

Above the wrecked plane, the sky was at last beginning to clear.

The Brigadier pulled himself painfully to his feet. One eye refused to open, and when he put his hand to his head, it came away sticky with blood.

He saw a huddled body, curled beneath a protective pillar of metal.

'Well, Professor,' said Lethbridge-Stewart, walking over. 'Two crashes in one day should be statistically impossible, so the chances of anything happening on the flight home are –'

The Brigadier stopped. Something was wrong.

'Dr Shaw!' he shouted.

Liz hobbled over, saw Trainor's body, and dropped to her knees. She checked for a pulse at his wrist and his neck, placed a hand over his grey lips, listened to his chest.

When she looked up, her eyes were streaked with tears. 'He's had a heart attack,' she said in a quiet voice. 'Even with the right equipment, I'm not sure I could do anything.'

The Brigadier rested a hand on her shoulder. 'I'm sorry. Had it not been for –'

Suddenly Liz grabbed Trainor's lapels and screamed into his dead face. 'Why did you have to go now? Why did you have to go when I hate you!' She collapsed, sobbing, on top of the corpse. 'You stupid, selfish bastard.'

Thanks to the skill of the Nedenah, the other occupants of the Cargomaster were able to pull themselves from the wreckage and walk away.

The Brigadier, Shuskin and Yates stood with the surviving UNIT soldiers close to Trainor's body, watching as the dark cloud overhead began to fade.

Liz and the Doctor sat on a small rise, their back to the wrecked plane. While the Nedenah walked calmly through sand in the direction of their own craft, the Doctor spoke in shocked whispers, his words only just audible above the screams of the dying Waro.

An hour later, the desert was silent.

FIRST EPILOGUE:
NO WIN SITUATION

'I hear the South American situation is worsening,' said the Brigadier gravely. He turned to the Doctor, and found him absent-mindedly throwing bread to the ducks in the lake. 'I said –'

'Yes,' said the Doctor, looking up. 'And I suspect it will get worse before it gets any better. Much worse.'

A walk in the park had seemed a ridiculous idea at first, but Lethbridge-Stewart felt curiously liberated, the horror of recent events beginning to fade. There were worse ways to spend a Sunday afternoon off duty. 'I don't know what the world's coming to,' he said with a resigned grin.

'Wish I could help you, old chap, really I do,' replied the Doctor, brushing crumbs from his trousers. 'But the future's as much of a mystery to me as it is to you. One of the things my people took from my memory, along with how to get off this planet of yours!'

The anger in the Doctor's voice surprised the Brigadier. 'It's not that bad, surely?'

The Doctor paused for a long time. 'No,' he said finally. 'It isn't. The planet has potential. If only you humans wouldn't go around killing each other so much.'

The Brigadier walked along the path surrounding the small boating lake. On the opposite bank a child was riding his bicycle, supported on either side by proud parents. The Brigadier noticed the Doctor watching the scene with detached curiosity. 'I always thought you said this was your favourite planet,' he observed.

The Doctor nodded, plunging his hands deep into the pockets of his voluminous coat. July was proving cold and strangely bitter. 'But there must be a better way for humanity to conduct its affairs,' he said. On the opposite side of the lake, the boy's bike wobbled alarmingly as his parents took their hands from his back for a second, then stabilised as they steadied him again.

'We've been saying that for years,' said the Brigadier.

'My point in a nutshell. Things must change.'

They walked back towards the main road, passing a group of boys playing football, their jumpers thrown down as goal posts. Another set of children, by the wrought-iron railings, were in the middle of a game of British Bulldog. The Brigadier looked at them fondly. It was all so simple back then.

'How was your meeting with the Prime Minister?' asked the Doctor.

'Went very well.' The Brigadier laughed. 'You know, he's not a bad chap, for a Liberal.'

'And the UN investigation of UNIT?'

'Just started. Hayes is refusing to talk, but some of the traitors have already been identified. US HQ is moving to Washington DC, and most of the Geneva paperwork has been recovered. But the CIA aren't saying a dickie bird. The Americans are protecting them, pretending nothing happened.'

'*Somebody* is protecting the CIA,' the Doctor noted. 'But there's more going on there than meets the eye.' He glanced at the Brigadier, but the veiled warning seemed to have gone unnoticed.

'I must say,' said the Brigadier, 'Those Nedenah fellows were very thorough. The American military combed the desert around the air force base, and didn't find a scrap of alien technology.'

'Do you think they'd admit anything to you if they had?'

'Well,' said the Brigadier, determined not to swamped by the Doctor's pessimism, 'I still say they did jolly well. Surprised to see them disappearing like that, at the end, but I don't suppose you can blame them. And the Waro were defeated. That's the most important thing.'

'It's a hollow victory for UNIT,' said the Doctor. 'There are still spies to be found. Still games to be played.'

The Brigadier reached down to pick up a discarded crisp packet, which he rolled into a ball thoughtfully. 'You know, I still don't understand what Rose hoped to achieve. The CIA are just idiots who think they're at war with the rest of the world. Hayes was misguided. Trainor was simply duped. But Rose? It seems he knew what was going to happen.'

'Indeed,' said the Doctor. 'Never underestimate people's desire for change. Rose was so disillusioned with humankind that he wanted Earth wiped clean, so that life could begin again. The Waro were his instruments.'

'Doctor,' said the Brigadier suddenly, dropping the crisp packet into a plastic rubbish bin near the park entrance, 'I know an excellent Chinese restaurant just a couple of miles from here. Would you do me the honour of allowing me to take you to lunch?'

'Yes,' said the Doctor, brightening at last. 'I'll even let you pay.'

Yates, Benton, and Shuskin sat in the lounge of the Barley Mow, drinking pints of Newcastle Brown and saying little. Shuskin was to return to her regiment the next day, and it had been revealed that Hayes had been behind the decision to place her in charge of UNIT. Of course, the return of the Brigadier had rendered that decision null and void, but Mike Yates was relieved to hear that the command that had so angered him was, in itself, tainted by the conspiracy.

'Curious weather we are having,' Shuskin said to no one in particular.

'Yes,' replied Benton. 'Brass monkey's, isn't it? That was the English summer, that was. A week and a bit in June!'

Yates grunted something noncommittal into his pint and stared out of the window.

Benton stood. 'If you'll excuse me, sirs, I must see a man about a dog, if you know what I mean.'

Once he was gone a moody silence settled over the table. 'I think that you dislike me intensely,' said Shuskin eventually.

'I'm sorry?'

'So you should be.'

'What?'

'I am a competent soldier, am I not?'

'Adequate,' said Yates, with a slight grin.

'And I am capable of making decisions?'

'I suppose so.'

'And you, Michael Alexander Raymond Yates, are a plank!'

'What?'

'A plank. It means –'

'I know what it means,' said Yates. 'It's just the stupidest insult I've ever heard.'

'You want worse?'

'No, plank'll do fine, thanks.'

Shuskin sipped her drink. 'Do you want to know what I think?'

'No, but I'm sure you're going to tell me.'

'I think you are a lonely man, Michael Yates. I think you are terrified of the pressure of command, but you cannot show this to anyone because you know they will think worse of you. I think you cover this up with sexist crap that would insult the intelligence of a four-year-old. I think you do not realise how lucky you are.'

'And how lucky am I?' asked Yates.

'Very lucky,' she said. 'You have many friends who care about you. This UNIT is like a family, protecting their own. There is only one thing you really need and that is a good woman.'

'Know any?' queried Yates, without thinking. Then he remembered the party at Cambridge, and the bedroom, and he wished he'd kept his mouth shut.

'Sadly not,' she said, standing and picking up her gloves from the table. 'They are hard to come by, and harder still to keep. But I have a feeling you will find one, sooner rather than later.' She saluted him as he clumsily stood, almost knocking the drinks over. 'Goodbye, comrade Captain,' she said and turned to leave.

'I'll see you around, Captain,' said Yates with a smile, causing her to stop.

'You may indeed,' she responded. 'And that would be a pleasure for both of us.' Then she pushed open the pub door, and was gone.

Benton returned from the toilet just as Yates sat down again. 'Has Captain Shuskin gone?' he asked.

'Yes,' said Yates. Then he shook his head as if to clear it of dead thoughts. 'Right, we'd better be getting back to HQ.' He paused. 'Business as usual.'

Thomas Bruce awoke, momentarily aware only of the sharp smell of antiseptic. His mouth still tasted of strong medicine and cheap liquor. Encased in crisp linen, Bruce felt safe and warm in his bed. He never wanted to get out of it again.

He had been hit by a stray piece of shrapnel in the early stages of the battle against the Waro. Collateral damage. Lying in a pool of his own blood screaming for his mother, and for Jesus, and begging someone – anyone – to put him out of his misery. When he had been found several hours later by one of the emergency medical teams, he'd fainted with the pain when they lifted him into the helicopter.

As in his tortured dreams, there was an almost permanent presence in the shadows of his hospital room. Sometimes it was somebody he knew, another badgeman from Control's stable. Sometimes it was just a faceless figure in a dark suit and sunglasses, reading the *New York Times* and ignoring Bruce's questions. Occasionally the man would blandly assure him that he was safe, that everything was taken care of, that he wasn't to worry – and, by the way, weren't Green Bay unlucky in the fourth quarter last night?

He was allowed one television station – NBC – and then only at certain times. It was as though they were keeping something from him.

When he was alone, which wasn't often, he remembered the crumpled UNIT file he had found in the wreck of the truck in Switzerland, completely by accident. It was a medical report from a group of scientists engaged in top-secret research on Nedenah DNA. The list of names included one he instantly recognised. Mary Bruce. His wife.

The report went on to suggest that quarantine procedures be tightened after the children of some of the research staff had died of leukaemia. That list of names included one he knew well. John Bruce. His son.

The file was dated three months after John's death. They had known all the time. They had known that they were playing with fire, that messing around with alien blood was likely to have some effect on those who came into contact with it. But people like Control and Hayes had just let the experiments continue.

He cried then. Not for his wife, nor his dead son, nor the marriage that had been torn apart by secrets and lies long before John's illness and the counsellor who'd done more harm than good. He cried for himself. He had played their game, and lost. And was damned.

Night time. Bruce got out of bed to find no one in his room. Softly he padded to the door to check on the corridor, but it was deserted. He looked at his watch. In the long, dark night of the soul, it is always three o'clock in the morning.

The gun was lying on the chair, obviously left there by Steve Cowper, who had been on shift until midnight. Maybe Steve was trying to tell Tom something – he was an old friend, after all.

Thomas Bruce picked up the weapon and felt its velvet touch in the darkness. He hobbled slowly across the room to the bathroom, and switched on the light. In this little cubicle, the shot would sound like a clap of thunder. It would be the last thing he would hear.

Bruce looked in the mirror and saw his own face reflected back at him. Tired. Haggard. Lost and alone. The last thing he would see. He spoke softly, to himself. 'Goodbye.' The last voice he would ever hear.

He put the gun in his mouth. He wanted to say something else, something relevant, something profound. His final statement to the world before he splattered his brains all over the white tiles. But he couldn't think of anything so he just pulled the trigger.

Click.

Bruce stared down, stupidly, at the gun in his mouth. He removed it and cracked open the chamber. No bullets. His mouth was dry and he felt sick. Behind him, he heard the door of the cubicle open slowly with a creak, like a sound effect from every bad horror film he'd seen.

'When you join the CIA, Tom,' said Control, 'you join for life. You don't think we'd let you take the easy way out, do you? *We* decide when it's over, not you.'

Bruce turned, his shoulders hunched. Ignoring Control, he limped back into his bed, and pulled the sheets over his head.

SECOND EPILOGUE:
FEELING SUPERSONIC

It was a bright, clear day in early spring. In the eight months since she'd left UNIT, many things had happened in the life of Dr Elizabeth Shaw. A return to Cambridge, briefly. Then travel, to Australia, the United States, Japan, and the Soviet Union. Her future as a scientific pundit had been assured when she stood in for an ill colleague during the televising of one of the Mars landings, and had charmed Patrick Moore into submission with her laconic wit.

Her first book, *Inside the Carnival*, had brought her money, fame, and death threats. UNIT, and Cambridge, were a million miles behind her now.

Except today.

She had been invited back to officially open the newly built Trainor Foundation building. As she arrived her attention was drawn to the plaque she was to unveil later in the day.

PROFESSOR BERNARD TRAINOR, 1916–1970

A LIFE LIVED IN THE PURSUIT OF SCIENTIFIC EXCELLENCE,
AND TO THE BENEFIT OF MANKIND
OPENED BY DR ELIZABETH SHAW, 24TH MARCH 1971

She smiled, imagining the horror Bernard would feign at the thought of having elements (trainorium, first found in rocks returned from Neptune) and buildings (the Trainor Institute in Maryland) named after him. People knew that he had helped to save the world, though few knew the circumstances.

'Hello, stranger,' said a familiar voice behind her.

'Mark!' she replied, turning and hugging him. 'I had no idea you'd be here today.'

'Wouldn't miss it for the world. How are you?'

'Fine, fine. Yourself?'

'Fine,' he said, with a cheesy grin. 'I saw you on television last night, making mincemeat of poor James Burke. What's he ever done to deserve that? You didn't use to be so beastly!'

'I've changed,' she said ironically, remembering old conversations and old arguments. 'You really wouldn't like me these days.'

'Oh, I don't know. You're much more interesting now,' said Mark as they walked, arm in arm into the building.

Just for once, Liz agreed with him.